SEX
$ELLS

Zazkia Lyndon

MT-ink.co.uk

Optioned by MTP in 2012
First published by MT Ink in 2017

© Zazkia Lyndon

ISBN: 978-0-9929397-2-4

Zazkia Lyndon asserts the moral right to be
identified as the author of this work

A catalogue record of this book is
available from the British Library

To Preston's grandmother...

'Stassy would come to realise that while the rules can change, the game always remains the same. Sex sells.'

1

Anastasia had never noticed the Michelangelo-esque design on the ceiling of her C.E.O's office, but that was probably because she had never even sat in his chair before...let alone been in this position.

She was hoping that the man who had appeared with some office parcels wasn't planning an express delivery service. She had time to kill today, and what better way to spend it?

As she was flipped over by the burly Argentinian courier and taken from behind over her boss's desk, her smallish naked breasts pressed against the cold glass top as she frantically shoved papers and stationery aside.

"Faster, harder," screamed Anastasia, teetering on her stiletto heels as her mobile phone rang and vibrated in the back pocket of her short denim skirt, which had now unceremoniously concertinaed halfway up her back, her knickers conversely halfway down her legs.

As she expertly reached around and up to grab her handset, the South American delivery man pounded away, not quite believing his luck...or Anastasia's flexibility.

New Year's Eve was a typically quiet day for business parcels. The Christmas shopping spree was well and truly over, and most offices shut down.

Of course he hadn't minded being shown around by a bored Anastasia, who had drawn the short straw of manning an empty advertising agency office on the last day of the year….and who was now attempting to talk to her housemates, Chloe, Sarah and Alexa, on speaker-phone. Classy.

"We're in the pub!" shouted the girls. "Where are you?"

"Stay there, I'm coming," shrieked Anastasia, quivering .

After taking delivery of his Latin-American load, Stassy, to her sniggering friends, offered her latest conquest a post-coital treat: two lines of cocaine, hastily chopped on the desk and quickly hoovered up by the pair. Then Rodriguez was dispatched.

"Ciao, postman Pablo," shouted Stassy, ignoring his name badge, as he scurried out the door…no signature required.

Her boss's desk and surrounding furniture rearranged, Stassy wet her finger and sucked up the cocaine debris as she left. Her girls would have expected nothing less.

Stassy was a later addition to a friendship group that met at secondary school. Alexa and Chloe went back the furthest…the first day of the first year. Sarah had become part of the gang when she had joined their class aged 13.

They were now in the prime of their lives, mid-20s, some money in their pockets and not a responsibility to their names. Their primary objective: to have fun, start a career and snare a man or…in Stassy's case… men.

On the career front, each had had varying degrees of success. Stassy had embarked on a career in advertising. Chloe was working in law as a solicitor. Alexa was desperately trying to become a model and/or a presenter…Sarah, an actress in the West End.

Now alone in the office, Stassy was hungry for more entertainment. She grabbed the newspapers from the front reception desk, and headed for the sofas. First *The Mercury* and its popular *Ladies That* supplement. Turning the pages, she found a relationship chart.

"I fucking hate this shit," sang Stassy, in a sarcastically high-pitched voice, as she started to read.

1) Occasional to regular relationship depending on time, location, sex drive and consumption of alcohol and/or drugs.
2) Unofficially seeing each other.
3) In denial; regarded as seeing each other by friends of both parties, but either or both parties' actual description of the relationship is regarded as 'nothing's happening'.
4) Seeing each other, but still seeing other people as an 'unwritten rule'.
5) Officially seeing each other exclusively; unofficially boyfriend and girlfriend.
6) Officially boyfriend and girlfriend.
7) Basically engaged or nearly engaged, without a visible ring showing from either party.
8) Engaged with ring.
9) Married.
10) Married and unhappy and either getting on (and accepting it) or seeking new partners.

"Ha ha," chuckled Stassy. "Numero uno, as always. That's me!"

Her mind immediately flicked to her housemates, her best mates, her closest confidantes. Alexa, the celebrity wannabe trying to hit No 8. Sarah, madly in love with the lothario, couldn't get past No 3. Chloe, the ultimate professional, trying to make romance work and probably only hitting No 4 at best on the 'love-o-meter'.

Stassy opened the Sunday Planet's annual sex

survey: 'START YOUR SEXY NEW YEAR WITH A BANG'.

Question No 1) How many sexual partners have you had in the last 12 months?

"Hmmm? This could be fun," she giggled.

As she began filling out the survey, Stassy's imagination ran wild and she cackled to herself insanely. At the end of her 'masterpiece' she read back the entries.

"Outrageous," she said triumphantly.

Before filling in the contact details section, Stassy paused for a few seconds, and then scribbled the name Preston Price, along with his phone number.

Preston Price's love life was far from that described by Stassy; perhaps that's why he became the perfect candidate for her moment of inspiration. He was the standing joke among all his friends in the most loveable way imaginable. In their student days, Preston had become the butt of all jokes - literally - suffering serious burns to his derriere when he passed out against a radiator at a party. Only Preston could find heating at full blast in a student house.

Stassy had a soft spot for Preston. His amorous angst towards her was fuelled by the various knock-backs she had given him along the way. She put the survey in her bag ready to post later. If anything came of it Preston would surely see the funny side of it.

~

Glancing at the clock, Stassy saw it was 4pm. An hour before she was meant to leave, but, "fuck them", she was out of there. "Nobody will know. Time to get the party and 2005 started," she shouted excitedly, locking up the office.

2

Chloe woke to her phone ringing and rattling and answered…begrudgingly.

"Oh my God! Oh my fucking God!" an excited voice bellowed at her.

"Hello," said Chloe, trying to place the distorted yet familiar excitable tones.

"He…has…got…the…biggest…cock!"

Of course. It was Stassy…her housemate.

"What the fuck – who has?" asked Chloe grumpily. "You have seriously woken me for this?"

"This guy Rui. He's a model and he has got the biggest cock I have ever seen and…and…I've been riding it all night like I was in the Grand National."

"Where are you now?"

"Up the Seven Sisters Road."

The phone went dead.

Chloe was up now.

Battle-weary and on the wrong side of slumber, Chloe was still trying to process Stassy's cock (and balls) story when she realised she had one of her own …just not so impressive.

"Have I got a huge cock?" asked Tom, stroking her arm.

"Well, it's okay. Just right," she assured him, rolling over to kiss his forehead.

"What's so great about having a huge cock any-way?" he reasoned.

"You know, darling, it really depends who it's attached to. That is just so much more important. Tea?"

Now it was all coming back to Chloe. After a fairly underwhelming New Year's Eve, she had collapsed into bed at around 4am on the first day of the year...a Saturday. The girls had all left the house together the night before and then, as often happened, proceeded to distribute themselves across various parts of north and east London, with various men.

Somehow, Tom had wormed his way into her bed... as usual. What the hell, she must have thought. It wasn't the best start to 2005, but it wasn't the worst, she convinced herself, as she lamented that it was Tom under her duvet, not some fantastically well-hung rampant stud. Last night was all still a blur. Would this year equal romance? Not at this rate...

In the trashed, morning-after kitchen, Chloe put the kettle on.

She had to get out of this thing with Tom, before he became a habit neither of them could shake. Was it just about the sex? It wasn't just the sex, surely? No, it was that 'approaching-30-and-wanting-to-settle-down-and-have-children' feeling...and, more than anything else, the security that comes with being truly wanted. Would their parents have accepted such a relationship? Was life simpler in their day?

This relationship teased Chloe. It had started so promisingly, the previous summer, when her old flame Pathetic Pete had introduced her to Tempting Tom in Highbury Fields. Romantically uncomplicated, they'd fallen into bed, repeatedly, for seven, no, eight months, without ever making it 'official.' Tom somehow managed to keep her just about interested enough, but the situation wasn't ideal.

Chloe believed you should always be looking for Mr Right; take relationships for what they are. To not make something good work for want of the right time...well, life is way too short for that.

At least Tom didn't parade around like a gigolo, like Sarah's 'love interest' Philippe. Well, not to Chloe's knowledge, anyway. In fact, Tom largely found it difficult, if not impossible, to pull due to his constantly stoned state. Unless it was the weekend, he was also shit at replying to texts and calls.

Chloe was actually really into him, but, like so many people around her, he wasn't 'looking for anything serious.' Well, at least not with Chloe.

She had to get out of it.

As Chloe stared vacantly through the kitchen window, Sarah appeared in her hazy vision and bent down towards the fridge.

"Morning babe," said Chloe. "Happy New Year."

"Hi," giggled Sarah.

"Could you pass the milk?" Chloe asked, as Sarah reached for some white wine and began pouring it into two oversized glasses. "Where have you been?"

"I don't know," sniggered Sarah. "I'm still off my head. Fucked, babe!"

Sarah's eyes were rolling in a way that went hand-in-hand with drinking white wine at 10.30 in the morning.

"Fucked...nicely fucked, though," she added, trying to reassure Chloe.

From Chloe's morning daze it slowly became apparent what Sarah was actually wearing: on top, a beautiful evening-wear number and on the bottom, a hand towel, her body swaying and rotating, just like her eyes.

"I'm so high. I'm really not sure where I've been," Sarah said, smiling inanely.

Sarah was never quite sure where she'd been. Generally one of the more reserved in the group, she was the mysterious one of the girls...a real dark horse.

A year earlier, at Christmas, Sarah and Stassy had travelled around Thailand. At sunrise one morning, as they'd been staggering back to the hostel from a Ko Pha Ngan full-moon party, Sarah had announced that she wanted a tattoo and, more to the point, she NEEDED this tattoo NOW. She'd stressed it was vital to have it done before the party drugs wore off: she just couldn't deal with the pain. It wasn't a rash decision, she kept saying. She'd wanted it for the past three years.

Sarah insisted on being inked in what looked like the worst Thai tattoo parlour on the island, amazingly and worryingly still open at 7am.

"I want Peace, Love and Harmony," she slurred at the Thai tattooist. Unashamedly pulling up her dress to reveal her commando status, she said, "Peace, Love and Harmony...in them Chinese letters."

"What you want? Where you want?" said the tattooist, shaking his head, clearly unable to understand his client's drunken slur.

"I like it here, I want it here...on my bum," said Sarah, pointing to her backside.

"You like it on the bum?" repeated the man.

"Yes, I like it on the bum...Peace, Love and Harmony," said Sarah, giggling at Stassy.

"Them Chinese letters" were unique, all right. Chloe got an eyeful of them as Sarah tried to hold up her hand-towel and carry two gigantic glasses of wine as she floated back to the bedroom. Shaking her head, Chloe turned her attention back to the tea.

Sarah steadied herself, approaching the stairs as if she were climbing a rock face...gingerly! Trying to keep her dignity while carrying the wine glasses, she was clearly hindered by lack of sleep and the previous night's excesses. She opened her bedroom door to find Philippe naked on her bed.

What a magnificent sight to start the year, she mused. He was tall and toned...and just gorgeous. Spread out on her duvet, his head propped up by her pillows, he was wearing nothing but a CD case, with two huge lines of white powder laid out across it. Handing her a fifty-pound note, he said, "After you, baby."

Sarah crouched down, tantalisingly close to his crotch. Shit, he is so fucking hot, she thought. But hey, concentrate on the line. Don't spill the line! She took the note and carefully hoovered it up.

Philippe reached for the hand towel Sarah was wearing and gave it a tug, exposing her tattooed bum. His fingers traced the lines of the strange script on her buttock.

"Remind me what this says," he smiled.

"Peace, Love and Harmony," purred Sarah, climbing onto the bed. "The words I live by." She sat astride him and took off her top, arching her back to give him a good show. "Peace, Love and Harmony."

~

As the kettle squealed, Chloe heard Sarah squealing too.

Back in the real world, Chloe found it refreshing to know how Tom had his tea in the morning. Not having to ask that question gave some sort of comfort to the relationship...a familiarity so often missing. Chloe stirred three sugars into his cup.

The phone rang. Alexa's exclusive ringtone on Chloe's phone was Kylie's Can't Get You Out Of My Head. Fitting, as she believed herself to be so unforgettable.

"Hi Alexa," answered Chloe.

"Hi babe – how's you?"

"Good. Pretty chilled. What you up to…you been to bed?"

"No, not yet, I'm having too much fun. I ended up coming back to this flat in Maida Vale. It's a pretty swanky pad. All a bit C-List, sweetie. Listen, could you do me a favour, babe?"

"Sure."

"There's a guy here chatting me up. He's coming on pretty strong. Can you go online and check his creds? He seems sort of familiar…maybe TV or something. Not sure. His name is Steve Keane."

"Keen like eager?"

"K.E.A.N.E," Alexa corrected her. "He must have a MySpace page or something…"

"Sure, darling. Call you back."

Tom had dressed, drunk his tea, and was rolling a joint. More Groundhog Day than New Year's Day.

"I'd better go," he announced purposefully. "I've got some work to do."

"Sure," said Chloe, knowing full well the spliff would leave him paralysed and unable to control his fledgling online business for the rest of the day.

"Bye," said Tom, sparking up as he walked out the door.

As Tom slipped out, he bumped straight into Philippe, who himself was sporting a lit joint and also making his escape.

"Happy New Year," said a beaming Tom, both chuffed and honoured he seemed to be hotfooting it from the house with IT-boy Philippe.

"Yeah, Happy New Year, mate. Time for bed, I think," said Philippe.

"See ya," they both shouted, just as a bedraggled Stassy wobbled past them into the house, her tights severely laddered and her skirt riding to a height exposing more than Philippe and Tom really needed to see.

The front door slammed.

"Hi Stass," exclaimed Chloe, greeting her haggard housemate in the hallway. "You look like you've gone 12 rounds with Lennox Lewis."

"Well, I'm on the ropes, babe. Feel like I've been shagged senseless. In fact, I have been shagged senseless. I can barely walk."

"Take the weight of your feet, hun. I'll put the kettle on…"

Stumbling in her stilettos, Stassy staggered into the lounge.

Sarah came teetering down the stairs.

"That fucking Philippe…didn't even finish his wine."

"Talking of whining," said Chloe, "you sounded like you were having fun."

"Oh yeah, sorry about that. Fuck, he was good."

"Tea?"

"Think I'll stick to vino. Need to sleep soon, but I'm flying."

Sarah was more appropriately dressed now, a dressing-gown covering most of her modesty.

Chloe made teas for her and Stassy. Sarah followed them into the front room with a glass of Sauvignon Blanc.

"Alexa called," Chloe updated the girls. "She's still out."

"Wow…she's normally tucked up by now," sneered Stassy. "What happens if she gets papped with bags under her eyes?"

"Or doing the 'walk of shame'?" chipped in Sarah.

All three girls roared. Alexa spent more time worrying about her appearance than anyone they knew… and was desperate to be famous. So much so, she had persuaded herself that she already was.

"She's currently out with Steve Keane," explained

Chloe. "Either of you heard of him? She asked me to do some digging."

"Isn't he that tantric yoga bloke?" said Stassy. "He's a bit of a player, I think. Always in The Jet Bar with a gaggle of gorgeous girls, with fake tits popping out everywhere."

Neither Chloe nor Stassy had noticed that Sarah was looking rather sheepish. "Steve Keane?" she mumbled to herself.

Chloe opened up her work laptop and waited for it to load so she could get online. She typed STEVE KEANE into the search engine, and waited...until they had their answer on the screen.

Stassy was right. The Sunday Planet had a picture of him coming out of The Jet Bar with a babe on each arm. Headlines included YOGA GURU'S A TOGA ROMEO...and KEANE'S TANTRIC POSITIONS WERE SEX-RATED.

They discovered that Keane had pioneered a revolutionary type of yoga. Acclaimed to improve sexual stamina, he had written a couple of books, including STEAVE KEANE PRESENTS – SEXUAL ATTENTIVE YOGA – THE ULTIMATE IN SEXUAL SUCCESS. And DOMINATING IN THE BEDROOM – HOW TO BE A SEXUAL DON.

"Shit, this guy is prolific ... in lots of ways," exclaimed Chloe. "He might even give Philippe a run for his money, Sarah."

They contorted their heads to better understand a diagram of how Steve combined sex and yoga together.

"Let me have a look," said Stassy, stumbling over to the computer. "Fuck, that looks both impossible and painful."

"Let's call Alexa," said Chloe, dialling her number.

"Really?" whinged Sarah. "Do we have to?"

Too late.

"Hi babe," answered Alexa, in a sultry tone presumably reserved for her new C-List chums.

"How you doing, darling?" asked Chloe. "Stassy and Sarah are here."

"Yeah, really good babe...really good."

"Can you talk?"

"Erm...no."

"OK, leave the room," said Chloe. "Blame the reception. I'll fill you in on Mr Keane."

"OK, will do...what's that you're saying?...ooooooh... I can't quite hear you gorgeous...hey, hold on there... let me just move a little...to...the...other...side...of...the ...room."

There was a pause as Alexa got into position.

"So...," she said, with anticipation and excitement in her voice.

"Well," began Chloe. "He is 'the King' or should I say 'don' of...well...I guess you would call it a type of tantric sex. He created this yoga which dominates in the bedroom. I would say he has a way with the ladies, and is pretty hot in the sack. He has been pictured in the Sunday Planet, and with loads of dollies."

Only weeks ago, the house's very own 'dolly birds' Alexa and Stassy had also been snapped by paps coming out of a bar in the West End. Alas, they were in the background behind any real celebrities, and very hard to make out in any of the publications the pictures appeared in.

"I'm putting you on speakerphone, hun," announced Chloe, moving her new Motorola Razr towards the others. Of course, Alexa had the gold limited-edition Dolce & Gabbana version, but then she would.

"Wow," whispered Alexa into the handset. "An audience! I'm honoured."

"Alright Lex, hear you've hooked up with Steve Keane," began Stassy. "Not sure you're cut out for tantric yoga, sweetness. Might be a bit hectic for you, oh delicate one. Don't want to break a nail now...or lose one of those hair extensions..."

"Haha, very funny Stassy," replied Alexa.

"He's definitely worth jumping, though," interjected Stassy. "I've never seen anyone achieve those positions before."

"Aren't most people worth a jump in your book, Stassy?" asked Alexa.

"Already had my first one of the year, babe...so, yeah, got the jump on you as usual, babe."

Cue more laughter.

"What...ever," said Alexa. "Gonna chip girls...thanks for the research...very useful. Ciao bellas."

"Happy New Year...see ya...all the best, darling... good luck," the others said in unison.

Chloe looked around the room at Stassy and Sarah, and thought about Alexa trying to snare Steve. All of them were hurtling towards 30, and none any closer to finding "the one." As she pondered what 2005 would have in store, she could see Sarah falling asleep on the settee, still clutching her glass of wine. Stassy had retired. "Come on babe, time for bed, the party's over," she said.

~

2005 got off to a fantastic start for Sarah. Only a few days into the New Year, she landed a West End part. Bursting to share the good news, she dialled Chloe's number first.

"Sarah," sighed Chloe unenthusiastically...out loud. "Hi, babe."

"How are you, sweetie?" asked Sarah.

"A bit left side..."

"Why, darling, what's happened?"

"It's been 10 hours 32 minutes since I texted Tom, and he hasn't replied."

"He's probably just busy," suggested Sarah, over-generously.

"Mmmm…," mumbled Chloe, before adding "busy getting stoned" under her breath. "Anyway, how are you?"

"Good, very good…I've been offered a part today!"

"Oh, that's fantastic," cooed Chloe. "What are you playing?"

"A neurotic bisexual nymphomaniac."

"Erm…right…OK…that's great, isn't it?"

"It's a bit sick," reasoned Sarah. "But it's work and quite high profile…and I only have to show my boobs and my left buttock."

"Well, that's good…isn't it? Where's it at?"

"It's West End, sweetie."

"Amazing. When are you starting?"

"Rehearsals, straight away…the show begins in March."

"That's brilliant Sarah, and it'll be good to diversify your portfolio a little. Shakespeare is cool and all that, but this will really showcase your talent."

"Yes, you're right. Listen, I am just catching the No 38. I'm shattered. I'll be home soon. If I don't wake up in Dalston."

"OK, babe."

Sarah rang off.

That really was great news, thought Chloe. Sarah had been a bit difficult recently…always the same when she was in-between jobs.

Chloe returned to what she'd been doing when Sarah rang: staring obsessively at her phone, like a night watchman. Why-oh-why hadn't Tom replied to her text? Over-analysing was a classic Chloe trait. She had tried to be flirtatious and funny. She had concentrated on every written word, trying to sound interested without appearing desperate...witty and punchy, but not cheesy or nauseating. "Stop it!" she screamed to herself. How could one man control her in such a powerful way? Especially one as flaky as Tom?

The phone rang and Chloe's heart leapt once more. She had now managed to convince herself it was all over, time to move on. Of course, though, she hoped it was him. It wasn't.

"Hey sweetie."

"Hi Alexa," sighed Chloe reluctantly. "What you up to?"

"I am just about to go on a date with Steve Keane."

"Really," said Chloe. "That's exciting. You're not hanging around with this one!"

"I know, I know, he's been chasing me all week. He's taking me to The Moss."

"Wow!"

The Moss was a restaurant reserved for real celebrities...difficult to reserve a table unless you knew someone.

"That's impressive!" added Chloe.

"I'm meeting him in this swanky five-star hotel for drinks first," continued Alexa. "I'm seeing this as a great career move."

Typical Alexa. Always putting her 'career' first: making it as a model/becoming famous was so important to her. Sure she liked to party, but her work ethic was also unrivalled. She was indeed the epitome of the term 'work hard, play hard' and, by the sounds of things, Steve Keane liked to play especially hard!

Fame was Alexa's goal, and she would do whatever was thrown at her to get there. As deluded as she often was, Chloe admired her for that; it certainly wasn't the lifestyle or career Chloe would choose for herself...and she liked food too much to let herself be super skinny. Her curvaceous figure and enviable bust were testament to that.

"Well, good luck, babe," announced Chloe, wrapping up the call. "I want full reports tomorrow...and get as much info on this tantric yoga lark - sounds fun."

"Sure thing, babe."

Like a security guard momentarily distracted by a flirtatious young lady, Chloe returned to her watch, waiting for Tom to call. Perhaps the New Year had scared him off. She hated the waiting-game. Had she played it wrong? Misread the signals?

She heard the front door. Thank God...something to take her mind off this endless, tedious, fruitless ordeal.

Sarah waltzed into the house, still high from the thrill of her new part, and plonked herself on the sofa, truly pleased with herself.

"Hi, babe," said Sarah. "I'm a West End actress! It's happening!"

"It's such fantastic news," smiled Chloe. "Well done, babe. Really well done. You deserve this." She stood up, went to the fridge, and took out the chilled bottle of bubbly that was reserved for an occasion like this.

Sarah kicked off her heels and let herself relax happily into the sofa cushions. Waiting for a new part can be so stressful for an actor, a yoyo of ups and downs and uncertainties...endless castings...a thankless task. It's hard to stay optimistic all the time, but it's Catch 22: if you don't remain positive in yourself, you will never find work. Sarah had been on this rollercoaster for a while. Her last role had been in A Midsummer Night's Dream as Hermia. It had been the break she needed, and she'd received several good reviews. However, when the run had come to an end, she had been at a loss. The anticipated work didn't come flooding in, causing Sarah so much self-doubt...until today.

"It's finally happening, babe," smiled Sarah, as

Chloe came in with the champagne. "I'm really going to get noticed this year. I can feel it."

Predictably, Alexa came in just as the cork popped. Never one to miss a champagne moment, Alexa.

Chloe turned off her phone – for good, this time – and the trio toasted Sarah's new part.

~

Sarah woke the next morning, rolled over, and switched on her phone. Maybe there would be congratulatory messages on it.

The familiar tone bleeped in her ear: "Message one – received…"

Sarah smiled.

"…at 4.32am."

Shit. No guesses for what was coming … just who?

"Alright mate," came the drunk, blathering sound of Stassy's voice. "I just wanted to let you know that I'm at Paul's."

"My name's Raoul," came a gruff voice somewhere in the background.

"Oh well, anyway, in case I get Rohypnoled, I'm at 430 Upper Street. So please come and get me."

The message went dead. Sarah rang Stassy at once.

"Alright mate," answered Stassy.

"Where are you??"

"I'm here, back at the house…getting ready for work."

"I got your message."

"Oh yeah, I was at Paul's…I mean Raoul's…or whatever he was fucking called."

"You going to see him again?"

"Naah, he was too muscly, too posh."

~

So, as far as '05 was concerned, Stassy Thomas was already well into her stride. Three shags in four days ... and the first week of the year wasn't even over yet. But then, Stassy was well known for being prolific in the casual sex department. She famously woke up in her bed one Sunday morning the year before with a used condom stuck on her forehead. Embarrassing enough, but nothing compared to the bloke lying next to her, looking up and saying: "Erm...we didn't use a condom last night..."

~

Sarah, a lady who couldn't afford to lunch, did so shamelessly anyway. On the first Friday of 2005, she lunched with Chloe at her favourite upmarket delicatessen on Essex Road.

Sarah, like Chloe, was also in a period of 'not looking for anything serious,' and had recently developed a penchant for black men. Her latest conquest, Philippe, was mixed race and drop-dead gorgeous ... the best of both worlds, she insisted. Stunning herself, the envy of any female, Sarah rarely had difficulty snaring young men.

In love with only himself, Philippe's female conquests were unparalleled, bordering on gigolo levels. Kissing his own knuckle had become his signature greeting when reaching out for the hand of the date in question.

Philippe had become Sarah's 'Everest.' To mere mortals, an insurmountable summit...at least that seemed clear to everybody else. They feared this frostbitten rock climber had peaked...bitten off more than she could possibly chew.

"What's happening with you and Philippe?" Chloe asked.

"Well, I guess we are seeing each other," replied Sarah, a brief smile appearing on her face.

"And is he still sleeping with the rest of his harem?" snapped back Chloe.

"Of course, darling. You know Philippe, he just can't keep his cock to himself…and given its size and ability and the body it belongs to, well, it's not actually that surprising."

"How very generous of you…I guess it would be a shame for others to miss out," replied Chloe sarcastically. "Do you mind if I have a go?"

"Well, I wouldn't go as far as that…"

"Exactly, because you really like him, don't you?"

"Well I guess I do, but anyway, I am just not looking for anything serious at the moment."

"It is all going to end in disaster," worried Chloe out loud.

"Oh shut up. It's all cool, I am fine."

Chloe wasn't convinced.

~

Sarah called Stassy. She needed a pick-me-up after Chloe and her moody pessimism. This year was off to a good start – new man, new West End exposure – she wanted to talk to someone with a sense of fun.

Stassy had made it into work on Friday…just. When Sarah called, she was twiddling her thumbs at work, waiting for anyone with any authority to actually make it back into the office after the Christmas break, and hoping her boss wasn't in any time soon so she didn't have to visit his office again just yet.

"How are you gorgeous?" she asked Sarah.

"Not bad, but still not fully recovered from New Year's Eve and New Year's Day. It seems to go on longer every year."

"Where did you actually go?" inquired Stassy. "We all seemed to splinter off fairly early on and I still haven't caught up with you properly."

"Everywhere...not totally sure. I know I ended up with the Shoreditch massive at 7am on New Year's Day in some dirty bar. All good, though...brought Philippe back with me. Somehow managed to drag him away from his posse. They were still going at 11 that night. I was fucked, babe, totally fucked – what did you get up to?"

"I ended up in Hoxton Square with this model guy ...Rui. He was hot. Went back to his and rode him all night."

"You going to see him again?" Sarah laughed, feeling happier already.

"Naah, probably not...if he calls me I'll definitely go on a date with him, but already deleted him from my phone."

"Good girl."

"Hey!" remembered Stassy. "I forgot to tell you. I filled out a Sunday Planet sex survey in Preston's name. Very amusing. Made up some funny stories. Doubt anything will come of it. I was just so bored at work."

"Stass," grinned Sarah. "You are soooooo naughty."

3

TWO MONTHS LATER

One seemingly innocuous Friday late afternoon in March, Preston Price was finishing up for the week at the recruitment company where he worked as a junior headhunter. His mobile rang.

"Hello, is that Preston?"

"Yes, speaking."

"It's the *Sunday Planet* here. My name is Raquel. We are interested in the sex life survey you completed at the start of the year," a female reporter announced in a gruff twenty-Rothmans-a-day voice.

"Oh?"

"Yes, well, it's taken quite a while to plough through them all. We didn't receive many entries like your one, sir, and we were wondering if we could interview you...your ex-wife, your gay lover and your ex-wife's gay lover?"

"Erm...right..." said Preston, trying to buy himself some time.

His mind was racing. This must be some kind of joke. He certainly didn't recall filling out a *Sunday Planet* sex survey recently, and he was sure he would remember a gay lover.

Then a moment of clarity came over him. Cartoon-style dollar signs flashed across his eyes.

"I take it you will be paying us for the interview?"

"Of course," the hack replied.

"How much?"

Preston was still picking up the pieces from his hedonistic student days, not to mention some costly private medical bills along the way. He had simply had too much fun, and a variety of jobs since leaving uni, which barely left him any money to play with.

"You could be looking in excess of £10,000," replied Raquel. "But it depends on the quality of the story, and if everyone plays ball."

"OK," said Preston. "Now I am interested. It isn't anything I am ashamed of, and it is very juicy. Let me have a little think and get back to you. I need to discuss this with my lovers and...erm...their respective lovers, as they are unaware about me completing this survey. I mean, I'd completely forgotten about it."

"That's fine, but I need an answer by Monday, as we will need all the copy by the middle of the week. We're hoping to run the feature in our *Ladies That* supplement magazine next weekend."

"Right," said Preston. "I'll get on the case. Do you have a contact number?"

Details were exchanged and Preston promised Raquel she would be hearing from him very soon.

Preston hung up, and started flicking through his contact list. Sarah was his first point of call.

"Hello sweetie," answered Sarah, in textbook thespian fashion.

"Alright Sarah, what have you been up to? Have you been filling out any *Sunday Planet* sex surveys on behalf of me recently?"

"You what? *Sunday Planet* sex surveys? Are you mad?"

A hysterical laugh boomed from the other side of the room.

"Stassy," exclaimed Sarah.

Stassy ran over to Sarah and snatched the handset.

"It was me, it was me," she said gleefully, still trying to speak through the uncontrollable hysteria that had arisen from memories of what she had written. "How did you find out?"

"I've just had a phone call stating that my entry was the most exciting the paper had received and that they would like to interview me."

"Fuck, fuck," shrieked Stassy. "Fuck, fuck, fuck... REALLY? Shit, I really didn't think there would be any comebacks...wowsers! How much Preston, how much?"

"Gee, you never miss a trick, do you, Stass?" said Preston.

"How much? How fucking much?"

"Well, she's talking five figures for a 'quality story'."

"Baby, I can give you quality...I'll be your wife for a cut."

It wasn't how Preston had ever imagined hooking up with Stassy, but if he were to go ahead with this scam, Preston realised he did not have much option but to accept her offer. In the next 48 hours he had to find an ex-wife, her gay lover and his own gay lover too.

"You will need to find a lesbian...erm...lady friend, but, ok...and you need to be available for the interview early next week."

"Cool," said his accomplice, happy to lie for a few quid, let alone a few grand.

"OK, keep in touch," said Preston. "In the meantime, I guess I need to find a boyfriend."

"And a girlfriend," chipped in Stassy.

"A girlfriend!" choked Preston on his words. "Just what did you tell them, Stassy?"

"Didn't they say anything to you?" said Stassy in the most innocent playful voice.

"No...what did you say?"

"Well, I just said that after I had left you for my gay lover, you had decided to try the other side for yourself...to see what you had been missing, but subsequently you discovered being gay just wasn't for you and you were back on the straight and narrow again now...and back in a relationship."

"Well, well, I have been a busy boy, haven't I?" fumed Preston. "Stassy, you need to have a serious think over the next 24 hours about what exactly you said in this survey. We don't want to be exposed as liars."

"Didn't realise you were so bothered about damaging your reputation?" countered Stassy.

"I am not. I'm more bothered now about not getting the cash. I've already spent it a couple of times over."

"OK," said Stassy. "Let's rendezvous at The Saddlers Arms Sunday night at 8pm. I'll bring a gay lover and find you one too. I have someone in mind! You find yourself a new girlfriend as well and we'll hatch a plan. Aren't I good? I am already getting into character, ex-husband... meeow!"

"See you Sunday at eight," said Preston, wondering what the fuck he was getting himself into.

"Bye-bye hubby."

Preston put the phone down and threw his head in his hands.

Stassy fixed her eyes on Sarah.

"Saaaaaa-rah," she whimpered. "Fancy being my gay lover. There's some cash in it for you."

"OK, but no tongues are to be involved...nor any groping."

"Agreed."

"Well, maybe a little bit of groping," giggled Sarah, giving Stassy a flirtatious kiss on the cheek.

"If you're lucky," replied her new 'girlfriend'.

~

Chloe's gut-busting trainee lawyer job at Smedley, Smith and Sweeney was rarely boring. In reality, Stassy's job in advertising should never have been so mundane that she needed to resort to pranking Preston or, for that matter, random character assassination. As Chloe wrapped up her own week in the office, her phone rang.

"Hi, it's Preston."

"Hello, lovely, how are you?"

"Well, I was hoping for a favour."

"Sounds ominous."

"Did you know Stassy had completed a *Sunday Planet* sex survey on my behalf?"

"No, I didn't."

"She wrote in saying that I had been married and my wife had gone off with a woman and I had then dabbled with my own gay relationship to see what it was like and then gone back to being straight."

"Right," said Chloe, raising an eyebrow. "And how exactly does this involve a favour from me?"

"Well, the *Sunday Planet* now want to interview me...plus my past and current lovers."

"You're joking. Oh my God!"

"And I was wondering whether you wanted to be my girlfriend. I mean, just pretend to be my girlfriend, my new girlfriend?"

Of course, Chloe was perfect for the role. She was very good at pretending to be someone's girlfriend.

"This is crazy - is it a wind-up?"

"There is cash on the table here. They're offering us at least ten grand if they get a decent story," said Preston enticingly.

"What would I have to do?"

"Well, I guess not a lot. I don't think they will really want to know much about our relationship. They'll be more interested in all these bisexual urges. I guess they will want to take a picture of you. I am happy to do all the talking. Please babe...I will love you for ever."

"I'm not really up for too much lying. Not in my game. I'm no good at fibbing either...too honest for my own good, but if I don't have to talk a lot, I guess I could go along with it," added Chloe, unconvincingly.

"No worries, that's fine, I really appreciate this. We are meeting in The Saddlers Arms on Sunday night to discuss it...at 8 o'clock. Now I just need to find my gay lover."

"See you Sunday, then, I guess," said Chloe sighing and shaking her head at the same time.

"Bye."

~

Later that night, Alexa returned to the house, stormed into the front room and glared at Stassy.

"Stassy, I was at the *Sunday Planet* offices today."

"Oh," said Stassy, thumbing through the latest copy of *Nearer* magazine. "Were you?" She didn't like the look on Alexa's face, but chanced her arm with: "Well Alexa, what were you doing there?"

"Never you mind, just some model shoot for the woman's section."

"Oh...''

"And anyway," stormed Alexa. "What I was doing there isn't the point. I got chatting to one of the reporters in the smoking room, put two and two together and made fucking four."

"Clever girl, just goes to prove you're not the dizzy blonde some people claim."

"So," continued Alexa, ignoring Stassy's catty comments. "They seem to have a hot new story they're working on. They've found a rather interesting individual, who appears to have had the most amazing sexual experiences...and guess what?"

"What?" said Stassy innocently, still flicking through *Nearer*, though no longer appearing to take any notice of the celebrity photos.

"This individual happens to be called Preston Price," continued Alexa. "Stassy, it's got your name and your work written all over it."

"Me?" offered Stassy, as if butter wouldn't melt in her mouth...the pages of the magazine now turning even faster.

"Yes, you," bellowed Alexa, snatching the mag from Stassy and glaring at her with her most frosty stare, the one she had perfected during an 'ice queen' photo shoot earlier in the year.

Stassy looked up at Alexa and grinned sheepishly.

"OK, well, alright, yes...it was me...and what a fucking masterpiece, I'm sure you'd agree?"

"Stassy," stormed Alexa, even louder, frustrated that her 'ice queen' eyes had failed to freeze Stassy in her seat. Why wasn't she as easily controlled as the men in her life?

"What were you thinking of? What if the press get hold of this? The fact is, Stassy, I live with you, you are my friend. One of my best friends. Preston is my friend too and you are lying. You are a blatant bare-faced liar ...a bloody fucking liar. I mean, you are bullshitting about Preston, aren't you? Preston hasn't had all those experiences. Of course he hasn't. He hasn't even been married for a start. Oh, Stassy, what have you done? You are going to ruin my career."

"Oh Alexa, please shut up...as if. Why would it ruin your career? I doubt anyone's going to find out and, anyway, how could they possibly connect it to you?"

"Stassy, the *Sunday Planet* doesn't give a fuck – they'll take any shit on anyone."

Stassy really hadn't taken any of this into consideration when she had written her little statement. She had not thought about how this would impact on anyone else. However, she was equally convinced Alexa could only wish she were famous enough to warrant the paranoia. Stassy had been bored at work. It was a giggle, and now it was going to make her some desperately needed cash. Couldn't Alexa just get a life...and join in the fun?

"I want you to call this off," demanded Alexa.

"No."

"Stassy...please."

"They will only pester Preston for the story anyway and then what's he going to say? He doesn't care, he needs the money and now he...we...have access to some real cash. Maybe we should ask for more if they're getting so excited?"

Stassy paused, composed herself and dared to put her arm around Alexa. She continued.

"Look Lex...it will be OK. C'mon, it's a laugh...and Preston and I are skint. It all started as a joke but now the money's not too bad...in for a penny, in for a pound, and all that. I promise I will not mention your name, let them follow me home or be so unconvincing that they will know it's a lie."

"Stassy, I promise, if this has comebacks to me...I will..."

Before Alexa could complete her threat her phone rang.

"Oh, hi darling. Yes, sweetie, of course, I am still on for tonight," she purred. "I'll just slip into something more comfortable. I'll be with you in twenty."

Alexa giggled, put the phone down and turned on

Stassy again, this time huffing and puffing, but no words came before she flounced out of the room.

As she was leaving the house, Alexa took Chloe aside for a quiet word.

"Babe, listen, I am really worried about what Stassy is up to," she whispered.

"Alexa," sighed Chloe. "What's wrong?"

"I don't want to be dragged into this thing. I mean, remember over Christmas, we were photographed together at The Jet Bar?"

"But sweetheart, you were really only in the background. It wasn't really you...it is all very blurred."

"Maybe...but what about in January?"

"Alexa, you could just about see Stassy's arm in that photo...only her arm."

"But, what if they have her connected to that arm...and anyway... there must be photos that weren't published," argued Alexa. "You would be amazed, darling, at what comes out of the woodwork. It's the wicked world of the tabloid...you can't blame me for being concerned. She can't do this. The money isn't that much. It's peanuts, comparatively. What's the point? This is my career we're talking about."

"Listen, Alexa. I am not saying that this is the most intelligent plan Stass has ever had, but it's not going to directly affect you. Hardly anyone will read it...a bit of cash for Stass and Preston. It will hit a small part of a big tabloid's largely unread supplement. There is so little association between you anyhow? Chill out. You sound like a paranoid freak."

4

The next morning Chloe woke up, rolled over and put her arms round Tom, who despite being AWOL ...again...for most of the week, had once more managed to find his way under her duvet during the cloak of night.

"Morning, babe."

"Grrrr...," was all he could muster.

Chloe cuddled him for a moment, fell asleep for a little while, then woke again soon after.

"What you doing today?" she asked.

"Working," said Tom abruptly. "Lots and lots of work...I have lots to do. Loads."

"It's a Saturday babe, and the weather is looking lovely," she replied, peering at the surprisingly sunny day outside. "Spring has sprung early," she added, confidently.

"I'm going home, I need to work," protested Tom. "I need to..."

"But you know you won't really do it...we could have a really nice...we never do anything together."

"What? It's not like you're my girlfriend or anything."

"Tom, you have been in and out of my bed every week for the best part of a year. How can you not consider me to be your girlfriend? Everybody we know sees us as being together. What is the problem with you? Get over it."

"Look, I'm sorry. I've always said I didn't want anything serious to happen."

"I know, I know," interrupted Chloe. "I never intentionally wanted anything to happen but we are where we are."

"I have always said..." repeated Tom, "...I never wanted anything serious to happen."

"Well, I am sorry, that's it then...,'' said Chloe calmly.

"What do you mean?" said Tom open-mouthed.

"...I am finishing it. That's it, we're no longer...well...sleeping together. From now on, this whole thing is over."

"Babe, OK, OK, calm down...," Tom said, rolling over and looking at her in his usual playful way. "One more for the road?"

"Get out of my bed please...and just go."

Tom dressed reluctantly and then left hurriedly.

So Chloe had finally managed to finish with Tom...and, of course, it is always incredibly difficult to finish with someone that you have never really been going out with. She showered, dug out a summer dress from the depths of her wardrobe and shuffled off to Highbury Fields.

This was where she'd first met Tom, in a magical encounter last summer. Alas, there was no fairytale to be found this time. It wasn't Summer or even Spring really yet. No starry-stoned feeling on the walk home. No irresistible spine-tingling, stomach-churning buzz when you meet some you really like for the first time. She felt miserable, guilty and alone.

Tom had left. Well, he hadn't so much as left, of course. She had asked him to leave. Yes, the man, who frequently left her distraught and desolate because he hadn't texted for the best part of 48 hours, had gone. She'd showed him...kicked him into touch, booted him out onto the street...told him to sling his hook, to jog on...do one. Don't you dare not text me or not want to hang out with me on a Saturday ever again.

Of course, Tom was more than happy to never text or hang out with Chloe again. The joke wasn't on him, it was on her. There were plenty more 'friends with benefits' in the sea...or the park...not that she would find one any time soon.

Chloe had finished with someone who didn't want to go out with her anyway. Now she had to remain strong, stand her ground and stick to the principles that were making her so miserably sad.

Back in the kitchen at the house, with an overpriced bottle of Pinot Grigio for one, Chloe sat staring into space, repeating over and over in her head: "Tom has gone, Tom has gone, don't text Tom, don't call Tom, Tom has gone."

The only 'action' Chloe had going on now was being Preston's pretend girlfriend. How had it come to this?

After a long morose night in front of the TV, she fell asleep on the sofa in the living room, waking at around 7am to the sight of two pairs of dirty feet, caked in a strange shade of black mud. They belonged to Sarah and Stassy, both staring at her with a manic calm that was infectious. Chloe's own misery was momentarily lost in their heady cloud of euphoria.

Sarah swayed and then, lurching forward, looked at Chloe in blind amusement.

Managing a faint grin, she asked them: "Where the hell have you been?"

"We'eeeeve been....to a party...in a forest...in west London."

"A forest party in West London? Are there any forests in west London?"

"Yeah, well, who knew?" said Stassy. "Somewhere near Shepherd's Bush....Shrubs Lane...Scrubs Lane...it was mental! Down by the canal. Heels weren't exactly the order of the day, though."

"How the hell did you find that?" asked Chloe.

"We all met at this amazing basement bar in Harlesden called The Lodge," continued Sarah. "With a Balearic garden at the back. You must go. They had a beach party going on and a band from New York playing live house music. Crazy."

"Sounds amazing..."

"Babe, it was surreal...next thing, we're following everyone out of the bar and down the road. We walked for about half a mile, went down on to the canal, along the tow path, and there's this proper party going off in the middle of a clearing...like a magical forest that time forgot. Hundreds down there...nice party people and a load of crusties. We bought some pills from this girl, and when the sun came up, turns out she was a 15-year-old gypsy traveller. God, there were some sights. It's like it was all a dream. We're still flying now. Aren't we Stass?"

"That's me," said Stassy, stirring suddenly, exhausted from her own brief description of their forest party adventure.

"Right, well, you'd better get some rest," said Chloe, all headmistressly. "Saddlers Arms tonight, hatching this stupid Preston Price thing..."

"Yes, we're there," promised Sarah. "We're 100% there...aren't we Stass?"

"That's me," said Stassy, slowly opening her eyes after zoning out again, the sudden realisation that the scam she had instigated was actually real, emblazoned across her gurning face.

Bookended, as it was, by the girls' return from deepest west London and Preston Price's tabloid scam meeting, another dreary Sunday was passing, which it often does if you're single, through sleeping, through being hungover, through nothing. Chloe was despondent about her ridiculous situation with Tom, but Stassy and Preston's ruse was at least distracting her. The whole thing was against all Chloe's ethics. She wasn't a liar, but then she wasn't going to lie...technically. She was going to pretend she was Preston's girlfriend and not say anything through this whole charade. Was that lying? Well, not exactly. Then she thought of Alexa. She wasn't doing her any favours... not if you bought into her paranoia. But you can't please everyone in life.

~

Preston called Chloe with military efficiency.

"Hi there...Saddlers Arms, 8pm: just checking you'll all be there?"

"Yes, Sar! I will be present and correct," she said obediently.

"And Sarah and Stass?"

"Yes, they plan to be there and they will be there," she assured him.

"Cool, see you then."

Chloe looked at her watch...fast approaching 7pm...time to get Sarah and Stassy up and out of their barracks. She moved slowly up the stairs to their rooms. Her aptitude for punctuality came from a deep resentment of her mother always meeting her late from school, ensuring she was a stickler for time ever since. This was something that Sarah and Stassy simply couldn't comprehend, whether they had been up half the night or not.

"Sarah," cooed Chloe.

"Urgh...," grunted Sarah.

"Let's be having you," she shouted.

~

Preston sat at the head of the table and dinged his pen against his pint, the sound resonating across the corner of the pub the group had commandeered. Everyone fell silent. He momentarily felt an unfamiliar feeling of power: rare, but exceptionally welcoming.

"Ok, guys and girls," started Preston. "There is ten grand on the table."

Preston pointed at the middle of the table, not full of cash, but of various drinks, and, still pre-smoking ban, a bulging ashtray.

"It will involve a small amount of everyone's time and a little white lying, but just imagine what we will all do with the cash."

There was still silence, so Preston continued: "Pay off our student debts? Start that deposit fund for a flat or just go on a hedonistic one: holiday/blow out/Ibiza?"

Chloe stared at Preston for a moment and then blurted out her gut reaction. "I'm sorry, I just don't think I can do it. I just have too much to lose. I know pretending to be your girlfriend is a small part of this puzzle, but my legal career is too important and, for the risk of sounding like Alexa, any bad press could be hugely detrimental to me. I am going to have to bow out. I am sorry to be such a prude."

Ralph stood up. Chloe stared at him...he looked like he was wearing make-up. She had nothing against guys in make-up, especially those in black eyeliner and a little powder puff, but it just wasn't something she generally encountered in day-to-day life.

Ralph spoke, his voice effeminate and cockney. "Well, quite frankly Preston," he announced. "I just don't give a damn. I will lie for you, baby."

It looked like Preston had found his man.

"So how do you know Stassy?" Chloe asked Ralph.

Ralph looked at her and flicked his long dark curly hair and flashed his mascara-coated lashes. "Well, darling," he explained. "Stassy and I go way back. We used to be quite something on the podium, at Hell a few years back. Didn't we Stass?"

Stassy nodded like she was head-banging to a house music track, offering an impromptu hand in the air as she fist-pumped and wailed: "Yeah baby."

Ralph continued: "Stassy knows that I'm pretty much game for anyone that bungs a few notes my way. And any mates of Stass are mates of mine."

Chloe was beginning to feel really pleased that she had already extricated herself from the whole situation.

Preston looked uncomfortable at Ralph's enthusiasm, but blustered on.

"Stassy?"

"Yes – I am in – in like Flynn...yes siree! It will be so easy to fake being married to you...and even easier to fake having a sexual relationship with this hot baby."

Stassy reached over the table and kissed Sarah on the cheek before licking around her left ear provocatively. Sarah let out a yelp and grinned back, licking her lips...almost excited.

"Right," said Preston, trying to bring some structure back to the proceedings, and looking more than flustered at 'The Stassy & Sarah Show'. "This is all shaping up rather nicely," he suggested.

"Quick question," interrupted Stassy, as the group settled itself. "Why do we have to give this whole tasty tale up at once?"

"What do you mean?" asked Preston.

"Well," reasoned Stassy. "There could be an advantage in milking the story. It may be less lucrative in the short term but more profitable in the long run."

"Please explain," asked Preston.

"Oooh, I love the smell of money," said Ralph. "Tell me more."

"So, let me break it down," said Stassy. "We all know this involves a few fibs, and white lies are easier to tell when there aren't so many people around. Less chance of tripping each other up. If Preston and I go for the initial interview we can get the ball rolling. If they like it we can offer more. Each time we give them more – more stories and more people – we can bag more money. Plus it will be easier for two people to tell this story from the get-go."

"It's not a bad plan. I can tell them that I haven't managed to get all parties to agree to be interviewed yet," said Preston, looking at Chloe. "But my ex-wife has agreed to it and we, the main characters as such, are happy to come in for an interview as soon as pos-sible. I will tell them that in the meantime I will do my best to secure the others for later."

Sarah nodded, happy with the plan of action.

"Great, let's see what they say," said Stassy.

Ralph pouted, clearly disappointed his fifteen minutes of fame had been delayed. "What...ever," he added.

Stassy leaned across the table, grabbing Ralph's hands. "Don't worry, darling," she reassured him. "Your day up in lights will come, I promise. This is the beginning of a lucrative journey."

Conversely, Preston was troubled by the Ralph part of the scam. He felt confident that, if he were gay, Ralph wouldn't be his type, but just thinking, "if he were gay" disturbed him, as un-PC as he knew that was. And it would be wrong to underestimate Ralph just yet. He might well still be useful.

5

Alexa cornered Chloe as she came back from the pub.

"Well, what's happening?" she snapped.

"I've been at the Saddlers."

"Who with?" grilled Alexa.

"Preston, Stassy, Sarah and some really random friend of Stass'... Ralph."

"What were you discussing?"

"Well, erm...you know...this survey that Stassy filled out..."

"And?"

"Sorry Alexa, but Stassy and Preston are going to do the interview," explained Chloe. "I've told them I'm not getting involved. Ralph is on standby and so is Sarah."

"Right, OK. Did anyone mention me?"

"No...why?" said Chloe, fibbing.

"Well, did anyone show concern for me and how this stupid stupid lie could impact my career?"

"No Alexa, that didn't come up. Look, talk to Stassy or Preston. I really don't want anything more to do with this. I'm going to hit the sack. I'm emotionally drained."

Alexa wasn't going to be able to confront Stassy tonight. She was off out with one of her regular squeezes, Oscar, and she wouldn't be back until at least the morning.

~

Chloe woke up at 3am, her mind racing in thought. She was glad to have got out of this ridiculous situation. Although not in practice, she had to agree with Alexa in principle. This sort of thing could so easily spin out of control. It probably wouldn't lead anywhere, but if it did, the repercussions could be immense. Certainly more so for her, than Alexa. Chloe's one-track path to carve out a successful career in modelling meant nothing would stand in her way. This great big fat lie would probably amount to nothing, but then with Stassy involved?...well, the words 'possible', 'is' and 'anything' sprang to mind.

~

Preston arrived at work on Monday morning at 9am, sharp...and after about 30 minutes went to the car park to make THE phone call.

"Hiya," said a husky Raquel.

"It's Preston Price here. You called me last week regarding the sex survey."

"Oh yes, thanks for coming back to me. What are your thoughts?"

"Well, I am happy to do an interview and my ex-wife will do it too."

"OK, what about the other parties?"

"Well, we have begun talks with them and they may well be willing to be involved. However, they are keen to see the tone of an initial article before they commit."

"OK, but are you sure you and your ex-wife can bring enough to the table first time around?"

"Yes I am. She is willing to tell everything for some cash and, to be honest, we could both do with the money at the moment, especially since the divorce. What do you think you can offer?"

"Well, when we discussed ten grand it was for exclusive access to all of you."

"I appreciate that, but we will give you the story you want."

"OK, leave it with me...can you hold the line?"

Preston waited for about 45 seconds, and Raquel was back on the phone.

"For full disclosure...for your ex-wife and you, I am prepared to offer £7,500," explained Raquel, before her tone darkened and she insisted: "But I mean FULL DISCLOSURE. If I don't have a story I won't run it and if I don't run it you won't get paid. Is that clear?"

"Yes," said Preston. "Crystal! Full disclosure. I understand. When do you want us?"

"Tomorrow...3pm."

"We will see you then."

~

Stassy got home from work. It was late...so hard to leave the office when you are in advertising. Shattered, she poured a glass of wine, heated some food in the microwave and started rolling a joint. She might just make an hour or so of mindless TV on the sofa, before crashing.

However, Alexa lay in wait in the lounge, like a dangerous cat ready to pounce. As Stassy stumbled in, wine in her left hand, plate of food in the other and spliff behind her ear, Alexa saw her chance and leapt at her precarious prey.

"Stassy," she raged. "What the FUCK?"

"What the FUCK you, Alexa?" said Stassy, as she pushed past. "What are you doing?"

"Sun...Day...Plan...Et. Lies, lies and more lies,"

shrieked Alexa.

"White lies and cash, Alexa...white lies and cash," responded Stassy. "Who gives a shit? Who are you? Mother Fucking Theresa? The truth police? The only thing that will stop me doing this is four grand. You going to give me that?...didn't think so..."

"You know I don't have that sort of money, Stassy," continued Alexa, much more calmly now. "I am trying so hard to make this work. I have such a short time to make this a success."

Trying to keep a straight face, Stassy burst into song. "You're beautiful, you're beautiful, you're beautiful, it's true," she wailed in a sarcastic attempt at the naff James Blunt ballad currently hogging the airwaves.

"Yes, well, my looks won't last forever, you know...however much I apply that miracle night cream to my face. I will still get old. Can't you see...look at the wrinkles starting to appear."

Stassy rolled her eyes and tucked into her 'spag bol' ready meal, slurping up her first mouthful noisily.

"Contrary to popular belief," said Alexa. "I'm struggling to make ends meet at the moment. Do you know how many castings I go to that amount to absolutely nothing? I am getting the odd bit of work here and there, it keeps me going, but I can't afford to be thrown in the gutter over something so ridiculous."

"Alexa, take a chill pill, mate," reasoned Stassy. "It's one day, one interview, one story. We will not mention your name. You will not be thrown into the gutter. Don't be so fucking paranoid."

"Well," hissed Alexa. "I better not be. I fucking better not be...or there will be hell to pay. I mean it, Stassy. You are messing with the wrong person if you think you can stand in the way of me and MY career."

Alexa stormed out of the room, slamming the

lounge door shut as she went.

~

Tuesday arrived. Preston went into work in the morning and then took the rest of the day off. Stassy did the same and the intrepid duo met in a pub in Whitechapel, where the famous *Sunday Planet* offices were based.

They had a pint of beer each – Dutch courage – and discussed their strategy.

"What's the plan Stass?" asked Preston.

"Let's go with the flow. Just let me do the talking," Stassy breezed, confidently.

"Fine," said Preston.

The pair checked into the *Sunday Planet* reception, and after a brief wait were whisked through security, taken up to the newsroom and marched into an interview room. *News 24* was blasting out on TV monitors everywhere they looked. The breaking news was that John Profumo, the man at the centre of the most famous political scandal of the 20th Century, had died at the age of 91. More scandal would be coming up fast, but first Preston needed the toilet, and turned to Stassy, mouthing: "I've got the shits."

While Preston hot-trotted to the toilet, Stassy started scanning her contact list. She was sure she could really do with a strong hard fuck after all of this...especially if she were asked to go into all the saucy tell-all details expected from a tabloid exclusive. But who would be the man for this particularly particular job? She picked out a couple of names randomly, and sent some speculative texts.

Preston returned from the toilet looking as white as a sheet.

God help us, thought Stassy.

Raquel collected Stassy and Preston from reception and took them to a meeting room where a young lady with a far too low-cut top asked if they wanted any drinks. She didn't have the gin and tonic Stassy requested so they settled for water.

Raquel spoke.

"It's fantastic to finally meet you face-to-face Preston...and you must be Anastasia?"

Stassy nodded and curtsied, inappropriately.

"So we will just begin, today, by running through your survey entry. Please expand as and when you see fit. Does that work for both of you? I must say, it's good to see you are still friends through all of this."

"Well, it's easy when you suddenly go off cocks," said Stassy, announcing herself in textbook fashion.

Preston almost gasped. Stassy had already taken this interview past the white lies phase, but why was he surprised?

"Are you OK, Preston?" asked a concerned Raquel.

"Yes, yes, I'm fine," he reassured her. "We are friends but at times like this I find the rejection of the male form painful, as it was the reason for our split."

"I'm sorry, but breasts..." continued Stassy, eyeing Raquel up-and-down for effect, "...they're just so much more appealing, sensual and tender. I now fail to see whatever drew me to cocks in the first place."

"OK, well, erm, let's get back to a happy place, shall we?" said Raquel, gingerly, instinctively fastening an extra button on her blouse. "So talk me through when you guys met, when you got married, etc..."

"We met at freshers' week at the halls of residence bar," recalled Stassy. "We were drunk. Annihilated, in fact. We snogged at the bar and then shagged in my room. I woke up with a huge hangover and with Preston in my bed. He claimed he was in love with me...and I have to say he was nice to have around, when neither of us really knew anyone else. The relationship grew. We met more like-minded people, partied together, had fun. We became like this double act...like *Starsky & Hutch*, *Cagney & Lacey*... Stassy and Preston."

"And then the wedding bells...," said Raquel, trying to speed things along so she could get to the crux of the matter.

"Looking back it was a little foolish," continued Stassy. "We came out of university and moved to London. We moved in with our Uni mates, but we just didn't have our separate identity. Everyone kept saying: 'Won't you put a ring on her finger?' So one day he produced one. How could I say no? Our wedding was relatively low key, but it seemed to seal our relationship."

"Talk me through the infidelity," said Raquel.

"It was me, all me," said Stassy, clasping her head in her hands and pretending to stifle a cry.

"Take a moment," said Raquel, feigning concern. "Take a moment."

Stassy took a deep breath.

"Sarah was like a dream," she enthused. "She just looked so amazing in the club...so hot. The moment I saw her I lost control. I wanted her. Preston had been working late. I was on my own. I walked across to her and introduced myself."

Preston stared impassively ahead. Inwardly cringing. Secretly perving.

"The moment our eyes met I knew I wanted her and I knew she wanted me," explained Stassy. "The desire was so intense. She made me tingle all over, I was so aroused. We began to talk, the air was electric around us. I wanted her so badly. We talked incessantly and slightly incoherently for about 15 minutes. I grabbed her, held her close to me and kissed her...kissed her hard. Preston went out of my mind, the desire for Sarah was so overwhelming."

This was good, Preston thought. Too good, in fact. How the hell had he found himself in this situation?

Stassy was relentless with her description of what supposedly happened that night. "Sarah had never had a lesbian relationship before," she continued. "And my only one had been a brief encounter in my teens and that only really amounted to a snog. That night I wanted more. Sarah suggested we went back to her place...which we did...and she totally blew my mind. The orgasm I experienced that night was the strongest I had ever experienced. It took me into a different world. I almost lost consciousness."

Preston undid the top button on his polo shirt, and mopped his brow.

"After that I could not keep my mind from Sarah. She dominated my thoughts morning, noon and night. Every minute I could, I spent with her. In the end it wasn't fair on Preston. He thought we were just mates. I had to come clean and tell him my heart was with Sarah."

Raquel looked at Preston and he dutifully looked glum.

"I can see this is all bringing back painful memories, Preston," she said.

"Very painful indeed. I loved Stassy. I still do, to be honest," said Preston, finally touching on some truth. "In my book marriage meant forever," he continued. "I worried maybe she would tire of me one day, find a new man, but to lose her to a woman was just soul-destroying."

"I can imagine, you poor thing," said Raquel, suddenly heartfelt, and momentarily forgetting the need for impartiality when both parties are present.

Composing herself, Raquel said: "So Preston, talk

me through how you met Ralph?"

Almost in a whimper at first, and far less fluently or confidently as Stassy had, Preston started to explain.

"Well, you see, what happened was...erm...when Stassy moved out to live with Sarah, well, I was in pieces...couldn't sleep, couldn't eat...I was inconsolable..."

Looking up at the ceiling, Preston wondered if he could do this. He poured himself a glass of water, and continued.

"I just didn't know what to do with myself. I was all over the place and actually began questioning my own sexuality. I went out one night and ended up in a gay bar, which is where I met Ralph. Our fling was short, but intense and I realised as much as I was drawn towards Ralph, I just wasn't gay...and that I had made a mistake. I feel terrible for hurting Ralph. I was confused...so confused. Looking back at it now, it was a dreadful way to behave."

Writing furiously, but looking very excited about the story that was starting to play itself out in her notepad, Raquel asked: "So where are you both now?"

"Well, Sarah and I are happy – really really happy," stressed Stassy. "We continue to be in a loving relationship."

"I am pleased that I have moved on," reflected Preston. "I now have a beautiful girlfriend, who I am very settled with."

"So a happy ending?" asked Raquel.

"Yes, of sorts," said Preston.

Raquel got some extra background information from Stassy and Preston. More and more immersed in the story and consumed by the web of lies their cash prize demanded, this time they fell effortlessly into the new characters they purported to be. Shaking hands with Raquel as they left, all parties said they would "be in touch."

The pub was calling. Stassy and Preston fell through the door of the nearest one, Stassy collapsing in a heap on a table in the corner...aggressively slapping her hand against it. "Oh my God, oh my God, oh my God," she exclaimed.

"You fucking crazy cow," declared Preston. "What the fuck have we done?"

They sank three pints each in barely twenty minutes, and tried to regroup. Stassy got the appropriate text back from fuck buddy option No 2, Rob, and shot off to his flat.

Up for a few more drinks with his partner-in-tabloid-crime, Preston had been dumped once more by his 'two-timing lesbian ex-wife', so sloped off home alone. Lucky old Rob.

~

Fully aware of the interview taking place at the *Sunday Planet* and the total apathy towards her plight from all concerned, Alexa was trying to keep herself busy, and Steve Keane had plenty to keep her entertained. Since New Year's Eve, they had been out together once, visiting various celebrity haunts, and she was delighted to be papped with him outside a private members' club in Piccadilly. Both playing it cool, they had gone their separate ways at the end of the date. Tonight, Alexa reckoned could be the night. It was a 'school night' and he had invited her to his place in Hampstead. He was going to cook.

Since Alexa had met the dashing, yet slight 'yoga sex guru' on New Year's Eve, Steve Keane had landed a presenter's job on the aptly titled lad's cable channel *Gary*. He was the last lad in town, but the channel had devised a smutty late-night tantric sex gameshow, *Tantric or Frantic?* Full of 'double entendres' and compromising positions for the show's predominantly twenty-something wannabe contestants, it was vaguely popular with students, but was probably only watched by 25 - 30,000 people...on a good day.

Alexa arrived at Belsize Chambers, a block of exclusive apartments. His was the penthouse. Fitting, she thought, for a sex God! She pressed the door bell. He buzzed her in and the lift took her to the 15th floor. His front door was ajar.

Steve Keane appeared, wearing a loincloth. The room smelled strongly of incense and the lights were dim. Scented candles were burning. In the background was Tibetan music. Rugs adorned the walls.

"Come into my lair," he teased.

Steve led Alexa into his front room. In the centre was a long, low coffee table with cushions all around it. "Sit down," he said. "Let me serve you."

Alexa sat down. Steve poured two glasses of wine and brought out mezze. He sat beside Alexa, his body gleaming.

After a little while Steve asked: "I call this 'Treat them mean, keep them Keane'. Would you like me to take you on an adventure?"

Alexa gazed into his eyes, almost pleading with him as she mouthed the word 'yes'.

"Take off all your clothes, except your panties," instructed Steve.

Alexa removed all her clothes, apart from her G-string.

"Are you aware of the downward dog, Alexa?" he inquired.

Alexa had undertaken a few basic yoga classes a few years ago. She knew what a downward dog was and nodded.

"Assume the position," instructed Steve forcefully.

Alexa placed her palms flat on the floor, her legs apart about a foot from her arms and her bottom high in the air. She pushed her head towards her chest, as far as she could manage. She stood on tip-toes and pulled in her tummy muscles by taking a deep breath.

"The downward dog utilises every muscle group," explained Steve. "Which is why it is such an iconic yoga position."

Steve observed Alexa's attempt at the position. "Bottom higher, legs a little further back, tummy in more and head further towards chest," he explained, and then gently guided his muse's head.

"Much better posture," he purred, brushing against her. "You have a wonderful body Alexa, so toned, so slim, so taut," he continued. "You need to be good to do it. I need you to be good to do it. Now you need to be a good student of mine, Alexa. Do you understand?"

Alexa would have nodded but was too concentrated on keeping her head close to her chest.

"Uh-huh," she agreed.

"Excellent," he said, running his hand tantalisingly over her backside. "If you don't understand, I will make you understand. I hope that is understood."

Alexa was beginning to wobble – it was a long time since she had practiced yoga – and it sounded like she would be spanked if the next position didn't go to plan. Wow, this Steve Keane was quite something.

"Keep in position," stressed Steve. "Keep in position."

Steve tantalised Alexa, running his fingers up her inner thighs.

"Keep in position," he reminded her.

Alexa was shaking, both from the maintenance of the position and the fact she was now incredibly turned on. Steve disappeared into the kitchen, returning with a pair of scissors. He carefully cut one side of Alexa's panties, which fell effortlessly to the floor.

Fuck, she thought. They were the most expensive knickers she owned.

"Keep in position, Alexa," he reiterated once more.

Alexa struggled to retain the downward dog as Steve continued to run his hand over her body, squeezing her nipples. She wanted Steve and she wanted him now. Eventually he commanded her to the floor. As she lay on the rug Steve made love to her furiously...again and again. Alexa orgasmed several times, and he seemed to do so internally on each occasion. After what seemed like an eternity he came and then led her to the bedroom, where they collapsed on the bed...no more than a mattress on the floor surrounded by wafting sheets, but with the effect of a low-slung four poster bed, and with a heady smell of more incense.

I could be in Thailand, not Belsize Park, thought an ecstatic Alexa, her body aching all over, but inwardly euphoric too, as she drifted happily off to sleep.

6

Alexa woke up around 8am in Steve's bed, but he was nowhere to be seen. She walked through to the kitchen to find a bowl of granola, yoghurt and fruit and some very green looking juice. Steve had left a note.

Left early for meditation. Last night was
awesome. I look forward to the next time.
I shall call you soon gorgeous, just pull the
door closed when you leave - Steve xx

Alexa purred. This was something she could see herself doing again. That was like no other night...ever.

~

Refreshed and on time, Alexa arrived in Wapping at the Headlines Global HQ burning with pleasure, to be interviewed for her pilot beauty column. She decided she would be advising the public on the benefits of drinking lots of water and practising yoga.

As usual, there was a flurry of activity in the newspaper's sprawling offices.

A casual smoker at best, Alexa – as usual, when she was stressed ahead of a shoot or column chat – hurried to the smoking room.

Rachel and a few of the journalists were sat there debating.

"So do you really think, if you are straight, like properly straight not bisexual..." said Raquel to another hack, "...that the trauma of a break-up could actually make someone have a gay relationship?"

"I think there is a bit of gay in all of us," responded the reporter. "It's feasible."

"Good enough for me," replied Raquel. "It's a great story. Let's run with it."

"Great, but if you are really worried about authenticity then ask for something that corroborates it."

"You're right, let's do that," said Raquel.

Alexa was frozen to the spot. Surely they couldn't be talking about...they were! She drew on her cigarette and listened.

~

Raquel called Preston.

"Oh, hi there, nice to speak to you again," Preston answered a little nervously, hoping the apprehension in his voice wasn't obvious.

"I've spoken to my superior, and we really like this story. It's definitely going to run this weekend. We love it, but we just want some old photos to go with it. Is there any chance we could have something from your wedding day please?"

Preston almost gasped, but managed to hold it together. He was never good at thinking quickly on his feet, and was beginning to wish he hadn't been able to blag it so confidently when the paper first called him. Should he say there weren't any, they were burnt in a fire, flood-damaged or eaten by his dog? Nothing that flashed through his mind sounded convincing.

"Wedding photos? Of course," he said. "When do

you need them by?"

"By the end of tomorrow?"

"Yes, of course, that should work...and you're running the story this weekend?"

"Yes, as long as we get the photos by tomorrow before I leave – 6.30pm – then the story will run this weekend."

"And payment?" asked Preston.

"It will be in both your accounts Monday morning, a 50:50 split."

"Great," said Preston. "Can you give me that in writing?"

"Yes, you will have a contract to sign when you bring the photos in...allowing us to run the story and committing us to paying you. I will need Anastasia to sign too."

"Fine," concluded Preston. "The photos will be with you by 5pm tomorrow."

~

Preston rang Stassy.

"D'ya want the good news or the bad news first?"

"Good News...natch," said Stassy.

"They are running the story this weekend and we will have £3,750 each in our accounts by Monday morning."

"That's great – and the bad news?"

"We need to be in Whitechapel at 5pm tomorrow to sign the contract and..."

"That's not such bad news..."

"...and bring our wedding photos with us..."

"SHIT, SHIT, MOTHER FUCKING SHIT. Preston, what did you say? Couldn't you have talked her out of the wedding photos?"

"Not without sounding like a complete fraud. What

did you expect me to say?"

"Perhaps they were at your parents' house...in South Africa?"

"Well, I am sorry Stassy, to be honest, I have never been as good at lying as you."

"We're fucked...how are we going to get ourselves out of this mess?"

"Well, you got us into this mess...I'll call you back in 15 minutes Stassy, by which time you need to come up with a fucking plan."

The line went dead.

Stassy paced around the car park at work. There had to be a way...there was a way.

She called Preston back.

"Meet me in The Islington Shed at 8pm," she rallied. "I will bring some troops, but we can't use Ralph or Sarah as we may need them later and they wouldn't have attended the wedding anyway. Sarah can come for planning purposes."

Stassy left work and managed to catch the charity shop as it was just closing its doors.

"Please let me in," she begged. "It's kinda important."

The manageress relented, and she crept in apologetically.

"I need a wedding dress," said Stassy. "Urgently!"

"Oh, I see, well, we have some lovely ones over here. Is this some sort of shotgun wedding or a Gretna Green affair?"

"Something like that."

Stassy settled on the only one that just about fitted. It was hideous but desperate times called for desperate measures. She gave the lady £20 and left the shop. She had a wedding to go to.

~

"Right," said Stassy, sat at a table at the Shed with a large glass of white wine in front of her. "We don't have a lot of time to plan this. Like, no time at all. We need to assemble a posse tomorrow morning. I suggest we all meet at 8am at Islington Town Hall? We're more likely to get people before work."

She looked around the table. Sarah, Preston and Chloe looked glumly back at her.

"We're not exactly a wedding party," said Chloe.

"And I can't even be party to this wedding, given I'm supposed to have met you in a club a few years later," Sarah reminded them.

"OK, so you can be the photographer, Sarah," said Stassy, leaping up, grabbing the pub landlord, Dave, and pleading: "Could you be my dad, please Dave?"

"What?" said Dave. "I don't need another daughter. I have enough shit off the ex-wife about our two."

Stassy, squeezing tighter on the landlord's hand, her face now inches from his, whispered: "C'mon Davey, wavey, you wouldn't let one of your favourite punters down, would you?"

"Now, I don't mind being your boyfriend, love...maybe we could come to an arrangement," said Dave with a glint in his eye and a raspy Sid James chuckle.

The familiar cackle reminded Stassy of her own dad, who tragically died from a heart attack two and a half years ago. His passing left a huge void in Stassy's life, and possibly explained her live-for-the-moment attitude. She paused to picture her father laughing at the bar in his own favourite pub, raised her glass to the ceiling, regrouped, and then returned to the moment.

"Dave, c'mon, less of that," she joked. "Will you be my dad? Yes or no. It'll be 30 minutes of your life, and you might even appear in the paper this weekend."

"Alright, Stassy, love, anything for you."

Stassy decided against asking Dave to bring his larger-than-life wife, Sandra, to act as her mother. She didn't want a stunt double for her mum, and certainly not one double the size. Her mother was still incredibly attractive for her age, slim, and prided herself on her appearance. Stassy knew that if her mother found out she had substituted her with Sandra she would never hear the end of it. Also, there just wasn't time to explain the ludicrous situation or to get her to London, so she would have to wing that one.

There was simply not enough time to convince everybody face-to-face, certainly if Dave was anything to go by. A scattergun approach was needed, so Stassy and Preston sent the following text to anybody they vaguely thought might be able to help and might be game for a laugh.

Please come to Islington Town Hall tomorrow at 8am, please wear clothes you may have worn to a wedding four years ago. Your photo may appear in the Sunday Planet this weekend. It's a long story, but you'll be helping us out immensely. We thank you from the bottom of our hearts and owe u one! Stassy and Preston x

Stassy sank back in her chair and stared back at Preston. "You need either a mum or a dad too...or both?"

"Thank you Stass, but I already have lovely parents..."

"Yes, but they live in South Africa," pointed out Stassy. "And I don't fancy their chances of making it to Upper Street by 8am tomorrow morning."

"I'll ask our next-door neighbours," said a resigned Preston. "I'm sure they will do me a favour. The old woman's got a soft spot for me. It's my only hope."

Preston left the pub to explain to a very confused Harry and Barbara what he needed them to do.

~

Around 25 people turned up to Islington Town Hall the next morning. A peculiar ensemble of guests, it must be said.

Stassy had plucked some flowers from someone's garden a few doors down from the pub and fashioned a bouquet as she walked down Upper Street.

Harry and Barbara, a sweet couple in their early '70s, had remarkably agreed to take part.

Stassy had even blagged herself a grandmother - a lovely old dear that drank at the pub who Dave the landlord brought with him.

"I do love a day out," she kept saying, during all 45 minutes of it.

Sarah took copious photos and got quite into the idea of being the official wedding photographer.

"Bride and Groom," she barked.

Somehow Chloe had managed to become one of the two bridesmaids, the other girl an old friend of Stassy's. It was decided that if they both wore a blue dress, of sorts, it would be OK.

"Bride and bridesmaids," bellowed Sarah. "OK, now I need bride with parents and any grandparents."

The photos went on. Sarah took shot after shot.

People on their way to work down Upper Street checked their watches and looked on in disbelief. The Islington Town Hall registry workers were particularly bemused when they arrived for work as the last few pictures were taken.

"We lost our wedding photos and wanted to recreate them," Stassy told them.

At just before 8.45am Stassy thanked everyone for coming, kissed each member of her new-found family and friends on both cheeks, and sent them on their merry way.

"Mwah, mwah...mwah, mwah..."

Lamenting the fact that Sarah hadn't upgraded to a digital camera yet, Stassy clutched the tiny black photograph film case in her hand like her life depended on it, reaching the local Quicky Pics store minutes after it opened. Later that afternoon she left work early – "migraine" – to pick up the photos on the way through to the newspaper offices to meet Preston. The best ten pictures were delivered, accepted and contracts were signed.

It wasn't the bridal look Stassy had imagined as a child, but beggars clearly couldn't be choosers here. And anyway, they were just out of uni back then...money would have been tight. It still was.

"It's been a pleasure working with you both," beamed Raquel. "I expect you'll be a little apprehensive in the run up to publication, but that's to be expected," before adding patronisingly: "For the record, I think what you've both done here is really brave."

"Thanks so much," said Stassy and Preston together, both oblivious to the faux-concern Raquel was showing.

The pair found the nearest pub and sat in the corner...shaking.

"What have we started?" said Preston.

"It'll be fine," said Stassy. "The papers are always making stuff up. You'll feel better when you get the money in your account on Monday. It will be one small story, in one weekend supplement, which hardly anyone will read. Tomorrow's fish and chip paper, they say. It will be forgotten in a week, and we will have the cash in our bank account. What on earth could go wrong?"

7

Saturday morning, and Alexa had been waiting for Steve's call, by now very much hoping to be invited to his place again that night. Her body was slowly beginning to regain its balance and she felt it might be time for her to begin her 'studies' again. There had been so much going on with Stassy. That had been stressful enough. Early yesterday morning there had been a huge flurry of activity as everyone left unusually early. She knew Stassy was in full flow with this *Sunday Planet* article, but she just couldn't bear to think about it. Just after lunchtime the text finally came through from Steve.

> *Hey gorgeous – can't stop thinking*
> *about you. Fancy coming over to my*
> *place tonight – 9pm. I want you x*

Alexa waited a good seven and a half minutes before she replied.

> *See you at 9pm x*

That evening she chose her outfit very carefully. She was conscious not to put on her second most expensive panties this time, eventually opting for a good day-to-day pair she could just about bear having torn from her.

Alexa left her house at 8.30pm in a taxi and arriving a little too early, she took a tactical walk around the block. Just after 9pm, now ten minutes fashionably late, she rang the bell. Steve let her up to the 15th floor.

As she walked through the door, he grabbed her, drew her close and kissed her passionately.

"You haven't been out of my mind for long, baby," he said, holding and kissing her excitedly. "Are you ready to come on another adventure with me, baby?" He looked at her longingly, adding: "I must warn you, this will be a journey of pain and pleasure in equal measures, but, as ever, I'll treat you mean, keep you Keane...and take you to somewhere only we know."

"Let's do it," said Alexa confidently, conveniently forgetting the physical torture she had endured after their last session.

"Good. Take your clothes off...all of them off for me now, baby. Do it slowly...really slowly."

Alexa complied, carefully removing each layer of clothing until she was standing in front of Steve completely naked.

"Before we continue," said Steve, with a glint in his eye, and pointing to the spiral staircase in the centre of the room. "I need you to go and sit on the naughty step."

"Erm...OK, but naked?"

"Well, that's why it's the naughty step," replied Steve.

Alexa did as she was told, trying to hide her modesty as best possible, as she sat perched on the third step up.

Steve circled around Alexa for several seconds, and then leaned in to kiss her tenderly on the lips.

"Right baby, I now want you in the Dhanurasana position - the bow."

Guided by Steve, Alexa laid down on the floor, and tried to assume the required position.

"Lie on your stomach," instructed Steve. "That's it...and now bring your chest up, arms behind your back, holding your ankles...that's right, baby."

Steve went into the kitchen and returned with a packet of nipple clamps, which he opened slowly, and expertly attached to Alexa's pert bosom. He then bound her hands to her ankles with rope, produced a wooden paddle and started to spank her behind...hard and forcefully.

The naughty step suddenly seemed slightly more mischievous.

Alexa gasped, but again she was also incredibly turned on.

Steve wielded the paddle again...and again...four times in total ...THWACK ...THWACK ...THWACK ...THWACK.

"Stay with me baby," implored Steve. "I must keep you in that position."

THWACK THWACK THWACK. Three more firm slaps.

Steve stopped only to grip Alexa's buttocks, massaging them at the same time. "Baby, now I will make you come. I need you to be a good student for me."

Alexa complied, spectacularly screaming and yelping, the ropes burning into her wrists and ankles as she wriggled and writhed. Steve took the clamps off and Alexa gasped again...some welcome relief. He then slowly removed the shackles holding her ankles and wrists together. Alexa was shaking, quivering on the rug. Steve lifted her up and took her to his bed and this time took her in a wholly more orthodox way.

~

Alexa woke around 8am on Sunday morning...this time Steve was still in bed.

"Morning gorgeous," he said, leaning across to kiss her.

"Morning," said Alexa, both groggily and happily.

Before she had a chance to say much more Steve had lifted her arms above her head, pinning her to the bed. Her wrists were sore from where the ropes had been, but as he pressed on them again it brought back memories of the night before and the mind-blowing orgasm that Alexa had experienced, so she succumbed to the 'power of Keane' once more.

"You ready for round two, baby?" asked Steve, relentlessly. Alexa was more than ready, but this time it was all over relatively quickly... well relatively quickly by Steve's standards, anyway.

"Let's get soapy," he said shortly after.

Alexa and Steve showered together in his huge walk-in wall-to-floor tiled wet room. Steve could not keep his hands off Alexa. "One last time for the road, baby?" Steve pleaded. Alexa could not resist him, so dutifully agreed.

~

Conversely, Stassy's Sunday morning began with another 'stranger' in her bed. She had been out in Shoreditch the night before, back pretty late, and was slowly piecing the night together in her mind when she realised she was not alone. She suddenly remembered she had dragged some bloke back...Andy or Ashley...and now she could feel him breathing next to her.

He was still asleep and, by carefully peeking under the covers, Stassy tried to assess what she had managed to pull. He seemed OK, maybe a bit more beardy than her usual type. This could be tricky.

Stassy was desperate to go and pick up the *Sunday Planet*. She had a date with destiny, and had butterflies in her stomach. She felt sick. She was also feeling pretty hungover and sleep-deprived. It was 10am and she hadn't got to bed until five.

She grabbed some clothes and went to the shower to wash away the sins of the previous night. She dressed and peered around her bedroom door. Aaron, Alan...or whatever he was called, was thankfully out for the count.

She went downstairs and called Preston. He answered the phone, sounding surprisingly bright and breezy.

"Morning Stass, how are you?"

"Hanging..."

"Seen the paper yet?"

"No."

"Well, we're in it. Congratulations...you should be very proud," said Preston, mockingly.

"Is it OK?"

"No, it's pretty bad."

"Right. I'm straight out now to grab a copy. Shall we meet at Highbury Corner for some breakfast?"

"11.30am at the Turkish greasy spoon?"

"See you there."

Stassy's head started pounding and she began to feel more nauseous...to make matters worse, there were sounds coming from her bedroom.

FUCK, she thought. This morning...of all mornings.

She tentatively opened her bedroom door.

"Morning," she said cautiously.

"Morning, beautiful," a gruff voice came back from under her covers.

"How are you doing?"

71

"Feeling a bit delicate, to be honest," replied her mystery man. "Last night was amazing, baby. You were hot, and I would love to do it again."

"Well, OK, great, but I have something I need to do this morning," explained Stassy. "But maybe call me? Shall I give you my number?"

"That would be good."

"Give me your phone," she demanded, grumpily.

He handed over his handset and Stassy punched in a number, vaguely resembling hers. "There you go...Sta-a-assy," she said, assuming he was also having name amnesia, and now standing hand on hips, and adopting a facial expression which screamed: "Time to go."

Sloping out of the bed sheepishly, as he assumed he was now expected to do, the poor guy slung on his clothes, kissed her on the cheek and left the room, bumbling out of the door.

Stassy's head was spinning. She stripped her bed and put the sheets in the wash, grabbed her purse, phone and coat, and left.

The convenience store was at the end of the road. She grabbed the paper and walked through Highbury Fields. The sun was shining. It was a lovely day, but Stassy just felt sick with anticipation, heavy with a dreadful hangover.

Preston was sat in the corner of the cafe when she arrived. Quickly ordering a full English breakfast and "lots of coffee" she opened up the paper. There was the article. Slap bang in front of her, a double spread in the magazine on pages three and four, with a headline screaming...OUR SURVEY SAID 'SEX'!!!... alongside the accompanying strapline...STUDENT SWEETHEARTS' CRAZY LOVE LIVES EXPOSED.

The piece was in Q&A format, with photos taken during the office interview dominating the right-hand page and a splattering of the stunted-up wedding snaps across the bottom.

This was no longer a joke, not that Preston had ever really seen the funny side of it. Stassy now had that cheeky smile on the other side of her face, hardly finding much to laugh about either. This was real now. They were in deep, in print and inked into millions of magazine supplements...Stassy and Preston's fibs, lies and fake love lives exposed to the nation.

"I would never look so minging on my wedding day," moaned Stassy. "I look shocking. That dress is so awful...and the flowers...urgh! The bridesmaids look dreadful too. It looks like some red-neck wedding you see on the internet."

"Yes, and they've embellished my love for Ralph," said Preston. "It's so embarrassing...how I dreamed about his stubbly beard and his long locks...I never said that."

The phone rang. Instinctively, they knew it was Sarah.

"Hi Sarah," said Stassy.

"I've just woken up. Shattered after the play last night."

"Did it go well?" asked Stassy.

"Yes," said Sarah. "Anyway, never mind that. How is the article?"

"A bit embarrassing, to be honest," admitted Stassy. "And a bit too near the front of the magazine for me...a two-page spread. You have nothing to worry about, by the way...you come across as a highly skilled photographer."

"Where are you?"

"Having brunch at Highbury Corner...the Turkish...with Preston."

"I'm on my way."

Stassy looked at Preston, momentarily dropping

her guard. "What the hell are we going to say when people start asking?"

There was an eerie silence for a few minutes as the realisation of the magnitude of what they had both done dawned on Stassy and Preston.

"Couldn't we be done for fraud?" said Preston. "I mean, we are being paid for this and we have signed a contract."

"Fuck," said Stassy, distracted. "How old do you think I look in these wedding photos?"

"In that dress...about 40. It's awful," said Preston.

"Well, I think we should say it was a long time ago."

"But we're only 26," argued Preston. "Just how long ago could it have been?"

"Well, nobody who knows us is going to believe I am a lesbian or in a long-term relationship with Sarah or that we've been married."

"No," said Preston. "We'll have to tell our friends we lied. Ask them not to tout the story around. We can't have the *Sunday Planet* coming after us...and what about work?"

"Well, if we don't get fired, let's just try and play it down," suggested Stassy. "Say it all happened a long time ago. Some reporter rang you saying he'd heard about it and wanted to run the story and we thought we might as well get some money...and we're bit surprised about the content."

"Just noticed," said Preston calmly. "The article is entitled 'As a result of our 2005 sex survey, the best entry was...'"

"Hmmm?" pondered Stassy. "Right, got it...the official line is...*we kinda bent the truth for a little cash.* Let people work out what is true and what isn't?"

Stassy ordered more coffee as Sarah arrived, clutching a copy of the magazine, and shaking her head.

"Well, well, Stass," she said. "Are you happy with your little masterpiece?"

"Hmmm?" replied Stassy.

"That's a fine little mess you've got us all into, isn't it, darling?" added Sarah.

"Well, at least you're only mentioned in name, Sarah," reasoned Preston. "Muggins here is plastered all over the piece."

"So am I..." said Stassy, indignantly.

"Well, it's no more than you fucking deserve, for coming up with that stupid survery in the first place."

"Well, you didn't have to go along with it, did you? Dickhead!"

"Guys, guys..." said Sarah, stepping into referee. "Come on, now, now..."

Stassy's mobile rang...followed by Preston's... helping further to defuse the bickering: various members of the 'wedding party', phoning in various states of hysterics.

After a while, Stassy stopped answering. It was just all too painful. Who knew so many of their friends and their friends' parents read the *Sunday Planet*? Calls from people she hadn't seen or heard from in years. This shit was powerful.

So far, though, no calls from either Preston or Stassy's family. Stassy didn't think she could cope with that today. Preston was pleased his family was in Africa where the *Sunday Planet* circulation was almost non-existent.

~

Later that night, after a day taking and dodging various phone calls, and largely drinking red wine to drown her sorrows, as Stassy was drifting off to sleep, a text came through.

Hey gorgeous, last night was fantastic. I would love to see you again, but I am concerned I might not be enough. As you should have noticed, I don't have any breasts? Also, how does Sarah feel about last night or doesn't she know? Adrian x

Shit, thought Stassy. She would respond tomorrow. She had had quite enough for one day.

8

Stassy traipsed into the office on Monday morning and walked to her desk, head bowed. It was like the whole team were staring and glaring at her. Her freelance contract fortunately meant she would be out of there in three weeks.

Avoiding eye contact and needless chit-chat, Stassy ploughed through her 18 overnight voicemails. Wow, they were all coming out of the woodwork now. A whole host of old school friends she hadn't spoken to since her teens...how on earth had they got her mobile number? University friends too.

Stassy checked her bank account. The money had cleared.

"Thank fuck for that," she squealed, vowing to escape on holiday as soon as possible. She was just about to start looking on the internet for suitable destinations when the phone rang from a private number. Reluctantly, she took it.

"Hi there, is that Stassy?" a deep raspy male voice said on the other end of the line.

"This...is...her," said Stassy hesitantly.

"I am calling from *Nearer* magazine."

"OK," said Stassy, well aware of the popular tabloid weekly. "Let me just go and find a quiet corner."

Stassy headed to the car park, one of her many second homes over the last few weeks. "I can talk now."

"Well," continued the voice. "My name is Marcello

and I am a features writer. I'm keen to have a follow-up interview with you from the piece that went out in the *Sunday Planet* yesterday. As our target audience is women aged 16-30, it would be fantastic if I could run a story with you and your current partner."

"Um? OK," said Stassy, before fibbing: "I have had quite a few calls this morning already, from a few of your competitors, can't say who, so the money would need to be right."

"Well, I have £5,000 signed off," replied Marcello.

"I think we'd need more than that," said Stassy. "My partner has been reluctant to get involved so far, so I'd need to twist her arm..."

"OK, let me see what I can do. I'll have to go back to my superiors. How would £7,000 wash?"

"I can probably convince her for eight..."

"That's a lot of money," said Marcello.

"I understand, but it's a good story and we will give you all the stuff that wasn't in the *Sunday Planet*."

"OK, I may be able to do it...as long as we've got the exclusive on this, if you don't do any other press before we publish."

"Let me talk to Sarah tonight and see what she says...call you first thing tomorrow," said Stassy, before adding like a true tell-all pro: "When would you need to interview us and when would you go to print?"

"Interview tomorrow or Wednesday for publication on Friday."

"OK," said Stassy, taking Marcello's number.

Within seconds she was on the line to Sarah.

"How do you fancy earning four big boys?"

"400 pounds?" said Sarah.

"No, four thousand, silly," said Stassy. "Four large ones, four bags of sand..."

"Bags of what?" asked Sarah.

"Four grand, you dopey mare...c'mon, get with it."

"Wow, four thousand...sounds great, but what do I have to do?"

"An interview with me for *Nearer* magazine."

"Right...," said Sarah, letting the idea take hold.

"Thursday or Friday."

"OK," replied Sarah. "I think I'm game. I'm just saying I am your girlfriend, right? It'll help me get into my role of the bisexual nymph in the theatre."

"Yes, a bisexual nymph is just what we need. Laters."

Stassy went back into the office. The stares seemed to be more plentiful and even more intense.

~

Alexa called Chloe. She was fuming.

"What the fuck have you done?"

Chloe closed her office door.

"OK, what's up?"

"Well, what do you think is wrong with me? The piece in the paper! I was meditating with Steve yesterday, so have only just seen it. I was doing my usual mid-morning scan of the weekend papers for any column inches of me and Steve...and there it was. So embarrassing...and absolute bullshit, just pure and utter bollocks. And what the hell is going on with those wedding photos? Fucking ridiculous. Why did you get yourself involved? You look like a very strange bridesmaid...and Stassy looks fucking horrendous. You all look like you are at some hideous trailer trash wedding. It's a total car crash...AWFUL, AWFUL, AWFUL."

"Please try and calm down, Alexa. They both really need the money. They still have loads of student debt."

"But at what price?" screamed Alexa. "At what fucking price? They are off their heads. What do they

79

think they are doing? They could seriously derail their careers, their reputation and drag the rest of us down with them. Aren't you concerned? You know, in your position?"

"C'mon, Alexa, it's not like we're associating ourselves with drug dealers, smack heads or the Mafia."

"No, just fucking fraudsters, shysters, con men...in fact, one big fucking bitch of a con woman," fumed Alexa. "Where are your ethics? That fucking code you are signed up to. Remember? The Hippocratic Oath?"

"I'm legal, not medical, darling," said Chloe, starting to panic all the same. Had she implicated herself by being involved in a fake wedding photo? Surely the risk was pretty low.

Alexa continued.

"I live and die by my reputation. Reputation is everything to me. It's what my career is built on. I can't fall back on a professional qualification or 9 to 5 experience. It is about ME...ME, ME, ME and I have spent the last eight years building my career and not associating myself with FUCKING FRAUDSTERS. Stassy is a TWAT and, at this moment in time, I could fucking KILL HER."

Alexa did have a point, not the killing Stassy bit, but certainly the potential implications of the scam. None of them had really thought it through, except perhaps Chloe, who had clearly opted out of any direct involvement at the start.

Surely, though, this would all die down as quickly as it started. It was one article in one Sunday paper. Nobody would remember it next week, let alone the week after. Would they?

~

Preston was used to dealing with office gossip. His antics on work nights out were pretty renowned. Like the time he lost his trousers when they had an away-day in Brighton and he had to come back in his sea-sodden underpants.

Now once more, Preston was the talk of the water cooler, but, even by his own standards, he had definitely upped the ante this time. This story took his tattered reputation into a completely different 'tatt-o-sphere'.

The article and its key points had been passed around work like wildfire and everyone had something to say about it. Preston had not come out of this looking at all good, and his bosses were starting to worry about client implications. At around 2pm, he was hauled into one of the director's offices.

"Well, Preston," his boss said, laying out the *Sunday Planet* magazine piece on the desk in front of him. "What have you got to say about this?"

Preston looked him square in the eyes and said: "C'mon Geoff, please don't believe everything you read in the press."

"Is that all you have to say, Preston?"

"Yes, that is all I have to say."

"Well, Preston, let's just say this might not be the end of the matter. I have not decided yet whether to launch an internal investigation. I may have no option. This kind of behaviour is not fitting of a recruitment manager."

~

Alexa woke up and went to her Tuesday yoga class: she clearly needed to practise some moves if she was going to keep up with Steve. The class started with the 'sun salutation' followed by 'downward dogs'. While in position Alexa couldn't help finding herself being taken back to Steve's penthouse. She let out a momentary groan and received a few odd looks.

"Purist yoga," mumbled Alexa to herself. "Purist yoga."

In any case, she needed to relax and take her mind off the recent press debacle. So far the links between her, Stassy and Preston had not materialised. A few close friends had picked up on the stories...please let that be the end of it...but she just fobbed them off...said she didn't really know what was going on.

After the 'downward dog' the class moved into 'the bow'. Alexa's wrists were still a little red from her lover's rope-trick and Alexa couldn't avoid pressing on them as she got into position. Again, it took her back to Steve and she felt hugely turned on.

"C'mon, Lex. Concentrate on the yoga position... con...cen...trate..." muttered Alexa. She left the class and went home feeling a little more relaxed, and made herself a salad for lunch.

She got a text from Steve around 2pm suggesting they meet later that evening at his apartment.

~

Stassy called Marcello.

Marcello agreed to give her and Sarah the £8,000. They weren't to talk to anyone else before the interview, which was scheduled for the next day, Wednesday afternoon.

~

Meanwhile, Preston reckoned he had diffused the interest in him for now. Director Geoff had a soft spot for him, so he was hopeful he would turn a blind eye.

He was still getting knowing looks at work and some of the juniors were fixing on him with intensity. He reasoned this period of anxiety was totally worth it for the best part of four thousand pounds. He desperately needed the cash. It was tough living in London with the legacy of his university high life.

~

It had been a couple of weeks since Chloe had finished with Tom, and so far she had managed to avoid his attempts to rekindle their 'romance' with a handful of bumbling booty-calls.

She needed more than a late-night lover who invariably treated her house like a hotel. She needed someone who didn't want to check out at midday, but wanted to take her on their very own 'city break' - to the cinema, the theatre, dinner...or to just hang out with some room service.

Chloe decided to call Will, who she hadn't spoken to in a while. He wasn't going to give her hearts and flowers, but he would give her the attention she hadn't had for a while. He was a good university friend and an on/off lover over the years. More recently, because of Tom, he had been firmly off.

She called him and they arranged to meet up for a midweek movie and some food and inevitably the follow-on. She knew it wasn't the greatest call she had ever made, but it made her feel attractive, wanted. It also felt necessary after her recent 'drought'.

~

Alexa arrived at Steve's place at 7pm. She was getting a bit bored with not actually doing anything with him outside of his boudoir. While the sex was great, well more than great – it was bordering ever so slightly on mechanical, like he was putting her through his textbook moves. She shouldn't complain, she had had more orgasms in the last week than she'd had hot dinners – but she wondered how long that raw physical energy would suffice. She wanted more than that...something emotionally deeper. She pressed the buzzer and entered.

As she walked through the door, Steve grabbed her and they embraced.

Steve hadn't prepared any dinner and suggested getting a take-out.

"Let's pop out for something," suggested Alexa.

"Baby, it's so hard for me to go out at night without being recognised. Too many paps."

Not with your meagre TV audience and niche yoga books, Alexa thought, but dared not say out loud.

"It'll be fine," said Alexa reassuringly, trying to stifle a smirk. "Let's just go somewhere local. Put on a hat and sunglasses or something."

Steve reluctantly agreed, but refused to go out in anything that covered his face. It was too late in the day for shades.

He walked down the street almost willing people to recognise who he was. Very few people did...only a handful gave a second look.

They went to a cocktail bar which was walking distance from Steve's penthouse and drank margaritas.

"This is a bit weird," said Steve.

"Why?"

"Well, I never really do this with a girl."

"What?"

"Well, you know."

"No, I don't know."

"Well, go out for a drink like this. I mean, I've met

ladies in exclusive style bars and, well, taken them home, but I don't usually take them to a normal place in the High Street."

"OK, right...well, how does it feel?"

"Good...different...nice, I guess...but I think that is something to do with the company."

Alexa smiled. Correct answer.

They finished their cocktails and went to the local Indian restaurant, again another departure for Steve Keane.

Halfway through their meal, a gooey-eyed waiter appeared with some extra naan bread and sag aloo the pair hadn't ordered.

"It's Steve, innit?" he said. "Steve Keane...from *Tantric or Frantic*?"

"Erm, yes," said Steve sheepishly, but also unashamedly.

"Loving the show...I'm a bit frantic and tantric too, bruvs. You get me?"

The waiter placed the extra dishes on the table and took out an order pad from the back pocket of his trousers.

"On the house, innit," the waiter continued. "Couldn't just grab your autograph, could I, bruvs?"

Steve duly signed the order pad, looking pleased as punch as he scanned the dimly lit, half-empty restaurant for quizzical looks from other diners.

Alexa and Steve stumbled home around 11pm, full of curry and beer and not a paparazzi photographer in sight.

Steve actually hadn't realised he might be able to go out in Belsize Park without being mobbed.

The viewing figures for *Gary* were tiny compared to the big terrestrial channels. The autograph-hunting waiter aside, he actually seemed slightly disappointed someone hadn't thrown themselves at him.

Alexa realised that her lover lived in a bubble of his own making, that wasn't completely real. However, there was still something powerful that drew her to him.

Back in the penthouse they were tired but buzzing from each other's company. They went straight to bed, the passion electric and furious, but less energetic than previous sessions. It felt more meaningful, well at least to Alexa.

Steve seemed to agree. "You are changing me, Alexa," he whispered, as they drifted off to sleep.

Alexa smirked. Bloody hell! As much as she was trying to stop herself, she was falling in love with this man. Could she be the one that tamed him?

9

Sarah met Stassy outside the *Nearer* offices in Farringdon. Getting into her role rather too easily, she pulled her friend behind a pillar, cupped one of her breasts and planted a sloppy smacker on her lips.

"Easy, tiger," exclaimed Sarah.

"You ready for this?" asked Stassy.

"About as ready as I will ever be," gulped Sarah.

They walked into the publishing house's main foyer. It was Wednesday afternoon and the offices seemed pretty quiet. They were taken to a meeting room on the top floor and asked to wait.

Marcello blustered in.

"Well, well ladies...thanks for coming in today. It's great to meet you both."

"And you," said Stassy, grabbing Sarah's hand and looking longingly into her eyes.

Marcello shifted excitedly on his seat. He had often fantasised about hot lesbians. Like many of his peers, it was his favourite fantasy and these were two really hot girls. He told himself to keep calm.

"So, let's get down to the interview?" he said, authoritatively.

"That's a good idea," replied Stassy, again gazing deep into Sarah's eyes. "We love getting down, don't we, babe?"

Sarah didn't know how to respond. There was no option, but to stare lovingly with desire into Stassy's eyes. This is just an acting role for money, Sarah told herself. I act well...I get £4,000.

Marcello felt extremely turned on: what fun he could have with these two.

"Stay focused...stay focused," he said to himself again and again. "Let's start from the beginning," he announced.

"Well," began Stassy, pausing, momentarily faltering from her script as she realised just how sexy Marcello was. He must be of Italian heritage; his skin was dark and his hair was so lustrous. Stassy looked into his eyes and there was an immediate connection.

Stassy dragged her stare away from Marcello, moving back onto Sarah and began: "Well, I was married to a guy called Preston Price. We were happy enough. We had been together since university and life was pretty much sailing along. Then I met Sarah."

Of course, Stassy was married. A lightbulb moment for Marcello, who had somehow forgotten she was into men as well...

"We met in a club," continued Sarah. "It was love at first sight. Stassy was eyeing me up from across the dancefloor. That initial look...and immediately it was game over for both of us."

"Sarah was hot," interrupted Stassy. "I mean really hot! Her nipples were erect through her sweaty top. I wanted her like I had never wanted anyone in my life."

"Preston was working away," added Sarah. "And when she asked me to go back to hers...well, I just couldn't say no."

"So you were both virgins when it came to this type of relationship?" inquired Marcello.

"I had kissed a girl previously," admitted Stassy. "But it was more for high jinks than for any sexual pleasure. That night after the club, yes, I guess you could say I lost that virginity...and it was amazing. So pleasurable – a woman knows a woman, if you get what I mean?"

Marcello said he could well imagine what Stassy meant and shifted in his seat, strategically placing his notebook over his crotch area.

"Oooh," muttered Sarah to herself, probably too loudly, suddenly realising how sexy Marcello was too.

His face was well-chiselled, with designer stubble and his hair styled with just the right amount of product. Also fixing her gaze shamelessly on the vulnerable reporter, Sarah could see the shape of Marcello's chest through his grey fine knit polo shirt...and she could tell he was becoming more and more aroused.

He needed to get this interview back on track, as Sarah was now coming onto him as well. These were two highly sexual ladies.

"So what drew you to Sarah, do you think, Stassy?" continued Marcello.

"Well, at first it was simple raw attraction," continued Stassy. "Then after a while I realised that Sarah was very much like Preston. It was just that she had tits."

Stassy let go of Sarah's hand and placed her arm around Sarah's waist, almost caressing the outside of her left breast, her fingers there slightly too long.

Marcello's face was turning red, his forehead perspiring. He undid his top button, still holding his pad over his 'nether regions', trying to write notes at the same time. Awkward.

"And how did Preston take the news?" asked Marcello, struggling to compose himself.

"He was understandably devastated," continued Stassy. "When I sat him down to tell him I was leaving him for Sarah, he thought I was about to tell him I was pregnant. He really wanted a child, but I wasn't ready for that. The news came as a massive shock. He was inconsolable."

"How long did you and Sarah's affair continue before you let Preston know?" quizzed Marcello.

"It was about six months," added Sarah. "We needed to be sure it was real. It was all so new for both of us, and Stassy needed to be sure she really wanted to leave Preston, and then she wanted to be sure I wasn't a cry for help, that she was really in love with me and that she really wanted to have a full-on relationship with a woman."

"And also Sarah needed to make sure it's what she wanted too," interjected Stassy, tightening her grip around Sarah, and drawing her close. "It was the first time for her as well."

These two were bouncing off each other like a well-oiled kiss-and-tell double-act.

"So what do you see as the future for you both?" asked Marcello.

"Well, we know we want to be together," insisted Stassy. "And that's our main priority for now."

"We have even talked about children," said Sarah.

"Maybe each taking sperm donations at the same time so we could have twins," added Stassy ambitiously.

Twins? What are these two on? thought Marcello, frantically trying to scribble down all he was being told.

"But we just want to enjoy ourselves at the moment," continued Stassy. "We should enjoy each other's bodies while we are young and flexible. Breasts drop after pregnancy. I want to enjoy Sarah's pertness for as long as I can."

Marcello didn't think he could take any more. He thought it was time they got a room, but he would love to be with them as well. However, if they needed to live out their hearts' desires, he needed to get back to pulling together next week's issue.

"Well, thanks, that's great girls. I definitely have enough for my article. If it's OK, I may be in touch if I need to follow up on any points. I will just buzz through to our photographer Mark so we can get some photos done."

"Great," said Stassy. "And the story will run next week...we will get our money straight after publication?"

"Yes," said Marcello. "First, my story needs to get approved by the overall editor and then, yes, you will get paid if it runs, but I have no reason to believe that this story won't get published."

Marcello shifted towards the phone, ensuring his notebook was still hovering over his crotch. He called Mark, but didn't stand up when he appeared.

Mark led Stassy and Sarah to a room for a photoshoot, and after much pouting and preening they were free to go, as was now tradition, to the nearest pub.

"Fuck, that Marcello was fucking hot," said Stassy, as the pair walked arm-in-arm.

"Fuck yeah," said Sarah. "Made it really hard to keep in character."

"Well, HE was really hard," added Stassy, as they both burst into a hysterical laughing fit.

"Think about the money," said Stassy. "Four big boys each coming our way, girlfriend."

"I know," said Sarah. "I kept telling myself it was just an acting role, but I could murder a big boy...right now!"

"Well, Sarah, you are a very talented actress," conceded Stassy, trying to control her laughter. "I have to say that the whole thing got me quite hot, you sexy lady, you..."

"Let me get us a drink, Stassy," said Sarah, trying to diffuse the situation. "We bloody need one."

Fuck, she was finding Stassy hot too.

~

As the *Nearer* magazine office wound down for another day, Marcello and Mark were ogling at grabs from Stassy and Sarah's photoshoot.

"Mate, what were those girls like?" said Marcello.

"Pretty damn hot, son...pretty damn hot," agreed Mark.

"I was struggling to keep my calm, mate," continued Marcello. "They were coming onto each other and to me at the same time. I'm sure of it. I think there's more to this story than meets the eye."

"Well, let your eye meet this, my friend," said Mark, showing Marcello another shot of the girls embracing each other for the camera.

"You get all the good jobs, you lucky bastard," said Marcello.

"Excuse me...they weren't coming onto me, mate," reasoned Mark.

"Now, now, mate, it's not a competition. Let's just say it was a nice little end to the day for both of us, but I'm done. Can't concentrate on any work now. I need a drink. Pub? Beer?"

"Fucking right," said Mark, shutting down his computer and grabbing his bag, as he locked up the photographic studio on their way out.

Marcello quickly returned to his desk in the newsroom, briefly looking at the scribbles on his pad to try and make sense of what he'd written down. He tossed it into a drawer on his way out, chuckling, when he realised it was largely illegible.

~

The reporter and his snapper had come to the right place. Stassy and Sarah were both three pints to the good, their jaws dropping as Marcello and Mark swept into the pub, nodding to locals and high-fiving the bar staff as they loudly announced their arrival.

Marcello couldn't believe his luck as he spotted the girls, perched on bar stools at the other end of the ramp, and strode towards them.

"Well, I never," he said to himself. "If it isn't Martina Navratilova and Billy 'fricking' Jean King..."

"Game, set and snatch," quipped Mark, scuttling after him.

"Drinks, girls?" asked Marcello, brimming with an inner confidence that always engulfed him when he stepped into the pub.

The relatively shy reporter had been transformed...and Stassy and Sarah couldn't help but find him even more irresistible.

"Sure," said Stassy, sidling up to Marcello as he grabbed the barman's attention. "Jagerbombs all round please..."

"Yes please," said Sarah, vying for attention and position as she appeared on Marcello's other shoulder.

Mark shook his head as he answered his mobile, and sighed as he assured his girlfriend he'd be on his way home shortly.

"Three, large Jagerbombs please, Paul," he said. "Mark, what you having?"

"Mate, I'm afraid I'm gonna split before this gets messy," whispered Mark in Marcello's ear. "Good luck son, good luck."

Mark left the pub, cursing his ever-attentive girlfriend. She had a late-night trip to the local

Scandavian furniture store planned: a night of flat-packing lay ahead for the under-the-thumb photographer.

With the first round of shots despatched, Marcello was in his element, as the girls struggled to stay in character. Two cheeky monkeys flouncing and flirting with their preening organ grinder.

"Now, I shouldn't really be fraternising with you two," said Marcello. "But I won't tell if you don't..."

"That's the name of your game, isn't it?" said Stassy. "Telling!"

"More like kiss and tell," added Sarah.

"Kiss and sell," bumbled Stassy.

"Didn't say anything about kissing, girls," replied Marcello, with a glint in his eye. "But it's not a bad idea. Right, who's going to kiss who first?...Paul, three more 'bombs' here please, mate..."

Stassy and Sarah winked at each other as Marcello paid for another round. Their overwhelming urge was to see who could pull this guy first. Their competitive streak was instinctively kicking in as they struggled to continue giving each other the attention this article required if it were to stand up.

The drinks flowed, as the girls both bought a round each. Sarah, black sambuca shots...Stassy, typically upping the ante, with a round of vanilla vodka, passion fruit and champagne-infused Pornstar Martinis.

Stassy struggled to sit upright on her stool as Sarah swayed from side to side, gesticulating with her arms wildly as she tried to impress Marcello with tawdry tales from her fledgling acting career.

With his interviewees now almost at his mercy, Marcello, himself nicely tanked up, swung into action.

"So, are you two still licking both sides of the stamp, so to speak, or have you given yourself to each other for good?"

"What an earth do you mean?" slurred Stassy.

"Yeah, what you trying to say?" swooned Sarah.

"Well, you both have been into men in the past," said Marcello, chancing his arm. "You can't go off us boys just like that, surely?"

"You'd be surprised, Mar...schello...," stuttered Stassy. "Have you noticed how beautiful my girlfriend is?"

"Yes, have you noticed how gorgeous I am?" agreed Sarah, resting her head on Marcello's right shoulder.

Yanking Marcello towards her, Stassy made Sarah collapse in a heap on the bar in front of her.

"Now, now girls...," said Marcello, helping Sarah back upright. "No need to squabble over little old me. I'll make sure you get your eight grand. I'll see you right."

"You better had," said Stassy, now snuggling up to Marcello herself, as Sarah glared at her.

"Yeah, we're having to bare all for this cash," argued Sarah, yanking Marcello back towards her. "You better not fuck us over."

"Chance would be a fine thing," said Marcello, a line which Stassy and Sarah couldn't help but applaud.

Now this was Marcello's moment, as he moved in for the kill. Slipping his arms around both Stassy and Sarah, he pulled them closer towards him as another round of Jagerbombs appeared on the bar in front of them.

"Now girls...how about adding some value?"

Stassy and Sarah weren't sure what Marcello meant but it didn't take much to imagine what he had in mind.

"And what might you mean by that?" asked Stassy.

"Let's just see how the night pans out," teased Marcello.

"Let me get this right? Are you talking about more

cash?" demanded Sarah.

"Maybe," sniggered Marcello. "Let's just let things play out, shall we?"

Sarah pulled Stassy to side and whispered vehemently in her ear. "What the fuck?...let's get the hell out of here...we're playing with fire...what the hell are we doing? I am telling you we need to leave and we need to leave now."

Stassy knew Sarah was right, completely right, but she was beginning to feel extremely attracted to Marcello. He was gorgeous, he was coming onto her and he was far too good...far too good...to refuse.

They seemed to have missed last orders as Marcello dived towards the bar...

"No more, no more," said Paul firmly from behind the ramp. He knew Marcello and he knew he was very drunk. He wasn't serving him again tonight, let alone his two lady friends, who were way ahead of him.

"Back to mine?" suggested Marcello. "I have booze and fun on tap. Come on ladies, you know you want to. I'm only ten minutes away, just off Liverpool Road."

"Well, it's almost on the way home," slurred a drunk Stassy. "C'mon, it makes sense, Sarah, a couple more drinks and we can head home from there."

"Perfect," said Marcello, grabbing Stassy's arm and leading her out of the bar as Sarah reluctantly followed.

"This is not a good idea," hissed Sarah, as they spilled out on to the street.

She had little option, of course, as she couldn't be seen to desert her 'girlfriend'.

Stassy was always a liability when you went out with her. It was likely to be a memorable night and this was already beyond memorable. Lying to a reporter about lesbianism and now rolling back drunk to his flat. What was the worst that could happen? she thought to herself sarcastically.

A nonchalant Marcello, now with a gorgeous girl on each arm, hailed a cab with all the swagger of a man living the dream.

As the black taxi pulled up, he bundled a bladdered Stassy and Sarah onto the back seat, plonked himself in between them, carefully placed his arm around each girl in equal measures, as to not appear to have a favourite, and demanded: "Home, James."

"Alright, smart arse," said the cabbie. "I know you think your luck's in, but I'm going to need a bit more information than that."

"Sorry, how rude of me, the Playboy Mansion please, boss," said Marcello, chancing his arm, before quickly adding: "Erm, just off Liverpool Road please, mate...Batchelor Street..."

"Batchelor Street? Fucking Batchelor Street?" slurred Stassy. "Taking us to your fucking 'bachelor pad', are you? Shit, you really couldn't make this up."

Before he could digest what Stassy was saying, Marcello felt a wet sensation on his neck. It was Sarah to his left, slobbering away at his ear lobe. Stassy joined in, leaning across to rub his chest. The cabbie gave the reporter a knowing look in his rear view mirror and Marcello winked back at him.

Life surely didn't get much better than this, although the old cabbie had seen it all before. By the state of his companions, this guy needed to get them home quick. They looked like they didn't have much left in the tank.

By the time the taxi pulled up in Batchelor Street, Marcello had briefly snogged Stassy, while Sarah's hand had progressed down to his stomach, circled clumsily around his right inner thigh and was about to see what he was really made of when the cabbie screeched to a halt and announced: "Right you randy lot...OUT!"

As Stassy and Sarah sat on the wall outside Marcello's five-storey apartment block he gave the cabbie a £20 note for the £8.60 fare and couldn't resist saying: "Keep the change, mate..."

"Brasses?" asked the cabbie.

"No!" said Marcello incredulously.

"Yeah, right...," said the cabbie, as he indicated and slowly pulled away, trundling off down the road.

Marcello shook his head as he turned around to see Stassy and Sarah staring back at him expectantly.

"This had better be a nice place," said Sarah. "We have standards, you know."

"And you better have some booze," added Stassy. "We're thirsty, you know."

Marcello could see these two were going to be a handful...and they had to negotiate the lift yet.

Keen to smuggle the girls in discreetly, so his mate 'Downstairs Darren' on the floor below didn't notice or hear there was a spare lady in his possession, Marcello flashed his key card at the intercom system and whisked Stassy and Sarah in. As he waited nervously for the lift to arrive, he prayed he wouldn't bump into Darren or, for that matter, anyone else in the block.

Once in the lift, Sarah wasted no time at all, comically slut-dropping to the floor as Stassy continued kissing Marcello. Still not quite sure exactly what she would attempt now her face was crotch level, Sarah toppled backwards, just as the lift door opened on the fourth floor, falling flat on her back, half in the lift, half out.

Stassy and Marcello, in fits of laughter, stepped over Sarah and then, with one arm each, dragged her the few yards across the corridor and into Marcello's flat as he expertly opened his front door with his other hand.

Fuck, what the fuck are we doing? thought Sarah, as she floated into Marcello's flat.

Marcello looked intensely at Stassy and offered her a drink. "Vodka and tonic baby, with a twist of lime?"

"Yes, perfect," replied Stassy.

"Sarah?"

"I'll have what she's having."

"Put some music on," demanded Stassy. "What have you got? I wanna dance."

Marcello had a big vinyl collection, and he started flicking through it.

"OK ladies, what do we fancy?" he asked. "I have some great house tracks..."

"Anything," said Stassy flippantly. "If it's shit I will soon tell you. Come on DJ, start spinning some tracks...they'd better be good."

Marcello grabbed a CD and said: "On the other hand..."

As Britney Spears' *Baby One More Time* blasted out, the girls couldn't resist getting up and dancing to it. Not many could. Marcello had played his ace card.

Stassy was usually far too cool to entertain Britney, but she was now pressing against Sarah, suddenly becoming cognoscent of the fact she needed to get back into character.

"Hey, lady, lady," said Stassy, squeezing Sarah. "Tell me, how much you love it."

Never the best at lyrics, Stassy warbled on relentlessly...then bent over and shouted: "Smack me, lady, please be mine."

Sarah slapped Stassy's backside and began to grind against her.

Marcello was getting extremely turned on and started thinking again about a revised deal.

"Maybe I could organise some more money ladies, you know, for a good performance tonight...sharing is caring. I reckon a decent show tonight could earn you girls another two grand."

Stassy was really fancying Marcello and the way she saw it, the offer of extra money would only help her pull him too.

"Are you offering us money for turning to the other side, Marcello?"

"You've already turned, though, haven't you?"

"You know what I mean."

"Yes, yes ladies, so another couple of thousand. I reckon I can swing it, if you two can as well?"

"Are you sure, Marcello?" said Stassy, taking Sarah to one side.

"Sarah, what do you think?" asked Stassy. "I love you and I don't want to destroy our relationship. It's a little messed up. Do you think we could involve Marcello for a little more money? He isn't that bad looking?"

Sarah could see that Stassy totally wanted Marcello.

"Well, maybe," conceded Sarah, as she and Stassy shuffled back towards the centre of the room, seemingly agreeable to Marcello's offer.

"Well, then..." said Marcello, brazenly, turning down the music slightly, and mixing in a house compilation, "...shall we begin?"

The girls nodded, almost reluctantly.

"Great," continued Marcello. "Right, take your clothes off. Everything apart from your underwear."

Both girls did as they were instructed, relieved they were wearing matching bras and knickers.

"Very nice," said Marcello. "My God, you are both looking hot. Do a little twirl for me ladies, please."

They both did as they were told.

"Lay down on the rug, girls," added Marcello. "I want to see how you girls roll."

Fuck, thought Sarah. Get into character.

She instructed Stassy to lie down and then sat astride her. She leaned down and they started to kiss. At first it was a little hesitant, then with urgency. She slipped her hand behind her back and undid Stassy's bra strap to reveal her boobs. They were magnificent and so pert. She licked each nipple and then ran her hand down to her crotch. Fuck, she wanted Stassy.

"Marcello, let's be having you," said Sarah.

"Yeah, you gonna get stuck in or what?" added Stassy, typically upping the ante.

Marcello started taking his clothes off, clumsily, and was soon down to his heaving Calvin Kleins. Stassy moved towards his bulge while Sarah caressed her.

Marcello was having the best blow job of his life and Stassy, as Sarah went down on her, was about to experience the most amazing orgasm too.

Marcello came explosively but he wanted more from Sarah and Stassy. "C'mon ladies...another two K...I want my money's worth."

Stassy took Sarah and went down on her. For another two grand, of, course, she thought, I'll make this girl come like she has never come before...and she did.

The three of them lay in a heap, sexually fulfilled and exhausted. Marcello had no reason to believe that these ladies weren't fully, unequivocally in love.

10

Stassy stirred...the morning after the night before. She ran to the toilet, vomited and sloped back to her bed, shivering under the covers. She felt dreadful.

Fuck...what happened last night? There had certainly been a lot of alcohol involved. Was Marcello really going to give them any extra cash for that performance or had they exposed themselves as fakes?

Stassy really wasn't sure. She conveniently had huge memory gaps of the night. After that Pornstar Martini and the shot of champagne that came with it, the night was a blur. She knew she had been trying hard to get into character, and she definitely remembered how gorgeous Marcello was...and the offer of extra remuneration. As for Sarah, well things had certainly gone too far there...how could she look her in the eye? This whole lying to the press was almost beginning to become a reality. Her head was spinning, but she also had a sense that she had tried something that had always intrigued her. Need more sleep, she thought...and a sickie...worry about it all later. She pulled the covers over her head and zoned out. At least she wasn't skint, for once.

Sarah woke up in a similar state – "Oh...my...God" – what the hell happened? There were the Jager-bombs, the Pornstar Martinis, the talk of bonus pay, the sexy reporter...and then Stassy. What the fuck was all that about? Would she be able to face her partner-in-crime today?

Their friendship was strong. She had met Stassy several years earlier in a particularly sticky situation... probably one reason why they had always been very open with each other about their sex lives, and maybe why they were able to even contemplate sharing this intimate liaison in the first place.

Sarah had pitched up at an east London address after a club with a few mutual friends who lived there. It was a huge property and at around 2am she felt brave enough to start looking for the toilet. Mission supposedly accomplished, she opened the door and burst in on Stassy, lying beneath a bronzed hunk with a very white bottom, which was moving up and down rapidly.

"Shit, sorry," said Sarah, the reality of what she had just walked in on engulfing her.

"Hey, don't stop," screamed Stassy at the man, who had taken time out to turn round and look at Sarah, like a petrified rabbit caught in the headlights.

"Don't look at her, look at me," barked Stassy brazenly. "I'm about to fucking come."

The man dutifully continued his bobbing up and down and Sarah decamped, mortified, quickly discovering that the door to the right was in fact the bathroom. Back downstairs, she mentioned it to one of the guys she knew in the house. "Shit, I just walked in on some people going for it...like really going for it...upstairs."

"Yeah, I think it's Rick and some bird he pulled tonight. She's pretty damn hot, from what I saw. He's one lucky boy."

About 30 minutes later Stassy appeared.

"Hey, sorry about walking in like that," offered Sarah. "I was looking for the bathroom."

"No problem, babe. Fancy a spliff?"

Sarah was confident they could come through this latest chapter of their relatively short, yet eventful friendship. It wouldn't have gone as far if it weren't for the whole interview and the lie, etc. As much as she had really felt as if she was acting, as if it wasn't really her, she couldn't deny that she was turned on by the whole thing too. Was it worth the money? She wasn't sure. And what on earth would Marcello put in his piece? Sarah suddenly felt sick to the stomach. She got up and had a shower. Stassy's bedroom door was shut and all was quiet...for now.

Sarah was on stage later that evening. Currently sharing the role of neurotic bisexual nymph with another actress, there had been no need to stay in character on her night off. She needed to get her head in order so made herself a bacon and egg sandwich, drank tea and took two painkillers, trying desperately to pull herself together so she could head to the theatre. She kept having flashbacks to the previous night, with all roads leading to her romp with Stassy. She wasn't sure she was ever going to be able to forget what happened. It was so different from any other experience she'd had previously. To be pleasured by a man and a woman at the same time was pretty amazing. Sarah groaned a little to herself, as various flashbacks popped into her head.

Her groaning became echoed by moaning upstairs. Fuck, it was Stassy. What was she going to say to her? Stassy appeared at the lounge door. She looked dreadful.

"Afternoon," said Sarah sheepishly.

"Erm...morning," replied Stassy. "I feel so dreadful. What the hell happened last night?"

"We had a threesome," said Sarah. "Do you remember? Surely my performance wasn't so bad that you've totally managed to erase the whole thing from your memory."

They both fell into fits of laughter. Typically, Sarah had managed to deal with the elephant in the room with humour.

"Now that, my darling, I won't forget in a hurry," said Stassy. "Do you think we let anything slip to Marcello?"

"I think we let plenty slip," sniggered Sarah. "But I don't think he had any reason not to believe that we are at least bisexual. It was a pretty damn fine performance, from what I can remember. I actually thought you were equally into me and Marcello. You couldn't seem to make up your mind."

"He did offer us more cash."

"Well, I reckon he got his money's worth," said Sarah. "Let's hope we feel the same when the dosh comes through."

"Anyway, what you up to today?" asked Stassy, in a feeble attempt to change the subject. "I've called in sick."

"Just trying to get my head together," mumbled Sarah. "Need to leave in a couple of hours for the West End...you?"

"I don't know – I'm meant to be meeting up with Oscar later for a few drinks. I'm not sure I can handle it, though."

"I guess we just have to wait now until Friday's issue to see what our dearest Marcello concocts."

"When do we get paid?" said Stassy, cutting to the chase.

"We're meant to get a transfer into our accounts as soon as it's published," remembered Sarah.

"Good...so we don't have to face Marcello again," said Stassy, relieved...and a little dismayed.

"Yep, that would be embarrassing. I hope not...I'm really not up for round two."

"Shit, shit, shit," said Stassy, suddenly remembering the severity of what they had done the previous night, let alone in the last few weeks.

"We've been pretty stupid," she reasoned in a moment of clarity. "Going back to the flat of a reporter's we've been lying to, let alone getting up to stuff with him. The last thing we want to do is expose that we've been bullshitting the press. Meeting up with him again would be really stupid. Are we agreed on that?"

"Yes, for sure. Yes."

Chloe appeared. She had a day off too. Pre-booked annual leave in her case, though. Stassy and Sarah were looking uncomfortable...guilty of something.

"Are you OK, Stass...you look pretty ropey?" suggested Chloe.

"Yep, big night last night. Sarah and I did an article for *Nearer* magazine...that comes out on Friday. We needed a stiff one after the interview and got a bit more than we bargained for."

Sarah and Stassy sniggered hysterically, then nervously.

"Well, I've never known you to pass up a stiff one before, Stass," joked Chloe. "Don't tell me one of you pulled the reporter."

Sarah glared at Stassy, who replied: "Er...kind of..."

"Where have you been, Chloe?" asked Stassy, again trying to change the subject."

"I just got back from Will's...went out with him last night. It was good to catch up. We had a giggle and some fun sex. I've had a dry patch since Tom left and fancied a bit of action."

"Going back over old ground is never good though, babe?" reasoned Stassy, who really wasn't in the best place to advise on these matters. She wouldn't know a dry patch, as Sarah could now testify, if it slapped her in the face.

"It's harmless enough," reasoned Chloe, "...and, anyway, not all of us are lucky enough to have a team of sexy men on speed dial."

Alexa walked into the room...beaming. She had stayed the night with Steve. Things were moving to a new level. They seemed really into each other.

"Stassy," she said calmly. "I want to put all this behind us. There doesn't seem to have been any fallout from the article...maybe I was overreacting. It's done now, let's move on."

Stassy looked nervously at Sarah and replied: "Yes, Alexa, let's move on." The pair hugged.

"Shall I make some tea?" asked Chloe.

The girls gossiped and giggled over several cuppas. Alexa was gushing about Steve and how wonderful he and 'it' was. It was rare for the four housemates to have such a good midweek daytime catch-up, certainly in recent times and under the cloud of Stassy's scam. Surely Alexa wouldn't be laughing when yet another 'exclusive', packed full of more lies, hit the shops.

~

Friday had come around very quickly. Stassy woke up with a sick feeling in her stomach. It is just a normal day, she told herself. It wasn't. There hadn't been one of those for a while. She got dressed and left for the office, physically unable to actually buy a copy of *Nearer* on her way in. It wasn't a magazine that was usually read at work, so she ambitiously hoped the day would pass without incident.

She had been in work for about an hour when the phone rang. It was Alexa.

Stassy didn't know whether to pick up the phone or not. She sat there blankly staring at the screen, willing it to stop. It wouldn't, ringing again and again. Halfway through Alexa's sixth or seventh attempt Stassy took the phone and went to the car park.

"Hello," she said gingerly.

"What the FUCK?" screamed Alexa. "What the FUCK? What the FUCK do you think you are fucking doing, Stassy?"

"What do you mean?" replied Stassy, clinging on to the slimmest of chances that Alexa hadn't seen the new article.

"Don't take the piss, Stassy," screamed Alexa. "Now you are making me really angry...and I'm sure you know exactly why I'm angry. You somehow failed to mention you had done another article. More lies...and now, God help her, Sarah is involved. How many times have I been photographed out with Sarah? She is acting in the West End. Why the hell is she so stupid as to get involved?...well, it's just beyond me."

"I haven't actually read the article yet," said Stassy.

"Well, I suggest you go to the corner shop and pick up a copy. That's what I have just done after my friend Rosanna called me and mentioned that my mates were in the latest issue...and did I know? You have managed to fill two or three pages in the middle of the magazine. There are some lovely glossy photos of you, with some of you kissing Sarah. I even got the impression that the reporter had first-hand experience of your antics. Why the fuck are you doing this? This is so cheap!"

"Alexa," pleaded Stassy. "I don't know - the whole thing has spiralled out of control. It all started with me filling out a silly survey and putting down Preston's details and then all these requests for interviews. The money is good and people's memories are short...it's just a bit of fun. Why don't I take you out for a slap-up meal...throw in some bubbly...try to make up for it?"

"Stassy, have you listened to anything I've been saying?" asked Alexa. "I am not going out in public with you for a long long time. I don't want to be seen with you. If these lies comes out it will be so detrimental to my career...Steve probably won't want anything to do with me, either."

Stassy changed tack. She wasn't going to beg.

"Well, so be it. I think you are being really OTT, Alexa," she added dismissively.

"This needs to STOP," shrieked Alexa. "I'm not sure how much more our friendship can take."

"I need to get back to work, Alexa," said Stassy.

"Goodbye," responded Alexa, slamming down the phone.

Stassy returned to her desk and kept her head down, focussing on anything else but the mess she was now in. No word from Sarah. Strange. And no more calls for the rest of the morning. It seemed nobody else had picked up on the latest article yet.

Sarah called Stassy at lunchtime.

"Have you seen the magazine?" asked Sarah.

"I can't, I can't face going to buy it. How bad is it?"

"God, it's a big piece. I haven't even been able to call you, I feel so sick, Stass. Three pages in total, probably the biggest article in the whole magazine, in fact. And it's pretty strong stuff. There are some lovely photos of us smooching and the reporter implies that he can personally validate the extent of our love for each other. On a positive note, I have checked my account and the money has cleared. Has Preston called you?"

"No, but Alexa has," said Stassy. "She is fuming."

"She needs to get over herself," said Sarah. "I still don't get why she is getting so stressed out about it all. I mean, so what...we live with her. What can it do to harm her career....or lack of one? If we did get exposed for lying, which I doubt, who would really care? We are nobodies and she is only slightly a somebody. She needs to get a life."

"I've got an answerphone message from Preston," said Sarah. "Saying that he didn't know we had done another article, and that his aunt had got hold of a copy and has been asking him if he's the same Preston Price."

"I will call him," said Stassy. "He should deny it, although there can't be many Preston Prices?"

"And there's a small photo of him in the article, lifted from the first story."

"Shit," said Stassy. "We really should have told him. Can you definitely tell it's him?"

"Darling, go and get a copy and see what you think," said Sarah, as nicely as possible. "You can't bury your head in the sand for ever."

Stassy said goodbye to Sarah, promising to go and get a copy. She went back into the office, grabbed her sunglasses and purse and went to the newsagent at the end of the road.

Stassy should have picked another newsagent. She was a regular in the corner shop near work and it was clear that the shopkeeper behind the counter had already read the article. He suppressed a giggle as Stassy hurried out of the shop, the offending item rolled up under her jacket like it was a dirty magazine. Back at the office she went straight to the ladies' and hid in a toilet cubicle.

The piece began....

Today we feature Stassy Thomas, who abandoned her husband when she fell in love with Sarah Phillips. Spouse Preston Price was thrown into such turmoil, so distraught she had left him for her lesbian lover, he too embarked on a gay relationship.

In this no-holds barred interview Nearer caught up with stunning Stassy and her partner, Sarah.

Stassy lifted the lid on her decision to dump hubby Preston for fellow good-time girl Sarah after a chance meeting in a fetish nightclub, explaining crudely: "We tried to stay loyal to our male partners, but it was just impossible...now we're both strictly vagetarians."

The pair certainly couldn't keep their hands off each other during our photoshoot.

Stassy explained: "I never realised I would feel so passionate about a lady, but when Sarah came along I found my soul mate. For me, she is an improved version of Preston and she has breasts. What more could a girl ask for? I love her and I want to be with her for ever."

Stassy, who has an unassuming star quality, is certainly gushing about her new lover, but does she think she would ever be with a man again?

Cuddling up to Sarah while looking longingly into her eyes, Stassy said: "This girl is plenty for me for now and there's certainly enough to handle, but never say never. Let's be clear, I am still attracted to men but it is more about the person than the sex. I really don't discriminate."

Sarah agrees. "I take life as it comes," she adds. "Stassy is more than any girl could ask for, but I'm keeping my mind open to what the future offers."

Wow, these sexy ladies are certainly more than this reporter can handle. I, for one, on behalf of all the men out there, hope they will once again return to the male form and, thankfully, from the glint in their eyes, I think that maybe one day they will.

And it continued...

11

Alexa couldn't wait to go out with Steve tonight. Their relationship felt like it was moving on from those early, heady, physical days. They were still pretty adventurous in the bedroom, but it was more than that now and Alexa was actually beginning to fall for Steve.

She was dancing around her bedroom when Chloe walked in.

"Hi Alexa, how are you?"

"I am great, darling. Really good. Going to Ubon with Steve tonight. We have been officially dating a month now so we are going to celebrate! He also says he has some exciting news!"

"You look fab, Alexa – really beautiful. Steve is one lucky man," added Chloe reassuringly.

~

Stassy felt sick about Marcello's article, after everything that had happened between the three of them. The fact he had then manipulated the story so badly felt like a pretty low thing to do. To compound everything, the money had cleared, but Marcello had only managed to find them an additional grand for their extra-curricular efforts, rather than the extra £2k promised. Arsehole. And vagetarians? They didn't say that. Or was that a typo?

However, for all her angst, Stassy couldn't deny Marcello's rogueish charm. It's not like she'd always liked a bad boy, she wasn't usually that fussy, but Marcello had got under her skin, in more ways than one! Stassy couldn't help feeling, if you wiped away all the sleaze, there was a real spark between them.

She hid the magazine in a drawer in her desk and tried to focus on work to take her mind off it all. Hopefully, not many people she knew would read the *Nearer* magazine article. She had been working for about 30 minutes when her mobile phone rang from an unidentified number.

"Hello," she said warily.

"Hello there," said a male voice, confidently. "Am I speaking to Stassy?"

"Yes," she said. "That's me."

"Great, my name is Bob, and I am ringing from *The Mercury*. I have just read the story in *Nearer* and I'm keen to do a follow-up article in this weekend's paper. I am keen to get a different angle to the story and was wondering whether Sarah, you, Preston and his ex-gay partner would be interested in doing an interview."

Now well-versed in how to handle this sort of thing, Stassy said: "I am getting so many calls of interest from your competitors right now, so the money has to be right. You are asking for all four of us, you want new material...it is going to come at a price. We need £15k, because I am getting a lot of heat from work and family for exposing these sensitive areas of my private life."

"Hmmm? That sounds steep," replied Bob. "A lot more than we would normally pay for non-celebrity articles."

"Well, that's our price," reiterated Stassy. "And I will still need to talk Preston, Ralph and Sarah into it."

Bob really wanted this story. It was definitely blowing the budget, but he knew his predominantly suburban female middle-class readership would lap it up in equal measures of shock and awe.

"OK, let's do it," he announced, sticking his neck out.

"Great," said Stassy. "When do you need the interview done?"

"Tomorrow morning, really," said Bob. "Certainly if it's going to make Sunday's paper. And we need to get it done this week, because I just about have the budget now, and that may not be the case in another week. Can we say 10.15 in the morning?"

"Let me confirm that with the others," said Stassy. "But I think that should be OK."

She put the phone down and rang Preston.

"Hi," said Preston, sounding royally pissed off.

"What's wrong, mate?" said Stassy.

"My aunt's been on the blower."

"And?"

"She is not very happy with me and she is threatening to call up my folks."

"Do you think she will?"

"I don't know, I'm hoping she'll calm down eventually."

"Well, you probably don't want to hear what I have signed you up for now?"

"No I don't. To be honest Stassy, I am pretty pissed off that you didn't tell me about *Nearer*, especially as I'm mentioned."

"It's my fault – I am sorry, Preston, everything has been happening so fast."

"It's a fucking joke, Stassy. Happening too fast? Nothing much was fucking happening until I got that call from the *Sunday Planet*. My life was plodding along quite nicely. Yes, I had a bit of debt, but I hadn't managed to completely rip the piss out of myself in the process or put my job on the line or be on the verge of family fucking crisis. Why me, Stassy? Why fucking me?"

"Look, Preston, I can only keep saying sorry. But we're in this now, we can't turn back the clock. And anyway, an opportunity has come up with *The Mercury* for their Sunday supplement. I have managed to secure us 15 big boys, but they need me, you, Sarah, and Ralph, and to see us all tomorrow morning to meet the Sunday press deadline. Shall we try and get together in the Three Crowns tonight straight after work, the four of us, to discuss?"

"Look," said Preston. "I need to think this through. For starters, I am sure my aunt reads *The Mercury*."

"Ok, well, you think it through, Mr Price...but the money is very good."

"I'll call you later."

"Ciao."

Stassy texted Sarah and Ralph.

~

Stassy arrived first at the pub and slumped down in a shabby chic leather Chesterfield sofa, as tatty as her reputation right now. Preston was the next to arrive. He looked tired and stressed. Sarah flounced in looking angry and Ralph floated in last, without a care in the world.

"That fucking Marcello," complained Sarah discreetly to Stassy. "I've read the piece several times now, and he has really bent our story and made us out to look like total floozies, who will do anything for sex."

"I wonder how he got that impression," smirked Stassy. "C'mon, it's done now, let's try and move on."

She then added wryly: "I didn't mind being called a wildchild, though. We're 26 years old, for God's sake!"

Sarah glared at Stassy, then her stare evaporated into a grin and she shook her head as she settled down beside her 'lover' on the Chesterfield.

"So…" said Stassy. "On to today's business…I have been contacted by *The Mercury,* and they want an article with all four of us for their Sunday supplement. They are prepared to give us £15k, but we would need to do it tomorrow first thing to make this Sunday's edition. Thoughts?"

"Yeah, baby," said Ralph, as yet to receive a penny or the limelight he so craved from this charade. "I'm in all the way – just tell me what to say and I will say it…"

Sarah sighed. "I just don't know…that *Nearer* article hasn't exactly presented me in the best light and I'm worried it could impact on my image, which isn't good in my line of work. Literally, the only reason I am considering it is that I could do with the money."

"My parents," said Preston. "They'll be so mortified if they get wind of this. Work is getting edgy…could even be out of a job soon…on the other hand, the cash just seems too good to refuse."

"Hmmm?…I know we are all getting in deep…very deep," said Stassy, winking at Sarah, who in turn blushed a little. "But when this is all over we can bank the money and it will all be forgotten."

The others nodded, Sarah and Preston begrudgingly.

"See you all at *The Mercury*'s offices in Notting Hill tomorrow at 10am," said Stassy, authoritatively.

~

As she left the pub wondering what to do for the rest of the evening on her night off, Sarah's head was still full of confusion about her feelings for Stassy...and that there was more 'press' to do the next morning ...when Philippe texted her.

> *Hey sexy, been a little while - I have*
> *missed you baby, fancy a late drink*
> *- we could head to the Ditch...? xx*

Perfect. Philippe would be the ideal way to take her mind off the whole situation...and also to prove to herself that she was still mainly attracted to men.

> *Sure, see you around 10.30ish -*
> *will call you when I get there Xx*

~

Alexa arrived at the restaurant about 8.30pm. Steve greeted her outside with a single-stemmed red rose, and kissed her passionately.

"Babe, you look hot, really hot. Shall we go inside? I have some exciting news."

"Oooh, yes, let's," squealed Alexa. "I can't wait to hear this."

They ordered sake and sashimi and gazed longingly into each others' eyes.

"So..." said Alexa. "Don't keep me in suspense."

"Well," announced Steve. "I have been asked to present a big Saturday night primetime shiny floor quiz show for *Channel 3*! It's big money and big profile."

"Wow, that's amazing baby," said Alexa jealously. "Really amazing."

Alexa couldn't help but feel total envy, but she was really happy for Steve. It was fabulous news.

The show he presented late at night on that obscure channel she had never heard of had so little viewing figures. It provided a decent income, but was no good for his profile...or hers. He currently struggled to get recognised if he walked down the High Street. This new show, however, was another level. Primetime Saturday was every presenter's dream. And, of course, this should be good for Alexa too. Being on the arm of Steve if he became a hot shot would be great for her own ambitions. Alexa perked up.

"When do you start?" she said.

"Pretty much immediately," explained Steve. "They want me to do some run-throughs in the next couple of weeks and then we go live soon after that."

"You are still going to do your late-night show?" asked Alexa.

"Ultimately no, but I have to see out my contract for *Gary* for the next month or so. I'll juggle the two at the start, and getting paid for both will be great while it lasts. Eventually, though, I will have to be exclusively primetime, which will be very nice, thank you very much."

"I am going to buy us a bottle of champagne to celebrate, baby," volunteered Alexa gallantly.

Alexa ordered a bottle of the house Bollinger. It wasn't the most expensive bottle on the menu, by far, but she was hardly going to fork out more than £600 for a bottle of Cristal. No, the £86 'Bolly' was a gesture, and more than appreciated by Steve, particularly as Alexa had not yet paid for anything in his company. Alexa would have rather spent the money on an afternoon in her favourite Spa in Covent Garden, and really should have used the money to pay off a small part of her monthly credit card bill, but she reasoned that the cost was more than worth the investment. She was sure she was about to make it to the big time vicariously through her man. Things were looking up.

As they clinked their glasses, Alexa's mind drifted back to Stassy and her antics. She had better not do anything to harm Steve's success...or her imminent rise to A-list celebrity status.

~

Sarah could see Philippe in the distance as she walked along Rivington Street, pacing up and down outside the bar he'd chosen, talking enthusiastically on the phone. He hurriedly wrapped up his call - "great, great, speak later, yeah, sure, bye" - and gave Sarah a quick kiss on the lips as they walked inside. It was slightly awkward, but he genuinely seemed pleased to see her. A drink to loosen up was definitely in order. They ordered mojitos and kicked off the small talk.

"So, how have you been, Sarah? What's been happening?" said Philippe, with a glint in his eye.

"Not bad, not bad...this new role is working out really well. Even had some good personal reviews. I've tried to ignore the negative ones, but in general the whole play is rating well, so I am pleased."

"That's great babe, really happy for you...and you deserve it. Could be the big break you've been looking for."

Sarah paused. This was agony. Did he know about the article or not?

Then she continued: "Well, we'll see, but I am hoping this will take my career to the next level or at least keep me where I am for a while. It's fantastic being in the West End. I'm loving that, and working with some great actors."

"And the other girls in that crazy house of yours?"

added Philippe.

"Well, Alexa has fallen in love with a guy called Steve Keane? Have you heard of him?"

"Name rings a bell, but not sure why?"

"Yeah, he created a new form of sexual yoga, which means you end up shagging in some very strange positions. Meant to be good for the whole pain-pleasure equilibrium and the concentration helps you delay orgasm or internally orgasm if you are a well-practised man...which by all accounts Steve is."

"Too much information, babe."

"Haha, sorry, but you get the gist. He is also hosting some late-night quiz show on a cable channel called *Gary...Tantric or Frantic*...it's got quite a cult following apparently, so he's a pretty good catch for our Alexa."

"That's it, *Tantric or Frantic*...think I saw that the other night when I was channel-hopping...but, c'mon, what's really been happening? A little bird tells me, you and the lovely Stassy have been causing a bit of a stir?"

"Yes...erm...Stassy...causing trouble, as always. She continues to have an endless supply of lovers on the go. She tosses them away, as soon as she has had her wicked way with them. I am not sure when that girl will ever settle down."

"OK, darling," said Philippe. "I'll spell it out for you...*Sunday...Planet...Nearer*...magazine...I mean, not the sort of rags or mags I usually go for, but my finger is on the pulse...what the fuck have you two been up to? I mean, it sounds...erm...intriguing. Need any other participants?"

Sarah, now blushing profusely, giggled coyly, and looked down at her drink.

"You know, I am available for weddings, Bar Mitzvahs and...erm...threesomes," added Philippe.

"Very funny," replied Sarah. "I'm sure you are. Look, it's just a bit of fun..."

"I bet it is...fun."

"It's just a bit of fun and something that got out of hand when Stassy tried to stitch up Preston Price with some sex survey in the paper. I'll talk about it in more detail when it's all died down, if that's alright?"

Philippe made a mental note that he would certainly be back for some more of this action. Sarah and Stassy, who he'd always fancied too, had certainly gone up in his estimation.

"Anyway, enough of me and the girls and that little situation," said Sarah. "How have things been with you?"

"Yeah, good thanks, I've been putting on some great parties. I'm working with some good DJs, making some decent dollar. It's all good, baby. Do you want another drink?"

Typical Philippe, glossing over his own personal situation.

"Sure," said Sarah.

She watched Philippe walk to the bar. He was so good looking and had such a great physique. Sarah knew he was no good and always had several lovers on the go. However, she also knew when he asked her to come back to his place later she would say yes... emphatically. It was inevitable. How could she say no to that body...like the cash currently on the table, he was simply too good to refuse.

It wasn't just Philippe's physique, though. Everything he did was so effortless. He always put Sarah at ease...had this way of making her feel like she was special. Feeling wanted by Philippe was a pick-me-up during times of rejection. Although Sarah was thick-skinned it was hard, both as a jobbing actress and single person, to be optimistic all the time, and that's when she would call Philippe.

~

Everyone was on time at *The Mercury*'s west London offices on Saturday morning: even a somewhat dishevelled and rather-pleased-with-herself Sarah. Bob greeted them all warmly, making a mental note of what sexy ladies Stassy and Sarah were in the flesh. The veteran hack immediately felt aroused at the thought of them in bed together.

"Right," said Bob. "Let's get in the interview room and get cracking."

Once inside, the lies began to flow effortlessly once more.

Much to Preston's dismay, Ralph, his luscious locks particularly flowing, got really into fabricating their relationship, which he described as passionate, intense and fulfilling.

Stassy and Sarah spent a considerable amount of the interview squeezing and ogling each other.

Preston even started to wonder whether there was actually something going on between them. My word, now that would be something, he thought. So much so, he had to think about Ralph to calm himself down.

Meanwhile, Bob was in his element, writing furiously in his notepad, listing the details of the various affairs. These people were certainly all very sexually charged, he noted, and up for anything and anyone. This was going to be a great piece.

After they had finished talking to Bob they were taken to another room for photos. They had a 'happy family' type shot where they were sat on a fluffy rug together. "Interlinked by love," said the photographer as he snapped away. Intrinsically linked and riddled by ridiculous lies, pondered Stassy.

Then she remembered the money. She was going to go on a long holiday as soon as she finished this latest production.

The photographer asked if he could have a wedding photo to add into the mix. Stassy said she would drop one off in the morning. Thank goodness they didn't have to pull that stunt again.

12

It was Saturday night. Chloe had managed to navigate another intense week at work and was looking forward to getting out of the office and having a drink. She was meeting an old university friend in a bar in Oxford Street. She was also single, so they planned to have a good catch-up and check out some eye candy.

Chloe ordered a bottle of white wine and the pair started gassing. They were halfway into the second bottle when random guys Simon and Nic came over and started chatting to them. They were OK looking, not gorgeous, but both had something attractive about them. They worked in the City and were suited and booted and said "yah" a lot. The foursome moved onto JD and Coke, and things became more flirty. Chloe, now seemingly on a roll, was paired with Nic and her friend with Simon. A couple more drinks in and they invited the girls back to their pad and after a final glass of wine, which Chloe only half drank, the couples disappeared into the boys' respective bed-rooms.

For the next hour or so the flat was filled with sounds of groaning and moaning. At one stage it seemed Nic was trying to outdo Simon. A bit of competition in the bedroom is always good, Chloe thought, as she laid back and enjoyed the show.

~

Sunday came round quickly and Preston was woken abruptly at 8.30am by the familiar ring tone on his Nokia mobile phone. Who the fuck is this now? he thought.

Shit, it was his aunt. He knew exactly why she was phoning, so let the call run out. He needed to be far more awake to deal with her normally, let alone with the ammunition she was surely armed with today. But he was wide awake now and he wasn't going to get back to sleep. He jumped in the shower and went to buy the paper.

Preston could see why his aunt was fuming. Her nephew and all these lies. The photo made them look as if they were in some strange polygamous set-up. Ralph was in his element in the article. And then there were the even more dreadful wedding photos.

Preston decided to go back to bed and actually managed to go back to sleep. He was woken up again at midday. This time it was his parents. He thought it was probably best not to ignore this call.

"Hello," he said hesitantly.

His mum was sobbing on the other end of the phone.

"Preston, why didn't you tell us? How could you have got married and not invited us to your wedding... and who are all those strange people that did actually go? I am sure we have met Stassy at some point over the years, but why didn't you tell us you'd got married? How come you didn't live together? It is most unusual. And why didn't you tell us you are bisexual? I feel like I don't know you? Your father is in pieces."

"Mum, mum, calm down," interrupted Preston. "Please let me explain. It's all rubbish, I have been telling lies."

"Lies?" said Mrs Price, her sobbing subsiding

momentarily. "But why?"

"Where to start...it's such a mess, Mum. It all started when Anastasia filled out a sex survey for the *Sunday Planet*. For some reason she thought it would be funny to put my name on it and then we got offered an interview and the money was good. I have debts, you know that, and it just seemed like a good way to pay them off."

"But this latest piece is in *The Mercury*? Your aunt called and has faxed me the article?"

"That's a follow-up piece. It was more money and it was just too attractive to refuse."

"Preston!" said Mr Price, jumping on the phone, after listening on another handset. "I am so disappointed in you. Why would you do something so stupid. If you had money issues, you could have talked to us!"

"I don't want parental handouts. I'm 27! And, it's not money issues, as such. It was just money for nothing, I guess," replied Preston, trying to somehow justify his actions.

"Nothing," bellowed his father. "Are you mad? Our whole family think you are bisexual and got married on a whim...and, worse, that you didn't even tell us?"

"And what about the wedding photos, Preston?" asked his Mum. "They look real...although it is a strange crowd?"

"We staged it?"

"This is preposterous...ridiculous," stormed Preston's father. "Why couldn't you have used your imagination in a more industrious and credible way?"

Preston's mother was now sobbing again, uncontrollably down the line.

"We need time to digest all this, Preston. We will speak later," stormed Mr Price, slamming down the phone.

~

Stassy's mum called at 9am, waking her as she answered the phone in a sleepy voice.

"Hi."

"What an earth are you doing in *The Mercury*?"

"It's a long story, mum. It started with me being bored at work, filling out a sex survey and putting Preston's details down. It turned into several press interviews. Basically, lies for cash."

"Well, that has made me feel a lot better," said Stassy's mum, sarcastically. "What on earth are people going to think, Anastasia? The cash surely can't be enough to put your reputation at stake?"

"Well, I am hoping this will be a small storm in a teacup," reasoned Stassy. "And when it all blows over I will have a nice pot of cash to get a deposit on a flat and go on a nice holiday. Maybe take me old Mum somewhere nice too."

"I really hope you know what you're doing, Anastasia. It seems a very risky approach to me."

"Well, it's done now, Mum. Guess we'll have to wait and see."

Stassy rounded off the call. Her mum had lived a colourful life and was the least of her worries. More pressing was the text that had just come in from Preston. Fuck, his parents had found out. That wasn't good news. They could be dangerous. Sarah was still asleep. This had all the hallmarks of a bad day.

Stassy's phone rang...an unidentified number.

"Hello," she said.

"Hi," said an excitable young lady. "I'm calling from *Channel 3*'s *Elevenses*. I run through all the Sunday papers looking for stories to feature on the show in the coming week. We would *love* to have you guys in for an interview. Preston mentioned in the article he was now in a heterosexual relationship. We would *love* to add his new girlfriend into the mix just to add a new angle to the story? What do you think? It would be a prime-time 'on-the-sofa' chat with our top presenters Will Blofeld and Polly Holloway."

"We need at least £3-4k each — so for all of us... that's...erm...£20k all in," said Stassy, calmly.

"OK, I can probably get that signed off for this story, but it has to be all of you. I need something exclusive, something different from the other stories and we need to move quickly. We will need to do this tomorrow morning. We shoot in Birmingham, so we will arrange a car for you to come up...picking up from 5am."

"OK," said Stassy. "This is all moving a little fast. We will clearly need to organise time off with work, etc. Does it really have to be tomorrow?"

"Look, I can live with Tuesday," said the researcher. "But if you can do tomorrow, I'll throw in another grand each, so £25k in total. Our programmes always have the most impact when the story is hot off the press."

"Let me see what I can do," said Stassy.

Twenty-five grand was a lot of money to turn down. She could probably take the day off work as holiday, although she would get some stick for the late notice. She could hardly call in sick and then turn up on *Elevenses*. Sarah definitely wasn't working tomorrow daytime and Ralph, a hair stylist, usually had Mondays off. She called Preston.

Preston answered the phone with a grunt. He seemed pretty forlorn.

"What?" he said.

"*Channel 3* have just called. They want us on *Elevenses*. With your girlfriend. And this girlfriend is an important piece of this puzzle now, as they want a new angle. They are prepared to give us £25k."

Preston's ears pricked up at the money. That would clear his debts significantly. Now he was so far in, there was no turning back. "When do they want to do this?"

"Tomorrow," said Stassy. "They want the story straight away. I am happy to call in for a day's holiday. It won't go down well, but, hey, I am freelance. It's not the end of the world and Sarah and Ralph don't work Mondays. What about you...and your girlfriend?"

"Well, I can take a day's holiday. I don't have client meetings. Like you, it won't go down well but I can live with that for this kinda money. We won't need jobs for a while at this rate."

"Sounds good to me!"

"So, that just leaves the situation of my girlfriend?"

"Well, the taxi comes at 5am tomorrow morning. You have about 18 hours to find the future Mrs Price. Even if she is a minger. "Get yourself out there and see what you can blag," demanded Stassy.

~

Stassy needed a friend to talk to, but not one of the girls. She needed someone independent, outside of her immediate circle, someone uninvolved with all this madness. She had been meaning to call Becky for a while. She had lived with Becky during her second and third year at university but due to her settling in south London, Stassy hadn't seen Becky half as much as she would like. As with many Londoners, most Islingtonites lived by the popular mantra, "don't go sarf of the river" so Becky might as well be living in Scotland the amount they saw each other.

Stassy poured herself a glass of wine and dialled Becky's number.

"Hey lovely," said her old friend a couple of rings later. "Nice to hear from you: how you doing? Been meaning to call you...I saw the..."

"Hi Becks. I'm good, well, OK...fair to middling, I guess. Been a hectic few weeks."

"Yes, well, wow...I saw some stuff in the papers...I couldn't stop laughing about the thought of you and Preston being married. He would have been over the moon with a one-night-stand, let alone a grope and a snog! And Sarah... what's all that about?"

"The whole thing started as a joke, Becks. I filled out a survey and then there was the offer of money and the lies have just escalated and grown...need to stop now, though, but people keep flashing hard cash in my face and I keep thinking what the hell. Plus I met this guy in the middle of this whole mess too, a reporter boy, I think I like him but it all feels a bit fucked up, and you know me, I am not a relationship kind of girl."

"Well," said Becky. "Relationships come to us all at some point, darling. Do you think he likes you?"

"I think he does, but what hope have we? I can't come clean now, because he will know he's been scammed. I wish I could get him out of my head, but I haven't felt like this before."

"I am sure after this has all died down nobody is going to give a shit, Stassy. Just bide your time. Good things come to those that wait!"

13

Preston needed a girlfriend. He headed to The Saddlers Arms. He'd never pulled in there before, so statistically it wasn't the best place to start, but it was as good as any.

He was on first-name terms with a couple of the barmaids...and he'd actually had a few chats with other females in there over the years. If nothing else, he needed a pint and a sit-down and a good hard think about what the hell he was going to do.

On the way to the pub he walked past his local chemist. Tina? Yes, what about Tina? Bubbly blonde 'Tina The Screamer' wasn't one of his 'best moments', but beggars couldn't be choosers. He took a deep breath and entered the pharmacy.

"Per-weston!" shrieked Tina The Screamer. Her reputation across the shared houses of Islington was formidable, her toe-curling cries of ecstasy renowned for rattling roommates' fixtures and fittings the borough over.

"How's it going, lovely?" yelled Tina. "You run out of lube, babe?" she quipped at the top of her excruciating high-pitched voice.

A middle-aged lady waiting for her prescription looked round at Preston and he immediately remembered why Tina could not be trusted in public places, let alone behind closed doors and certainly not on live TV.

"Alright, Teen?" said Preston. "How are things? Just

passing, babe, thought I'd say hello," he lied.

"C'mon, Pricey. What's the real reason for this visit? You got a nasty rash you can't shift?"

Preston shuffled awkwardly along the counter as another customer, this time a male of his own age, gave him a weird look.

"Ha, ha," screamed Tina, unforgivingly. "Look at him, he must have crabs, that's why he's walking sideways."

It was time for Preston to abandon this particular line of enquiries and he slowly walked backwards out of the shop, meekly acknowledging wary customers as he left.

Preston definitely needed a drink now, and ordered a pint as he crashed through the doors of the Saddlers..

Shit. Behind the ramp tonight was Preston's least favourite barmaid, Blanka. Grim and moody and of Czech origin, she always blanked him and rarely checked if he needed anything. She was a complete non-starter and so Preston took his pint, went over to the jukebox, and started flicking through the song lists for inspiration.

Fittingly, with the ordeal that lay ahead of him, he picked out *Blue Monday* by New Order and slumped into a chair in the corner of the pub. As he wondered how he was going to find a heavenly person today, Preston cursed devilish Stassy for dumping him in this predicament and pictured his mum and dad sobbing and fuming in equal measure halfway across the world.

As he racked his brain for someone stupid and irresponsible enough to become his girlfriend for a live prime-time TV appearance that could soil their own reputation forever, he realised he was both those things and had done exactly that.

If he had a little black book, he'd thumb through it

and pick out a foxy ex with a free spirit, happy to oblige an old flame, but few of Preston Price's old flames were in any way obliging. In fact, most had blacklisted him. Did people even have little black books, these days? Now it was all about an accommodating contact list on your mobile phone ...and Preston was sparse in that department too.

He needed to put his thinking cap on, venture further afield and find himself a 'girlfriend'.

Perhaps 'Suz The Flooze', who did the cloakroom at The Cellar Bar on Upper Street, was worth a punt? Perhaps he needed someone without a dubious nickname? He wasn't even sure he and Suz were even on talking terms yet, not after the incident in the back of her Fiat Punto...

The slap round the chops that Suz delivered when he tried to put his jacket in at The Cellar Bar barely half an hour later was not exactly a surprise. She even came out from her position inside the cloakroom cupboard and kicked him hard, down the stairs and into the club...straight into the arms of a pungent hippy chick, who, to put it politely, was 'a couple of crusties short of a demo'. She hung on to him for dear life and tried to stick her tongue down his throat.

Unfortunately for Preston, Serendipity - by name, but no means by odour - was, in technical terms, in need of a good wash. Preston reminded himself that he was a girlfriend short of a lucrative TV interview, and running out of time...fast.

It was now 10.30pm and a car from *Elevenses* was due to pick him up at his flat at around 5.15am. The chances of finding anyone else available to go to Birmingham at the drop of a hat, in the next seven hours or so, were slim...but he was confident 'Dipity', as he would quickly nickname her, didn't have a job...let alone a schedule.

"Hey man," said Serendipity. "Did that freaky cloakroom girl attack you too? She's got some bad karma coming her way...almost didn't let me in..."

"Yeah, well...erm...we've got history," said Preston. "Anyway, sorry about knocking into you like that. Let me buy you a drink to apologise?"

"Great...a pint of snakebite and black please," said Serendipity, a cheesy smile wafting over her grubby face. "I can't remember the last time someone bought me a drink," she added.

"...or you had a nice long soak," mumbled Preston, as he gulped and turned towards the barman, trying not to breathe through his nose.

"A pint of snakebite and black please, barman... actually, make that two...and a couple of white sambucas, please, mate, as well..."

Preston paid for the drinks, downed both the sambucas and handed his 'conquest' her pint of, what students affectionately call, 'Diesel'. "Get that down ya," he added, inappropriately, as he quickly cut to the chase, desperately trying to ignore the emissions wafting his way.

"Look Dippy, or Dipity, or whatever your fucking name is? You look like someone who believes in fate, someone who is happy to seize the moment, grab whatever opportunities come your way...and all that shit..."

"Yeah, man, that's absolutely right," said Serendipity, gulping at her snakebite like a woman possessed.

"Look, I'm going to get to the point. I'm working on a TV documentary right now," fibbed Preston. "It's part of a new reality show and we're off to Birmingham in the morning. We need a few extras for the shoot tomorrow. D'ya fancy coming along?"

"Sure..."

"Sorry?" said Preston, amazed that someone, a female...well, of sorts...had actually agreed to his ridiculous request, well sort of...

"Yeah, dude, I'm in...if you buy me some more of this 'Diesel' for the rest of the night, I'll do whatever you fricking want."

Preston was in. He had fulfilled his remit. He had secured the services of someone to play the role of his new girlfriend...and right now, she was his girlfriend, for the next 24 hours at the very least.

"Two more snakebites, please, mate!"

~

It had been decided that the taxi would stop first at Ralph's, then onto Preston and his 'girlfriend' and finally, Sarah and Stassy.

Ralph leapt into the taxi at 5am. He was so excited about his first TV appearance he hadn't really slept. He had drunk an espresso: well, a double double, in fact. He would be fine. Most importantly his hair looked good, the conditioner, product...all was in place. His luscious locks were thick and gleaming and he was ready to rock.

Next to be picked up were Preston and his 'girlfriend'. And as Preston rarely had a girlfriend in tow, Stassy and Sarah were desperate to see what he had come up with. The car pulled up at Preston's place and the driver called his mobile.

A light on the first floor flashed on almost immediately. The driver leaped out and rang the bell and more lights in the flat came on. A whole six and a half minutes later Preston tumbled out of the property, with a young lady...kind of like a female spaced-out version of Pig-Pen from Peanuts. Her hair was wild, unkempt...well, dreadlocked, really, and she also looked high...really high. That would be the LSD tab she had taken barely half an hour ago for breakfast. She didn't have shoes on and wore a vest top and cargo pants. "OMG!" screamed Ralph to the taxi driver. "What the fuck?..."

As 'she' got in the cab there was an immediate odour. Ralph almost vomited. Jeez, he had spent the best part of the morning getting ready, beautifying himself for his first TV appearance and now he was having to share his taxi with 'Swampy'.

"What the fuck, Preston, what the hell are you doing? Are we really going to have to go on TV with this mad woman?" he squealed.

Ralph sprayed himself with his emergency bottle of Chanel No 5, and it really was only for emergencies, and closed his eyes. Maybe now was time to get some sleep.

The taxi rolled up outside the girls' house and the call was made to Stassy and Sarah, who came out relatively promptly, giggling and squeezing each other. Shit, thought Preston, these girls really have taken this too far. They jumped in the car. It was 5.30am, really too early for anything. The stench was immediate.

"Preston," began Stassy. "Where the hell did you get her?"

"Guys, this is Serendipity."

Serendipity was vaguely focussed on the taxi ceiling. Her eyes appeared to be rolling everywhere.

"Serendipity?" pressed Stassy.

Serendipity jolted from a trance like state. "YES," she boomed.

"Are you OK?" asked Stassy.

"Yes fine, flying along baby, flying along."

Stassy glared at Preston and mouthed..."What... the...fuck?"

Preston smiled and lifted his hands up, giving

Stassy a knowing look that said: "You always knew this was going to be difficult."

The three-hour car journey to the Midlands was suffocating. At the first services the group had a whip round and bought a handful of magic tree car air fresheners, and hung all of them above where Serendipity sat. "I love trees…" she said, as she relaxed back into her seat, to stare up at them swinging gently above her. She'd never smelled so good.

~

Marcello arrived at the *Nearer* offices early on Monday morning. The phone rang about 8.30am.

"Marcello," answered the reporter.

On the other end of the phone was a disgruntled ex-lover of Stassy's. She had snared him, had her wicked way with him, failed repeatedly to remember his name, and then callously cast him aside. She wasn't responding to his texts or taking his calls. Adrian had really liked Stassy. He didn't take well to being rejected. Normally women flocked to him. He thought there was a connection. Now he felt used. The ego had landed. Then he saw the *Nearer* article at his sister's flat and couldn't believe what he was reading. It just didn't seem like the Stassy he had been with. He was pretty sure she hadn't been married, nor Preston, who was a friend of a friend of a friend. The more people he spoke to and the more he had dug into the story, he was certain that it was all a bunch of lies.

"Hi, my name is Adrian," he told Marcello. "Did you write that article about Stassy Thomas, Sarah Phillips and Preston Price recently?"

"I did indeed, how can I help you?" said Marcello,

his ears pricking up.

"I think you will find it's all bullshit," continued Adrian. "You only need to scratch the surface and find you've been had."

"And what makes you think that?"

"Well, Stassy has never been married. Check the marriage records and you will find no wedding between Stassy and Preston Price, or either of them separately. And if she is in a devoted relationship with Sarah, it is funny that she slept with me the weekend before last. She certainly didn't seem to be more into breasts that night, I can tell you. I suggest you do a bit of homework and you'll probably come to the same conclusion."

"Right, and you said your name was..."

"Bye, mate."

The phone went dead.

Well, well, thought Marcello. He needed to do some digging and then have a think about his next move. He didn't relish the idea of admitting to his bosses he had paid money for a dud article, despite the old mantra of never letting the truth get in the way of a good story. Maybe there was another way he could benefit from this information. That threesome had been one of the best moments of his life and he would love a rematch. He had been fantasising about it ever since, and this could be a way to make sure it happened again. First he needed to establish that this 'whistleblower' had his facts straight.

~

The taxi arrived at the studios at The Biscuit Warehouse complex in Birmingham where *Elevenses* was filmed. The car rolled into the back of the studios, the group exceptionally pleased at the opportunity to stretch their legs and remove themselves from the vehicle. Ralph had spent nearly the entire journey with his head cocked up against an open window, breathing in polluted motorway air, his hair all over the place.

Serendipity had fallen asleep against Preston and was dribbling on his shoulder.

Sarah and Stassy had been trying not to gag the whole way, the smell even intoxicating in the back of the people carrier.

The group were ushered into the studio by Liz, the bubbly young lady who had called Stassy on Sunday, and taken to make-up. 'Wardrobe' took one look at Serendipity and said she should go on as she was. No one wanted to deal with her and there really wasn't enough time to make any improvements. This wasn't a make-over show.

The group were soon on the couch where the famous daytime presenting duo, Polly Holloway and Will Blofield, sat opposite them.

"So, welcome all of you," announced Will, wondering what the overpowering odour was. "You have recently been in several newspaper and magazine articles about your different relationships and how you have all been exploring your sexuality. We are delighted to exclusively welcome Serendipity to the programme. She has yet to be interviewed so this is a first today. She is the new girlfriend of Preston Price. How does that feel, Ralph?"

"It breaks my heart to see Preston and Serendipity together. I am still in love with Preston, and I just don't feel that she is right for him," answerered Ralph.

"Yes, I am," slurred Serendipity, putting a grubby hand on Preston's shoulder...somehow picking up the gist of the conversation.

Preston was actually beginning to wonder whether

Ralph was a better catch than Serendipity. The stench seemed to be getting worse. He had essentially been drunk for most of the journey but was now sobering up. The extent of what he had 'pulled' was really becoming apparent and being on TV with her was horrendous. Would he ever live it down?

~

Preston's grandmother lived in a care home in the north of England. She was walking past the day room, when her friend Donal called her. "Edith, isn't this your grandson on the wee TV box?" he asked.

Edith eased herself arthritically into her well-worn armchair and started watching the TV.

Stassy was reflecting about how she and Preston had first met at university and started talking about getting married. A photo of their wedding day appeared on screen. Stassy had now told this story so many times she was starting to believe it herself.

Donal said: "I didna know ya grandson had got married, like?"

Edith was looking quite pale and whispered: "Neither did I."

Sarah then went into full swing about how she and Stassy had met, and explained how their relationship evolved.

"Goodness," exclaimed Donal. "This is all a bit racy for daytime TV."

Edith had gone almost as white as sheet.

Then Ralph began...talking of his love for Preston, detailing their intense and passionate relationship and how he was devastated when it all came to an end. Preston was shifting uncomfortably on the sofa while Serendipity clumsily draped herself over him, trying to act in a reassuring way, but instead mauling him like a large cat.

Donal was in a state of shock now. Edith's grandson was certainly a dark horse. What was the world coming to? This would have never happened in his day. You found your sweetheart and you stayed with her. Sure, there were some people who were attracted to the same sex, but people didn't chop and change and go around shouting about it.

Edith had gone very quiet. Donal took his eyes off the TV and looked back at her. She had collapsed in the chair and was motionless.

"Oh my goodness," he screamed. "HELP SOMEONE HELP...NOW!"

~

The *Elevenses* interview lasted about ten minutes, in which all the gory details came out. If not a little perturbed by the lingering smell, Polly and Will looked thoroughly pleased with their work on this hot scoop. It had certainly spiced up Monday morning.

Their subjects were all ushered back into a car, grabbing croissants, pains au chocolate, muffins and anything else they could lay their hands on as they were led through the green room and out to the rear of the building. They would be dropped back at the nearest station, with first-class train tickets in their hands and their reputations in the gutter again. They had all earned another load of cash and managed to get through the whole thing without Serendipity even knowing she was getting paid, so there was her share to divvy out between them too. This amounted to another grand or so each. Not to be sniffed at...just like Serendipity, in fact.

The more he sobered up the more Preston cringed at the result of his impromptu date night.

Preston turned to Stassy, waggling his finger and insisted: "This is the last one, Stass – the last one...we have got another nice lump sum coming, but we have to call it quits now – agreed?"

"Agreed," said Stassy, as her phone rang. It was the *Sunday Planet*.

"Anastasia, it's Raquel from the *Sunday*..."

"Ah, yes, hi there...please call me Stassy."

"Just saw you on *Elevenses*, Stassy, and I was wondering whether you would be interested in doing a follow-up article. We would keen to do a piece with all of you this time, highlighting the fact we broke the original story – what do you think?"

"I will talk to the others, but we feel we have done enough press, really," said Stassy, as Preston glared at her, nodding his head slowly and defiantly.

"OK, let's talk in a bit," said Raquel, ignoring Stassy's resistance. "Now this story is building, I'll be able to get you better money. You never know what might come of it? These situations have launched careers!"

Stassy asked for some time to "think about it" and put the phone down. It immediately rang again.

"Hi," said Stassy.

"And how is the dynamic duo?" said Marcello.

"Oh, hi, rat face. Are you calling up for a follow-up article as well?"

"What lies do you have this time?" hissed Marcello.

Fuck, thought Stassy, this cannot be happening...

"What on earth do you mean, Marcello?" she replied brazenly.

"Well, I had an interesting call this morning from someone that clearly isn't a fan of yours. A male conquest, who hasn't taken too kindly to your lesbian-claims. He has called you a liar and, you know what... the more I've dug the more I realised he was correct."

"Well, I'm not sure you can prove that, Marcello."

"Well, I believe I can," he sneered.

"And even if you could...what the hell are you going to do about it?"

"Well, I have two options... a) write an exposé article or b) maybe you and Sarah could somehow talk me out of it? I really enjoyed the other night; you were both superb. Seems such a shame for it to be a one-off experience and now, well, maybe it doesn't need to be?"

"Holy fuck, Marcello," exclaimed Stassy. "Are you trying to blackmail me?"

Sarah looked at Stassy...anxiously.

"Let's not call it blackmail," said Marcello. "That's such a strong word. Let's think about it as you're trying hard to prove the story and keeping me pleased so I'm not tempted to dig even further. I just saw you on the TV. I am sure you wouldn't want to jeopardise your payment for that, now would you?"

"Fuck off, wanker..." interrupted Stassy.

"So I take it you and Sarah will be round my place at 8pm, then? I will text you the address in case it has slipped your mind."

Marcello gave a loud cackle and put the phone down.

"Fucking hell, Sarah," exclaimed Stassy. "Someone called Marcello and told him I was a liar and now he wants us both to go over to his flat tonight for a repeat performance."

"REPEAT?" yelled Preston. "What does that mean?"

Sarah looked at the ceiling of the car, desperately trying to find the spot Serendipity found so interesting, while Stassy bit her lip and stared out of the window. Headphones now on, Ralph was oblivious.

"Oh, I get it," continued Preston, the penny

dropping. "I knew you two had been behaving a bit weird recently. You've been getting it on, haven't you? Lies become truth...fuck, what is happening to us?"

"I don't know," said Sarah. "We can't let him blackmail us, he could play this game again and again."

"Yeah, but it's this time that's so critical," argued Stassy. "We can't afford to be exposed as liars this week. We have a lot of money riding on it."

"Lucky bastard," muttered Preston, with the only scant consolation, the fact that by not protesting, he was essentially pimping Stassy and Sarah out to save his own cut of the latest round of cash. But, boy, did he wish they were coming round to his place tonight instead.

Before Preston could protest further, his phone rang...

There was silence in the car as Preston listened intently, horror slowly engulfing his face.

"OH MY GOD NOOOOOOOOOOOOOOOOOO," he exclaimed. "FUCK FUCK FUCK. Dad, I am so sorry...so so sorry...how could I know she was going to watch it? OK, I'm on my way. I'm in Birmingham so I'm halfway there. It won't take me long. Have you managed to get a flight from South Africa?"

Preston looked like he had seen a ghost...and asked the taxi to pull over. He opened the door and threw up on the pavement.

"What is it, Preston?" said Stassy, as Serendipity tried to hug him again.

"Fuck off, you smelly bitch," screamed Preston.

Everyone in the cab momentarily giggled, also acutely aware this was no laughing matter.

"Grandma watched the programme this morning," wailed Preston, uncontrollably. "She's had a heart attack and is in intensive care. I need to get to Hull...as soon as possible."

The cab went silent. Stassy tried to console Preston. This was all her fault. How had something so futile turned into this?

Nobody spoke. They got to the station, helped Preston get connecting tickets to East Yorkshire, and saw him onto the train. He was in pieces.

The rest of the party took the train to London. Fortunately Serendipity had been banned from first class as, apparently, you needed to be wearing shoes to sit in that carriage. The mood was sombre and everyone felt dreadful for Preston, his poor grandmother and his parents.

As Stassy and Sarah attempted to mentally prepare themselves for another threesome, Preston's mental anguish was just gruesome.

14

Alexa had heard a commotion at dawn. Sarah and Stassy had been awake unusually early and a car had arrived...or had it dropped someone off? Alexa had gone back to sleep, and woke again just after 11am. She had turned on the TV and choked on her rice cake when she saw them all sat on the sofa with Polly and Will. Who on earth was Preston with? She looked like she should be hugging a tree, not him.

Alexa was raging, but what could she do? At least she was trying to find fame through honest methods, good looks, a good figure and a relationship with a genuine celebrity. This sorry lot were just lying their way towards their dubious infamy, not that they had craved any fame in the first place.

Alexa decided to go to the gym, clear her head and work off some steam. "Anger is a driving energy," she reminded herself.

As she came out, Steve called.

"Hi, baby," he said tenderly.

"Hiya," said Alexa.

"Are you OK, gorgeous?"

"Not really."

"What's wrong, baby?"

"It's Stassy...that stupid cow and her never-ending campaign of fucking lies, and her idiot cronies," spat Alexa. "That lot seem to go along with every move and agree to anything she says. I'm just not sure where this ridiculous story is going to end. She was on *Elevenses* this morning lying her tits off...yet a-fuck-ing-gain! I am fed up of her lies, their lies. Now you're about to go prime-time, this is bad news for us."

"Look, baby don't worry about it," said Steve calmly. "They are stupid, yes, and they shouldn't be messing with the press like that, but they won't bring us down. Never. What is it they say? No such thing as bad publicity...and I can't see you hanging out with them once we're both A-list."

Alexa sighed, dejectedly. "Oh, Steve, I don't know."

He continued: "Look, why don't you come over tonight, baby? I'll cook some dinner and show you some moves you will never forget. It'll take your mind right out of this nasty place it's in...and into another world. Are you up for it, baby?"

"Sounds good, darling. I need to take my mind into that place, wherever the fuck it is. I can't wait. I love you, Steve. I don't know what I'd do without you right now. You always make me feel better."

"I love you too, Alexa, and can't wait until tonight, hot stuff."

~

Alexa arrived at Steve's penthouse. He had laid out an array of food, mostly raw and salad based. Alexa didn't mind. She needed to keep a count on calories. Putting on weight was bad for business. It was nice to be with someone also on that level. After they had eaten, Steve led her into the bedroom and placed a yoga mat by the bed.

"Right," he announced triumphantly. "This position is called 'the plough'."

He continued: "Lie on your back and put your head on the mat facing the bed and arms down by your sides. I want you to swing your legs up and over your head and rest them on the bed."

Alexa acrobatically did as she was told, and Steve then bound her arms together and put handcuffs with a bar into the middle onto her ankles.

He left the room and came back with a bottle of champagne. Pouring some into Alexa's open mouth, Steve then doused her naked torso with the rest. The fizzy 'Bolly' cascaded down across her breasts, the various strands of liquid gathering on her stomach into one flow, which ran expertly towards her crotch and in between her legs.

"The pour-fect way to ingest champagne, my dear Alexa," said Steve, bending down to lick at her sticky nipples.

Wow, thought Alexa. This is amazing.

Steve then lay on top of her on the bed, carefully positioning himself so his weight was on his arms rather than her. Alexa was indeed taken to a better place, and she momentarily forgot the worries her flat-mates and best mates had thrust upon her and the threat to her and Steve's careers...and relaxed.

"Oh, my fucking God, Steve," she screamed, as she came in an explosive frenzy. "You are so fucking good at fucking."

~

Stassy and Sarah gathered themselves as the train pulled into Euston and they staggered onto the platform. It had been a helluva day. They had briefly talked to Preston as he had arrived at the hospital. His grandmother was in intensive care and not in a good way. Preston was by her side and, with his parents on their way from South Africa, he was mortified and petrified in equal measures.

148

The girls took the tube from Euston to Highbury & Islington and walked back through Highbury Fields, an eerie silence descending on their favourite stomping ground as they made their way home.

As they neared the house, Stassy's phone rang. It was Marcello. She answered it reluctantly.

"You still ready for tonight, baby?" he inquired.

"Not really," said Stassy. "We've just had news that Preston's grandma is in intensive care...because of the shock of the story."

"And..." responded Marcello ruthlessly.

"Well, believe it or not...wanker...when one of your best friend's relatives is ill...from your own doing...you don't exactly feel like a threesome."

"Well," sneered Marcello. "I would have thought a threesome was the perfect way to take your mind off all that..."

"Well," fumed Stassy. "That just shows what a bunch of fucking cunts you reporters are, doesn't it?"

"Now, now," reasoned Marcello. "You should have thought of that before all those lies, darling? There is an awful lot at stake here? Your lies have now delighted the viewers of *Elevenses*...you've had your mid-morning brunch with Will and Polly...and now it's time for mid-evening munch with Marcello."

"Adios," said Stassy, slamming down the phone, as she stifled a smirk. "What are we going to do, Sarah?"

"You started this, Stassy," pointed out Sarah sternly. "You need to deal with it. I don't exactly want to sell my soul to the devil either, but last time was good sexy fun. I enjoyed being with you and Marcello. He is pretty hot, and you are one fine-looking lady."

Sarah was now blushing profusely.

"So you're saying we should just go and have some fun?" said Stassy.

"Totally. It's been a pretty incredible day - for good

and bad reasons. Let's go and let our hair down. I could certainly do with a drink, whatever happens."

"Fuck it," said Stassy. "We haven't got much choice. Shower, change, lippy and out again. I'll order a taxi to Marcello's for half an hour."

The girls slipped into the house and did the necessary turnaround in 30 minutes flat. Beep beep, trotting out the door in their heels, and on their way to Marcello's. Stassy wore a silky black dress with plunging neckline and Sarah, a fitted black chiffon blouse which clearly revealed a silver sequin bra underneath.

"Wow," said Stassy. "Dressed for the part I see, darling."

Little was said in the cab. The silence broke only for small talk and nervous giggles. Each passenger spared as many thoughts possible for poor Preston.

Buzzed in via the intercom system, this time the duo made their way up to the roving reporter's apartment in a rather more sober fashion...albeit, for Sarah, with the faint flashback of that drunken slut-drop.

The conniving hack opened his front door, sporting a huge grin...holding a silver tray boasting three gigantic lines of cocaine. Nose candy for his candy girls.

Fittingly, hot off the press, blagged from the Music Editor at *Nearer*, 50 Cent's new album *The Massacre* was playing.

"Nose-up, ladies?" he asked. "And champagne, of course. Don't tell me I don't treat you right. I might even invite you to *my* candy shop...let you both lick my lollipop.

Stassy and Sarah looked on despairingly, but they couldn't deny that Marcello had prepared well for his erotic evening's activities, with a raft of extras to ensure this night went off with a bang. Ever since the last encounter he had been obsessed with the thought of it happening again. He had fantasised about it continually, dreaming about how he could do it even better than the last time. When the call had come through, effectively exposing them, his mind had gone into overdrive. This was his ticket. If nothing else, this could guarantee him a steady stream of Stassy and Sarah.

He handed the girls half a Hi-Agro tablet each. Octagonal in shape and typically green in colour, the Hi-Agro had quickly become a big player in the legal high scene, and synonymous with improving your sex drive. Marcello necked one himself, and filled up his guests' champagne flutes.

"Something to wash it down with?" he suggested. Those last lines already hastily devoured by the girls, they obediently swallowed the broken little green pills and gulped their bubbly down.

But Marcello was not being upfront about everything.

Plunging the whole sorry episode into new depths, he had set up a series of covert cameras and audio mics throughout his flat, hoping to capture Stassy and Sarah - and particularly his favourite Sassy Stassy - in all their glory.

Since dropping out of film school to major in journalism, he had always fancied himself as a director and now his time had come.

"Lines, champers, action," he whispered to himself as he leaned around the back of the shelving unit in his lounge to activate the master switch for his crude covert audio-visual creation.

He had test-piloted the intricate set-up a number of times, since he bought the system from a surveillance specialist website some years before for an investigative job he was working on. This was too good an opportunity to miss, especially as any admission of guilt he could capture would be priceless, and give him even more leverage.

He was sure the result would be amazing, better than the porn he normally got off on. He would record a show he could watch at his own pleasure...and leisure. Just the thought of pressing 'record' sent a tingle all over his body.

Button pressed, hopes high, as Marcello spun around he could tell the girls were starting to loosen up, so he topped up their glasses some more and laid out some more lines.

Was the Hi-Agro starting to kick in now too? Did it work on women? Neither Stassy or Sarah were quite sure, but there was a unmistakable whiff of sexual tension in the air. Marcello had quickly assumed the role of leader.

"So then, ladies," he began. "Do you want to start by telling me what on earth is going on?"

"Do you know anything about tumbleweed?" sniped Stassy.

"Isn't it a Mexican bush that keeps on rolling?" said Marcello.

"Exactly, and that's kinda what happened here," explained Stassy. "I filled out a sex survey. I was bored, I lied, I put my mate's number on it and then the phone started ringing...people throwing money at us. It just kept rolling."

"For lies?" clarified Marcello.

"Well, for..." stuttered Stassy.

"Lies," insisted Marcello.

"Yes, for lies..." admitted Stassy, her defences down.

"I see," said Marcello, excitedly. "Well, I think it's time to pay your dues, then, you naughty girls."

"And why should we do that?" demanded Stassy, incredulously. "You made up a load of shit too. I mean, vagetarians? C'mon?"

Sarah glared at Stassy. She had just admitted to lying to Marcello in return for thousands of pounds. Surely she knew why they needed to have some fun...to defuse this situation. Why was Stassy trying to wriggle out of things at this late stage of the game? And, holy shit, didn't she realise how hot she was looking right now?

Marcello was playing the role of dominant master, but was also mindful not to incriminate himself. The key purpose of this recording was obviously for his own pleasure, but, in the wrong hands, the footage could leave him exposed. His bosses would not be impressed he had paid so much for a fraudulent story.

As much as his magazine didn't want the 'truth to get in the way of a good story' – more an unwritten rule than a mission statement – the powers that be hated paying for blatant lies. Breaking the fact that the story had been fabricated was hardly going to make the medicine go down, either. Marcello should have done his homework before interviewing these two chancers, and definitely before paying for their nonsense. Right now, he still needed to keep them on side.

"Well, I am a relatively easy man to please," he continued. "It doesn't take that much to keep me quiet."

"OK, cards on the table," insisted Stassy. "It's one more time and more time only, right? I have never been at anyone's 'beck and call' and I am not about to start now!"

Attempting to call Marcello's bluff further, she added fiercely: "If you want to expose that you paid so much money for a bunch of shit, then do it."

As much as the coke was helping to dilute the severity of this sordid situation, it was also giving Stassy a warped clarity...and a bravado which meant she could still give as good as she got. Unfortunately for her, she didn't know she had already handed Marcello far too much.

As the latest line of cocaine took hold and gave Stassy a familar sensation at the back of her throat, she glanced at Sarah to assess her reaction to her latest outburst. Her housemate grinned back at her forgivingly.

The more time Stassy spent with Sarah in such intimate situations, the more she actually fancied her. This really wasn't the worst evening she'd ever had. Marcello was plying them with free champagne and coke. If she were honest, she was quite enjoying the tension with their host. It was the ideal way to take her mind to off poor Preston. At least for now.

Stassy wasn't known for her conscience. However, she knew full well she had brought this on Preston. Although he was a bit of a fool, she adored him and, although she would never admit it, she saw him in the role of 'annoying younger brother' and she always had his back. Even if the chance of Marcello exposing them was slim, the fallout for Preston, especially with his parents on the next plane to London and his grandmother on the edge, was horrific.

Back in the room and Marcello didn't want it to be the last time, he really didn't, but he was realistic. He might never have enough sway to engineer this situation again. He knew that the procurement of this video, as underhand as it was, would let him relive the next few hours for eternity. If tonight was going to be the last time, he was going out with a bang!

He racked up more lines. Stassy and Sarah were flying.

Marcello pulled out some clothes from a bag: he had prepared, and prepared well.

"Something I made earlier," he exclaimed, holding

out two schoolgirl outfits.

"More like something you laid earlier, you dirty sod," replied Sarah.

"C'mon, you devious hussies," he pleaded. "Why don't you give them a go?"

Each outfit had tops that were tied at the waist and shorter-than-short skirts.

Stassy and Sarah looked at each other. The heady cocktail that Marcello had supplied was really taking effect.

"Do you have a cane?" teased Stassy.

"Really?" asked Marcello, his face lighting up.

"Well, naughty schoolgirls..." continued Stassy, effortlessly getting into character again, "...if that's what we're meant to be? Aren't we meant to be in your office, sir? For being very naughty, sir?"

Who exactly was the actress around here, thought Sarah?

"No, Stassy, I don't own a cane," said Marcello, grabbing a Nike Air Max trainer from under his coffee table. "But I do have a gym slipper here. You both deserve to be spanked. You know cheats should never prosper."

Marcello paused. He was starting to regain confidence in his role.

"Time to get dressed, ladies...NOW! I won't ask again. Please don't make me angry..."

Marcello produced two white shirts that were pretty much see through. "I need to see your cleavage, so not all the buttons please."

Marcello handed out fishnet stockings and suspenders.

"Right, take your panties off...definitely no panties."

Stassy and Sarah dutifully complied with Marcello's demands, and nodded in approval at each other's 'finished product', both feeling very sexy in their new outfits.

"Bend over, ladies," perved Marcello.

Stassy and Sarah giggled, then both knelt on the wide leather sofa that dominated the front room, simultaneously thrusting their backsides towards Marcello.

"Let me give these lovely things a squeeze," said Marcello, before momentarily dropping his guard and then, able to resist no more, slapping both their bums firmly.

Stassy groaned and started to kiss Sarah. She pushed Sarah onto the sofa, tugging at her skirt.

Marcello was really enjoying the action. Shit, he thought, I am a lucky boy, as he watched his students go for it. This would make a great film; he couldn't wait to watch his work.

After 'observing' for a while, Marcello decided he wanted a bit of the action.

"Come on, ladies, make room for me."

Stassy and Sarah parted and let Marcello in on the fun, as he nestled in between them. Hell, those girls had gone for it. With him...with each other...with that strap-on he had produced from nowhere. And, significantly, with Stassy on her own while Sarah fixed more drinks. There had been no holding back. It was frantic. The girls both collapsed in his bed and he retired to the front room...officially, the happiest man ever to spend the night 'on the sofa'.

He couldn't wait to relive that night tomorrow, the next day and the day after...all thanks to 'lines, champers, action'.

15

Stassy left Marcello's around 9am and went straight to work. Sarah took a taxi back two hours later. She was exhausted from the night's activities. Her head was spinning as the cab weaved its way through north London. She hoped things wouldn't be awkward with Stassy. Her mate was on fire last night. She had really got into this latest 'performance'...or maybe it was just that Sarah could remember more this time around. Stassy had an insatiable sexual appetite – the rumours were true – so much so that Sarah had gone to bed while Stassy and Marcello carried on in the lounge a bit longer.

She wondered whether she would ever get together again with Stassy...without Marcello in the mix. Would it be as good? She felt confused. She knew she was definitely attracted to men. She had never felt attracted to another girl before and she wasn't sure she would have even looked at Stassy in this way if the lies to the press hadn't started, but now she could no longer deny an increasing infatuation. Stassy was a beautiful woman...stunning...and being with her in that way had opened Sarah's mind, frazzled as it was through all that cocaine and booze, to a whole new world.

~

Preston had hardly left his grandmother's hospital

bedside since she had been admitted and he was there, looking particularly sheepish, when his parents arrived. His dad welled up the minute he saw his own mother, tubes and wires consuming her.

Preston had never seen his dad cry and it made him emotional too. His mother glared at him and, not for the first time in the last few weeks, her son buried his head into his hands.

"What have you done, Preston? What have you done?" she blubbed.

"I am so sorry, Mum...I really am. How could I have known it would lead to this?"

"I am so ashamed," said Mrs Price. "I brought you up to always tell the truth, Preston. I just don't understand it."

"I can't believe how I was drawn into all this. It all started as a bit of a joke. I am SO sorry."

"Lying never pays, Preston," his dad fumed, wagging his finger at his inconsolable son.

Preston was probably at the lowest point of his life. He had hardly slept. His grandma was on death's door and his parents were suddenly back in his life with a devastating bang. His workplace had not reacted well to his *Elevenses* appearance or his subsequent unplanned leave, and it looked like he was in the firing line, fully expected to be accused of bringing the company into disrepute.

~

Marcello had called in sick at work. There was no way he was making it in today. He felt sluggish but extremely satisfied. Stassy had been on formidable form last night and he had really felt a connection with her. He decided to text her. He had to see her again.

The conniving reporter planned to spend the rest

of the day in his dressing-gown watching what he had recorded, and would then start work on an initial edit. The explosive footage had been stored on an external hard drive, so he connected it to his gleaming white Apple iMac computer, and fired up the iMovie progamme that would help him create his murky masterpiece. He needed a version which was mainly centred on Stassy, purely for his own pleasure. Sarah was OK and seeing Stassy with her had been amazing, but he wanted a movie of Stassy on her own. It was going to be an enjoyable day off.

~

Stassy arrived at the office and made a beeline for her desk, head down. Shattered and sheepish, she felt everyone from the receptionists to the office staff to the cleaners clocking off from their nightshift were staring at her...whispering to each other....giggling.

Thank goodness this contract had almost ended and Stassy could leave and start a new position, where hopefully people would not recognise her. Fat chance...she was both drained and deluded.

Yesterday was a crazy day. Up at 4.30am, she hadn't crahsed out utnil at least 4am the following morning...at a conservative guess. Against all odds, the potent cocktail of alcohol and drugs had got her firing on all cylinders, as she pushed both her mind and body to the limit. Marcello was one sexy man...and as for Sarah? Well, she cringed thinking how far things had gone again with her pal. Hopefully, their friendship was strong enough to withstand all this.

Stassy's phone vibrated.

Hey baby, you were super-hot last night...super-hot! I felt so much more of a connection this time

- I would love to take you out sometime...just the two of us, let me know baby - Marcello xxx
Stassy put her phone down. She just couldn't think about him or any more of that right now.

~

Marcello's boss, Jack, took an agitated call around 2pm that afternoon. Worried his impromptu chat with Marcello hadn't had any impact, spurned lover Adrian decided it was time to take things up a notch by calling the magazine's editor. He had now also gathered more evidence on how he could prove Stassy's story was all lies.

Marcello's boss was livid. He had paid a lot of money for a story his flamboyant reporter had insisted was a scoop they couldn't resist.

This irate caller really seemed to have it in for Stassy, and didn't care who knew. With this fresh evidence surely about to do the rounds, Jack was sure that these lies would be exposed somehow, and then he would be in hot water with his own superiors. He was fuming. It was careless. Marcello should have done some basic research before he presented the story to him. The furious editor was indignant when he further discovered Marcello had called in sick that morning.

~

Unaware of the drama unfolding back at the office, Marcello was really enjoying his stint at video editing. He felt this could be a new vocation for him and, boy, might he need one. Stassy was looking even hotter than he had remembered. He really focussed on his star's best positions. As he scanned back and forth through the recording, the more he had to relieve the rising bulge in his boxers. The after-effects of the Hi-Agro was still fuelling his insatiable lust...the relentless footage of Stassy compellingly addictive.

Back in the real world, Marcello was upset Stassy hadn't returned his text. It had felt like she was really into him. He was like a man possessed, constantly checking his phone to see if she had replied.

It had been several hours since he had messaged her. Frustrated, he turned back to 'virtual' Stassy. He was in control of her.

~

Marcello made it into work the next day. A memo on his desk ordered him to meet with his boss at 10am. Not good. He was even more alarmed when he arrived at his editor's office to see the company HR Manager sat next to him.

"Shit," he said under his breath. "This looks ominous."

"Hi Jack," he said tentatively as he entered the room.

"Sit down, Marcello," said Jack impassively. "As you know, this is Rebecca from HR."

"Hiya, Rebecca," said Marcello, as positively as he could muster.

"Well," his boss began, shifting on his chair, looking furious. "I had a call yesterday from an angry young chap who claimed that the Stassy/Sarah story we printed last week was completely untrue."

"Right," said Marcello. "I don't know anything about that."

"Well, from our initial investigations, it looks like it may have been fabricated."

"Really? Well, erm, I don't know about that."

"Well, you know the protocol at this magazine is to check all the facts before we go to print. You know that - it has been drummed into you enough times. Can you explain what you did to verify the facts on this occasion?"

Rebecca from HR was poised with her pen.

"Well, I interviewed them. I had no reason to believe they were lying. Why would they lie? And anyway, the story had already been in the *Sunday Planet.*"

"Marcello, you paid them almost ten grand for this story. Could that have been a good incentive for them to lie? And when did we ever take the *Sunday Planet*'s word for it?"

"Yeah, but..."

"I can't believe you are comparing the quality of our magazine to that trash," shouted Jack. "We pride ourselves on how accurate our stories are. The *Sunday Planet* has no morals, you know that too. For a top story at that price I expect some basic investigation."

"Basic investigation? I always cover the basics," countered Marcello.

"Yeah, right. Like checking whether Preston Price and Stassy had actually been married?"

"They gave me wedding photos? Surely that is proof?"

"Well, a marriage certificate may have been more conclusive. I dug around for about ten minutes earlier and discovered it doesn't exist. Don't give me basics."

"How often have you known lying interviewees to go to such great lengths...actually faking a wedding?" hit back Marcello.

"People do a lot for ten grand and ten grand is a lot of money for this magazine. I have no doubt the real story will come out and then where will we be? I be? I signed this off as I believed you had done enough work to verify the authenticity of this story. You know I place my total faith and trust in my reporters and I've always looked out for you."

Historically, Jack and Marcello had always been close - Jack the deputy editor when Marcello joined the magazine. Both London United football fans, Jack was always generous with corporate tickets for matches that came his way.

"Yes, Jack, and I've always done my best for this magazine. I expect more support from you on this, though. It's impossible to get it 100% right all the time. You know that."

Rebecca from HR decided it was time to step in. The conversation was getting both heated and personal.

"Look Marcello," she interrupted. "We already have good evidence to suggest this story is fake. It was a big deal for the magazine and we paid top whack for it. Your training has instilled in you that working for this magazine requires a high level of investigative journalism to ensure that we are not exposed for printing incorrect information. We pride ourselves on the truth. I am therefore telling you that you are under a disciplinary investigation. You need to go home now while we investigate the circumstances. I will write to you with the minutes of this meeting today and tell you about the next steps. You will be paid during this period and we will meet in around two weeks to conclude what we have found from our investigation. I will be in touch."

Marcello was in a state of shock. Jack had his back no more.

Rebecca from HR accompanied him back to his desk, suggested he collected any important personal belongings, and then escorted him out of the building.

Marcello stood motionless outside in the street for

a few minutes. He was stunned. This was not what he'd expected when he had turned up to work that morning. He staggered down the road, crestfallen. The pub was opening. He crashed through the doors and ordered a pint and a tequila shot.

"It's a bit early...even for you, Marcello?" said the barman.

"Today has been a dreadful day, Paul," said Marcello. "Same again."

"Steady, Marcello. It's only midday."

"There has been enough of today already for it to be a truly dreadful day, Paul. Same again, please."

Stassy still hadn't replied to Marcello's text. Fuck her, he thought, as he downed another shot, at virtually the same spot he had seduced her and Sarah after that initial interview. Mourn-Star Martinis all round this time.

Meeting Stassy Thomas had been a disaster. She was a temptress, and he had been callously lured into her lair. The one good thing to come out of it was the sex tape he now had.

Marcello sank his pint, did his third shot of tequila, and slammed both on the bar for another round. He wanted revenge.

16

Marcello got home about 4pm. Intoxicated. He had stayed for several more solo rounds at the pub, until Paul started suggesting it was about time he left. 'They' decided that meeting his colleagues, or potentially ex-colleagues, in the pub as they finished work was probably not his best move. Drinking manically on your own is never a good look, whatever the circumstances.

He poured himself a pint of tap water, ordered some pizza and returned to his editing. He felt he had nothing to lose now. Sure, the magazine was 'carrying out an investigation', but as far as he was concerned the whole thing was futile. It was pretty clear from Rebecca that it was game over. He would have to go through the motions...reconvening in a couple of weeks' time for a sign-off meeting.

He needed to think of No 1 now. The work he had done on the edited version of Monday night's sex-fest was action-packed. He had captured Stassy in all her glory. She looked fantastic, and was unwittingly immersing herself in the role.

He thought about a new job in editing, specialising in adult film. He would need funds to buy himself some time following his 'disciplinary'. These chancers had cashed in...why shouldn't he? But he needed to move fast. Stassy's antics could soon be yesterday's news.

Marcello poured the half-full pint of water into the kitchen sink and cracked open a cool can of Stella. Fuck her, fuck them, fuck everyone right now. Now firmly back on the sauce, and determined to devour the rest of the beers in the fridge, Marcello threw caution to the wind and bowled back into his living room. He started to research online, quickly finding a website that specialised in 'celebrity' sex tapes called *All-Star Porn-Star*. How fitting, he thought, although he may well have shared his last Porn-Star Martini with Stassy and Sarah.

Hardcore homemade footage of a footballer's W.A.G, a hard-up reality TV star and the estranged daughter of a famous actor were all advertised on the site. Download a 30-second teaser clip for free or watch the full unadulterated action for a fiver. A flashing banner across the top of the screen announced....WE PAY HARD 5-STAR MONIES FOR HARD ALL-STAR HONIES.

Marcello gulped. This was serious, but there was no time for sentiment. The porn world took no prisoners and, if nothing else, he had also been well-schooled in leaving his scruples at the door. His mentor and editor Jack was right. Someone would expose Stassy any day soon. It might as well be him. He needed to beat her other spurned lover to the prize...be ahead of this particularly sordid game. Before another irate 'ex' jumped on board.

There was an '0898' number on the contact page of the website. Marcello composed himself and made the call.

"*All-Star Porn-Star,*" answered a lady in monosyl-labic tones befitting such an enterprise.

"Hi there. I have got some rather delightful footage that I think you may be interested in. And there's a nice little twist, a topical exposé story that involves an infamous bisexual babe, the UK's biggest tabloid newspaper, and a prime-time daytime TV show."

"OK, interesting...very interesting," said the voice perking up on the other end of the phone. "Tell me more..."

"Ring me back and I will tell you everything," replied Marcello, with half a thought on his impending sacking. "This seems to be a premium-rate number."

"OK, what's ya number, doll?"

Marcello gave his details and hung up. Within a few seconds his phone rang.

"So what do you have to offer us?"

"Well, there has been the story of this most amazing scandal in the papers, magazines and on daytime TV over the last couple of weeks which is, shall we say, a complete lie. It's like a bisexual love triangle, but with five sides...and each one completely fabricated. More like a twisted love pentagon, really."

"A love penta what?" asked the lady.

"Well, you know...a filthy, conniving debauched love pentagon," continued Marcello, getting into the part far too easily himself, the lager fuelling his bravado. "And I have the leading lady on tape admitting the whole thing is a shameful sham. She then indulges in both lesbian and heterosexual activities – it's in-depth – if you get my drift? I want to sell it for cash, but I won't accept a stupid offer."

Ears pricked, the woman on the other line of the phone was clearly interested.

"OK, so let me just get this clear. You have a sex tape that will expose a tabloid slash daytime TV story and has some extremely explicit content involving both women and men."

"Well, two women and a man, but in a nutshell ...yes!"

"Well, this seems like something we would be more

than happy to take a look at," confirmed the woman. "Can you visit our offices in Soho tomorrow afternoon to show us the footage?"

Marcello took down details of the address, just off Old Compton Street, and wrapped up the phone call. "Great, I look forward to meeting you tomorrow," he gushed.

He then spent the rest of the day and evening ensuring the tape was just right. It needed to expose Stassy's lies, but also be up there with the best sex tapes out there. It was all about Anastasia. He would be careful to edit out any sign of drugs, reduce Sarah to a bit-part and make sure he couldn't be recognised or implicated whatsoever. He was confident he had enough footage of Stassy to pull this off...to pull anyone off!

~

When Marcello woke the next morning his head was throbbing. The grim reality of his suspension was really taking hold. But he knew what he had to do. He grabbed the blank DVD, scribbled on it the slightly revised title of '*Lies, Champers, Action*' in marker pen and left his house for Soho.

Striding along Old Compton Street, then taking a left into Greek Street, Marcello shuffled into an alleyway, entering the backstreet offices through the sort of nondescript side door befitting a shady porn empire.

Once inside and up two flights of a steep, grubby, carpeted staircase, Marcello pushed through a set of double doors and found himself in a surprisingly plush reception, manned by a brassy buxom mature lady, aged in her late '40s, oozing an unmistakable MILF-like-chic that said 'been there, done that, worn the wet T-shirt.'

"Hi, I'm Linzi," she purred. "We spoke on the phone yesterday. Please take a seat, darling, I'll just buzz through to Jerry."

Marcello heard Jerry Jerkoff booming down the corridor before he actually saw him. He had already noticed a huge framed publicity poster of him on the wall for a film called 'Jerking Girl', which, if he wasn't mistaken, also featured a certain receptionist in her heyday.

"Hi, I'm Jerry," said a portly man in his early '50s, with dyed jet-black 'Only For Him' hair. "Jerry Jerkoff...pleased to meet you, son."

"Hi...Marcello."

Clearly not his real name, as per any porn star worth their salt, Jerry Jerkoff had lived a colourful life since those heady days of the mid-80s, when VHS was king, and his core hardcore business flourished...long before the internet finished off many of the traditional porn barons, 'actors' and 'actresses'. Sex sold much better back then. Sex sold well. Sex was solid gold. Sure the worldwide web opened up the whole industry and made porn more accessible than ever, but it had proved fatal for many too. Jerry had striven to move with the times, and embraced the internet, but he was largely out of his depth, an X-rated dinosaur ...a 'pornosaur'...'porn-anaras-anus-X', in fact. X-rated, but almost extinct too. The measly five pounds he could charge per download, if he was lucky, was a drop in the ocean compared to the price of a 'video tape' back in the day. Now it was all about volume, a profile and celebrity...and selling 'sex tapes' on the back of notoriety – preferably of celebrities on their backs, in their entirety.

"Right, son," said Jerry, encouraging Marcello to follow him back down the corridor. "Let's have a look at what you've got."

Jerry showed Marcello through to what he described as "the boardroom." Sure it had a huge table in it, but there were no chairs, a whole host of cameras and tripods in the far corner, plus what looked remarkably like a casting couch.

Jerry beckoned Marcello to sit down in a soft-seating area with hard stains at the far corner of the room, where a huge state-of-the-art flat screen TV and DVD player stood.

Marcello handed over the DVD. Jerry put it into the machine and pressed play. Marcello had also brought copies of various newspapers and magazine articles from the past few weeks and a tape of the *Elevenses* interview.

Jerry scanned the press as the footage started. The film began with its star confessing that her story was all lies. Next she was passionately kissing another lady, stripping her down, kissing her breasts and then taking off her skirt. She moved onto a mystery man. From the footage it wasn't possible to tell who the man or other girl was, but, bloody hell, this lady, who was totally identifiable, was giving them both the most amazing times of their lives. This lady was hot...really hot. Insatiable, in fact. This was one of the hottest supposedly non-scripted scenes Jerry had seen for a long time. He tried to contain his excitement as he needed to get a good price for this, but he knew instantly this was going to be lucrative for all concerned.

"Right, son. I want this but I ain't going to pay a huge price. Presumably you have consent from both the unsung and sung heroes in this footage?"

Marcello blushed.

"Rightio, well, that definitely pushes the price down as that presents a lot of risk for me."

"Well, give me your best price," said Marcello. "I watch a lot of porn on the internet. I know that even without the exposé to run alongside it, this is strong material."

Jerry knew this was true, and he believed this sex tape could be game-changing for his website. It was rare that something that ticked so many boxes came along. Stassy's performance had the potential to ensure everybody concerned did very well out of this, thank you very much.

"Look mate, I don't want to give you a bad deal. I'll give you £12,500 for all rights you have to this DVD."

"Sorry pal, that's not going to cut it," said Marcello. "I need at least £25k for this. I'm out of work soon. You know this is a gem. If you don't want it, I will find someone else."

Marcello, well-versed in bargaining tactics from his experience negotiating tabloid scoops, began to stand up as if he had been insulted and was about to walk out of the room.

Jerry could sense a good deal was slipping from his hands. He looked Marcello square in the eyes and said: "I'll take it now...twenty grand. That's my final offer."

It was a big deal for Jerry's company. This material was of the highest possible level, though...and fast-paced enough for today's cut-throat, competitive world of porn. He was sure the infamy already generated by this scam meant *All-Star, Porn-Star* could ride on this publicity pony for some time.

Marcello agreed to Jerry's revised offer and left the building with £1,000 in tatty £50 notes stuffed in his pocket...and an agreement promising the payment of the remaining £19k within three days.

Linzi winked and pouted at him as he skipped down the stairs. "All in a day's jerk," joked Marcello to himself. "All in a day's jerk."

Out in the seedy Soho air, Marcello suddenly spared a thought for Stassy. Just fleetingly, but a concerned thought all the same...did she really deserve to become an unwitting pornstar?

Then a moment of clarity. Fuck it! That bitch deserves anything coming her way. Her lies would probably cost him his precious job. She had already sold her soul to the tabloids, and the stunt he was about to pull had her modus operandi all over it. Stassy had earned good money from her lies. Why shouldn't he?

Marcello strode purposefully down the street, as ever, looking for the nearest possible pub in which to wax lyrical. The drinks were definitely on him.

17

Stassy was glad Sarah was out working when she got home. Emotionally and physically spent, she didn't feel like facing her just yet. She kept having flashbacks and again, post-getting it on with her bestie, she struggled with the aftermath of such intense and irregular intimacy.

As if by magic, and to give her something else to think about, Alexa stormed into the kitchen as Stassy was making her dinner.

"So Stassy, don't you think you might have gone a bit far this time? Your parents must be so proud of you lying like that on national TV...and who the hell was that Serendipity? She looked like she'd been found in a bush, let alone dragged through one!"

"I know, Lex...goodness knows where Preston picked her up from? She reeked and really let the side down."

"Oh, and you have such high standards, do you? You're pretty grubby yourself, Anastasia."

"That's a bit low, Alexa. When did you start being so prim and proper? Aren't you shagging a tacky yoga-sex-guru?"

"Yes, I am, thank you very much, and in the privacy of his tacky luxury fucking penthouse apartment..."

"Alexa, I am knackered. I've had a difficult 48 hours and I just want to eat some food and go to bed."

"And is this it?" asked Alexa. "What's next? Your

own sleazy reality show?"

"Listen," argued Stassy. "Preston is up north. His grandma is in intensive care. She had a heart attack watching *Elevenses* yesterday. I feel shit about the whole thing, if I'm honest with you. I don't think we will be doing any more press. It's pretty much game over. Please leave me alone, Alexa. I just want to sleep."

Alexa could see that Stassy was upset. For once, she decided not to push it any further. So far the fallout hadn't impacted her, and the news of Preston's grandma was genuinely devastating. She ordered a cab, and headed to Steve's.

~

Over in theatre-land, the TV interview didn't seem to be doing Sarah any harm. It was as if her fellow actors held her in a higher level of esteem because of it. Fame-hungry 'luvvies', one and all, deep down they were envious of the prime airtime Sarah had secured. Any TV exposure was good for an actor's career. Ticket sales were up slightly and she could also hear murmurings in the audience when she came on stage. However, Sarah was finding it hard to put Stassy to the back of her mind. She felt a weird tingle, just thinking about her...a tingle she had never experienced before. She called Stassy to check she was home, and grabbed a bottle of wine on the way back to the house...

~

Stassy was about to slope off to bed when Sarah arrived with two bottles of rosé, determined to cut the ice and lighten the mood.

"I forgot to ask whether you wanted red or white,"

said Sarah, sheepishly.

There was a distinct air of apprehension in the living space currently, as if all of the housemates were having relationship troubles...except this involved two of them, and with each other, not to mention Stassy's own issues with Alexa.

Sarah sat awkwardly on a kitchen stool, wondering how she could possibly open this conversation, but she needn't have worried.

"So..." started Stassy. "I know this is not going to be the right thing to say..."

Sarah wondered nervously what was about to come out of Stassy's mouth.

"...I just can't get Marcello out of my head," continued Stassy. "I know he has been an absolute shit, an complete bastard to be honest, but I just get this feeling he could be the one. I feel so mixed up."

"Hmmm?" mused Sarah, partly relieved, partly disappointed because of her increasing feelings for Stassy. She had seriously wondered whether something more could develop from this. Life imitating art! She had thought a lot about Stassy over the last few days.

"Well, I guess we do always tend to go for bad boys," reasoned Sarah. "I'm not sure Marcello can come good, though."

"He came very well, if you remember rightly," laughed Stassy. "But then he was in my expert hands; I'm pretty hot stuff, I'll have you know."

"Stassy," screeched Sarah. "You know what I meant."

As the laughter subsided and Stassy continued, Sarah stared lovingly at her housemate, her mind flitting back to Stassy going down on her...the amazing multiple orgasms she had experienced. If she was honest, she hadn't felt like that for years, maybe ever.

"What should I do?" begged Stassy. "It's a hopeless situation...it's totally the wrong start to a relationship, although at least he's one man who knows the truth."

"Yeah, who knows? Bad boys can change...and we haven't really given him the chance to be good yet, have we?"

"Agreed," said Stassy. "You could even argue that we led him astray in the first place."

"Look..." said Sarah, quickly coming to terms, somewhat frustratedly, that there would be no further discussion about their own romantic affairs, "...maybe you and Marcello can make it work one day. It is all a bit raw at the moment, but in time this will probably be an amusing story, a great tale. Maybe deep down he has a heart and a heart that will treat you right. You deserve that, Stassy. You deserve to be loved and loved the right way. We all do."

~

Preston woke up early on Friday at The Vacation Lodge, Hull. He was not doing well. He decided to call up work and quit...and started to look at how he could sublet his room. Sure, he'd earned some decent money in the last couple of weeks, but his hotel (and bar) bill was racking up. He was convinced he was going to be fired and it was probably best to jump before he was pushed. He might even get a decent reference that way. It was unlikely he was going to be able to leave the north for a while, and work were not going to let him take any more extended leave. To compound matters, his parents were still barely talking to him.

He called the office at 9am and told his boss he was very sorry for any offence he had caused, but he wouldn't be coming in again.

~

Also about to be 'unemployed', Marcello was not entirely enjoying his new-found freedom. In limbo waiting for his own judgement day, in front of the jury that was essentially toffee-nosed Rebecca from HR, he felt there was a huge vacuum in his life. There was only so long he could spend in the pub getting hammered.

The doorbell rang as he was mooching around in his dressing gown. It was the postman with a 'to-be-signed-for' recorded delivery envelope. Inside was a bankers' draft for £19,000. The void was filled. It was time to take a slow, smug, stroll to the bank.

~

Stassy had woken up feeling a lot better, after her chat with Sarah. Her own payment from *Elevenses* had cleared, and her bank balance was looking the healthiest it had ever been.

I am now a woman of means, she thought. Surely, all this shit will blow over any day soon. Yes, she felt dreadful about Preston and his poor grandma, but the old dear was probably on her last legs anyway, she tried to convince herself. She started thinking about Marcello. He was gorgeous...and she felt a definite chemistry between them. She should text him back, she decided.

> *Marcello – I am up for a one-on-one*
> *rematch – let's start with Sushi on*
> *Sunday and see where it takes us? x*

~

Marcello was in the bank about to deposit his banker's draft when the text came in from Stassy. Fuck, he thought, that's put the cat among the pigeons. He pondered for a moment, the cheque in his hand, the cashier looking expectantly at him. What price loyalty? What price the truth? He defiantly slipped the cheque under the counter and then simply replied...

Sushi Sunday is perfect - see u then baby...look forward to dessert x

With his bank balance about to climb heavily into the black, Marcello wondered what was about to become of Stassy and if there was any possibility they had a future. He really liked her, enough to consider starting a relationship with her, but surely when *'Lies, Champers, Action'* went live, any romance would be short-lived. He could have ripped up the cheque and blindly followed his heart, but it was too late for that now. Twenty grand was a lot of money for someone who was about to lose their job...

~

As the cheque cleared, the sex tape began to go out for its 'theatrical release'. Marcello had been checking allstarpornstar.com all day Friday, roughly every ten minutes or so. Finally, when he logged on late afternoon, there it was in all its glory. A flashing banner announced 'WORLD EXCLUSIVE – 'LIES, CHAMPERS, ACTION' – *the fake lesbo fakes it no more.'* Hot off the press, Marcello happily paid £5 on his credit card for the first download. Cha-ching!

~

It took Raquel at the *Sunday Planet* a matter of hours to pick up on the story, and the availability of the sex tape online, and to naturally connect it to her original article. She called news editor, Rob, over to her desk, and gestured towards her computer screen.

"What are we going to do about this?" she said. "This is Anastasia Thomas, the girl who I originally interviewed with her ex-husband about her lesbian affair, and his own gay fling. Remember?"

Rob nodded. Otherwise motionless, he looked intently at the hardcore footage. Stassy was really hot, but she had blatantly lied to the paper. Lied on the survey, lied at interview, and stunted up wedding photos to further corroborate all those lies.

The *Sunday Planet* had to print this reveal. If they didn't, someone else would. They needed to get a story together and a story together fast. If they tackled this head on, in their own inimitable style, they would come out looking like the victims and their readers would look like they had been duped too. Priceless.

But who were these people in the sex tape with her? In particular who was the girl with Stassy? Whatever the case, there was a great story to be had here, and with the tape going viral very quickly Rob quickly assembled a team of his sharpest reporters. "We need to get our facts together and get a story ready by the morning, and get something in the paper for Sunday," he barked. "A quote from Anastasia too. We need to give her the right of reply."

~

Saturday heralded Steve's big prime-time debut and the launch of his new show *Date With Destiny*. Alexa was excited – maybe more than Steve himself.

This was also her moment to shine, she thought...the start of her hitting the big time too.

First stop was an early appointment at the hairdressers. A three-hour stint - highlights, cut and blow-dry. Next a manicure, pedicure and eyebrow shape. Alexa was home for a quick lunch consisting of rice cakes with low fat cream cheese and slices of cucumber.

It took her around 40 minutes to find an outfit fitting of a TV presenter's girlfriend. She had been careful to choose something that was both stunning, and slightly unassuming – not easy – so she wouldn't outshine the host.

By 3pm Alexa was ready to go to the studio. A beep from a car outside the house sounded Steve's arrival and she ever so carefully trotted down the staircase that dominated the hallway of the house. The driver got out of the car, a black Mercedes S-Class, and opened the rear door. Steve, suited and booted, was sitting nervously inside.

"Gosh," he gasped. "You look gorgeous...absolutely stunning. I'm one lucky man to have you on my side tonight."

Alexa got in the car and Steve reached over and kissed her.

"Watch the lipstick," she giggled. "Are you ok?"

"To be honest, I am absolutely shitting it," admitted Steve. "I don't feel ready. The run through yesterday took hours. I'm not sure the crew are ready to do the whole thing live either. There's no chemistry yet. What if I mess up the autocue? This could be a very short stay at the top."

"Stay positive," stressed Alexa. "Really darling, it will be fine...you have just got to think it is no different from the other little quiz show you have been doing."

"Yeah, apart from the live audience and about four

million more viewers...yes, you're right, baby, it is absolutely the same."

"Hey, hey...c'mon, I meant standing on stage reading an autocue and presenting a quiz show, forget the audience at home...and in the studio...and do what you do best. That's why *you* are standing on that stage, baby. You have what other people don't have."

"You're right darling, you are right. Sorry I snapped, I'm just tense. I'm so pleased you're here. I don't think I could do this without you."

Alexa smiled coyly.

The car arrived at the studio and the driver leapt out and opened the rear door on Alexa's side. The couple got out and were greeted by a young female production assistant, holding a clipboard, with a headset on.

"Steve has arrived," said the lady into her mouth-piece. "I'm taking him through to the green room."

He has arrived indeed, thought Alexa. And so have I.

"Hiya, I'm Katie," said the production girl. "Let me show you through and give you a wristband."

Alexa was given a VIP wristie that was quickly and expertly fastened by Katie. No need for Steve to wear one. His face was plastered on all promotional material for the new show in the studio's foyer. He was automatically access all areas.

Inside the green room, Steve and Alexa settled down into a sumptuous leather sofa.

"We will come and get you for hair and make-up in about 20, Steve," said Katie. "There are some snacks and drinks here. Help yourself."

"I'm too nervous to eat," said Steve, the moment Katie had left the room.

"You'll be OK, my love," said Alexa soothingly, as she caressed the back of his neck. "Let me get you a Diet Coke."

It seemed liked an eternity before the hair and make-up artists arrived. Alexa was relieved when they did. She was running out of calming words to say to Steve, his nerves building rather than receding. Clichés like "it will be all right" were neither appropriate or effective.

While Steve was in hair and make-up, Alexa called Chloe.

"Hey babe, how are you?"

"I'm OK, babe, a bit bored...," said Alexa listlessly. "Just waiting around at the studio for Steve to go on. He's really nervous."

"He will be OK once he's up there," reassured Chloe.

"I know, but the waiting is endless, it is so tedious..."

Alexa could be such a diva at times.

"Isn't that the life of a TV star, Lex?" inquired Chloe. "There's bound to be lots of waiting around...unless you are really famous and then maybe you get helicoptered in and straight out again."

"Yes, I don't think we have quite made it that far yet," conceded Alexa, even managing a small chuckle.

"At least it's live and you'll wrap at a reasonable time," reasoned Chloe.

At that point Katie walked in and signalled to Alexa.

"Listen, lovely, I've got to go," she said. "Looks like I need to take my place in the audience now."

"Well, please pass my best on to Steve," said Chloe. "I'll look out for you...going to tune in now."

Katie took Alexa to her seat in the audience. And it was a good one, great view, although she wasn't so sure she would be in shot when they panned to the audience.

The audience 'warmer-upper' was in full swing as Alexa sat down. The jokes were dreadful, but the audience was on good form. They all seemed very excited to be there. Alexa turned off her mobile, anxious not to be responsible for anything that might distract Steve on his big night.

Finally, the countdown to Steve's entrance. Now Alexa was feeling nervous too. But then he appeared, her man, her boyfriend, her hero. Within minutes he was in his stride...

Alexa watched with delight as Steve charmed the contestants and faultlessly read the questions from the autocue.

Every ten minutes there was a pause for a commercial break, and everyone had a chance to breathe before they were counted back into the live show.

The set was glistening and the quiz had the audience gasping as two contestants went head-to-head in the final.

It was a hard-fought contest. When the eventual winner was announced, the audience clapped and Steve said: "That's it folks….join us again next week, for another episode of *Date With Destiny*."

And cut...

Katie came out and ushered Alexa back into the green room and Steve soon appeared grinning from ear to ear.

"That was amazing, baby," cooed Alexa.

"Thanks, hun. I feel so much better now that the first one is out of the way."

The executive producer came sailing into the green room with a bottle of champagne.

"Well done, Steve. You did really well, mate. Let's crack this open."

Glasses were poured and clinked to the sound of success. Several hours later Steve and Alexa stumbled into their car, and were taken back to his penthouse.

"What a night," exclaimed Alexa, as the couple stumbled into the lift.

"Yes, babe," drooled Steve, pressing her against the wall as he instructed the lift to rise.

"Now I want to celebrate in the best way I know how..."

~

Raquel rang Stassy. No answer. On seeing the reporter's name appear on her phone's screen, Stassy, who was holed up in her bedroom, decided she'd had quite enough of the *Sunday Planet* for the time being. She would deal with it next week.

~

Sarah's phone vibrated.

"Hi, babe," began Philippe. "How are you doing?"

"Good," said Sarah, trying to hide the pleasure in her voice that a call from Philippe always produced. "I'm not working this evening," she continued. "I have the day off, so I'm just chilling."

"Ah, good. I wanted to see if you fancied an early dinner before I start my club night? You can come to the venue after if you want to? Maybe see if any of the other girls want to come down? You know what it's like when I'm working...but be great to see you for dinner first, baby, whatever."

Sarah was a little taken aback. It was unusual to be asked out on a date in a primetime slot with Philippe. She wasn't going to complain, though. She was ecstatic, in fact, but determined not to let on.

Maybe she should pretend she already had plans? Did it look sad that she hadn't already made plans this Saturday night? What the heck, she told herself, this was too good an opportunity to refuse.

"Dinner would be good. About the club after...can

I take a view on that later on?"

"OK, sure," said Philippe.

"I did have some plans for later," lied Sarah. "But, it's nothing I can't get out of."

"OK babe...shall we go to that new fusion place near the club?"

"Sounds good...what time?"

"Let's do 7.30pm... I need to be on the door by 10-ish."

"Coolio, see you there."

Sarah spent a good couple of hours preparing for her impromptu Saturday night date, not that any date with Philippe wasn't fairly short notice. She wanted to look irresistible. Recent events had been emotionally confusing and it was good to be going out with Philippe...a real man! She lived in hope that he would realise he was in love with her and bring all his other suitors to a close. She settled on a low-cut black and gold cocktail dress, which was far shorter than it needed to be.

Philippe was waiting outside when Sarah arrived.

"Shit, baby – you look hot...red hot."

"Thanks, hun," replied Sarah, chuffed to bits. "I haven't really gone to too much effort, to be honest."

"You have effortless beauty, Sarah," said Philippe, a line even she knew was bordering on nauseous. What was he after?

Philippe took Sarah's hand and led her proudly into the restaurant. "So, how are things?"

"Good, really good," smiled Sarah. "Been a crazy few weeks actually, but life's pretty good right now."

Philippe nodded and gazed intensely into Sarah's eyes. She found his demeanour a little strange, almost unnerving. Philippe just seemed so much more amorous than usual.

"What you drinking, baby?"

"Wine would be good – white?"

"I'll order a bottle…"

Philippe walked to the bar, consumed by the Sarah and Stassy situation, a subject matter he had obsessed over for the past few weeks. What was Sarah like? Not coming clean last time about the stories in the press and her involvement…and now THE sex tape. Did she think it really could have passed him by? Did she realise the footage was currently the talk of the internet? Well, it was in the circles that Philippe mixed in; as a regular subscriber to *All Star Porn Star* he had received an email informing him of an imminent release linked to recent press activity. He knew it was Sarah immediately, and the familar tattoo confirmed it. He instinctively decided not to tell her about the tape.

He had now played the download umpteen times, though, and hadn't stopped thinking about Stassy and Sarah together since. He had to find a way to get Sarah and Stassy back to his flat. He had experienced a threesome before, but those girls weren't on the same level as Sarah and Stassy and definitely didn't have the skills he had witnessed on his dirty download.

Philippe and Sarah ate, drank and laughed, Philippe paying her compliment after compliment.

"Come to the club with me, baby…I want you by my side tonight. Help me by being the hostess with the mostess…and are any of the others around, anyone else you'd like to ask?"

"Well, I'm not sure…the others are all busy doing stuff. They weren't up for coming down."

Philippe's heart sank. Tonight would not be the night, but he wanted to keep Sarah on side. He was sure he could engineer a rendezvous with Stassy in due course. He must not mention any knowledge of the sex tape just yet.

"Please come," said Philippe. "I promise to make time for you and introduce you to a few people I know who are coming down."

Sarah was taken aback yet again. Philippe had hardly introduced her to any of his friends before.

"OK, let's do it then."

"Great baby...let's go."

For the rest of the evening. Philippe took her on his arm, paraded her around the club and introduced her to his friends as his "lady". Sarah felt the belle of the ball.

At the end of the night, instead of going back to his loft apartment in Shoreditch, which would have been the easier and nearest option, Philippe engineered retreating to 'the house' instead, in the hope that Stassy might be home.

"I really like you," purred Philippe in the cab back to Islington. "I can't quite put my finger on it, but I feel different about you, Sarah, and you look delicious tonight. I want to taste every bit of you..."

Philippe always looked tasty, but Sarah wasn't going to tell him that. She was just going to enjoy a seductive side of Philippe she rarely knew....and see how long it lasted. She was more than happy for him to put his finger on it.

But there was one huge reason that Sarah appeared different to Philippe...and her name was Stassy. Finding Stassy home was always a long shot, especially at 4am on a Sunday morning.

Unusually, Stassy was home, and even stranger, she had tucked herself in for an early night, ahead of her date with Marcello.

Philippe would have to regroup. Sarah would do for tonight, but next time he had to snare both of them. He was obsessed and possessed in equal parts with the very thought of it.

~

Marcello spent the whole of Sunday checking the *All Star Porn Star* website. The 'downloads' were already into the nine hundreds, and the film had only been up for 24 hours. This sex tape was about to blow up and already had all the hallmarks of a self-perpetuating viral sensation. Marcello momentarily bemoaned that he hadn't secured any extra royalties based on downloads, but the £20k buy-out he had negotiated did reflect that consent from all parties had not been secured.

Hugely impressed with the quality of his work all the same, Marcello smiled to himself, then automatically cringed that he was about to go on a date with Stassy. She couldn't know about the tape yet. She would have been in touch by now, surely. How had she not found out by now? He secretly hoped the date was a disaster so he wouldn't have to feel guilty about selling her out. He never usually risked dates on a Sunday; he was normally recovering from something or other. He was sure, where Stassy was concerned, he would never recover from his sly sordid subterfuge.

Marcello styled his hair back, cleaned his teeth and put on his favourite aftershave. He winked at himself in the mirror. Looking pretty damn good, he thought. First to arrive at the sushi restaurant in Hoxton, he went straight to the table and waited. Stassy arrived moments later, looking gorgeous, in a dress, her hair flowing. If she didn't look a million dollars, then she certainly looked more than the tacky twenty thousand pounds Marcello had sold her out for.

"Hi," he said anxiously.

"Hey," said Stassy, flicking her locks. "How you doing?"

"All the better for seeing you," said Marcello

reaching over to kiss her, acutely aware that he needed to make the most of this moment, this meal, and any resulting action later on in the proceedings.

Unless Stassy really didn't have any morals, there was no chance she was going to forgive him for the impending furore.

"Mmmm," said Stassy, blissfully unaware of the traitor in her midst. "That was nice."

This actually might turn out to be quite a pleasant date, thought Stassy. The flashbacks from the other night were still there, and she could feel herself blushing, but she was going to make the most of this night away from the spotlight. It would certainly be her last for some time.

They each ordered a beer and started talking, the conversation flowing freely. They discussed their childhood, their interests. They realised they had a lot in common. The food arrived, they ordered more beers, then sake, and talked incessantly.

In the end Marcello suggested they go back to his place, and Stassy eagerly agreed.

Giggling and holding hands, they piled into a taxi and began kissing. The taxi driver asked them to "come up for air" to tell him where they wanted to go. No wisecracks this time.

As they got into Marcello's flat and sat on the sofa, the double-crossing hack grasped Stassy's face and looked into her eyes. More Clark Cunt than Kent.

"You know, I really like you, Stassy," said the rogue reporter as genuinely as possible. "There just is something different about you...and, of course, you are stunningly gorgeous."

"Well, you are definitely more than meets the eye Marcello. I am enjoying myself."

"Would you let me take you to bed and show you a different side of me?"

"Please...show me the way."

While Stassy was in the bathroom, Marcello went back into the lounge and quickly logged on to *All-Star Porn Star* on his laptop. The downloads had jumped over the 10,000 mark. Shit, he thought, better make the most of this while I still can.

18

Stassy had set the alarm on her mobile for 8am. Another Monday morning...what surprises would today hold? For starters, she was surprised Marcello wasn't stirring too...maybe he had a late start? She grabbed a shower, got dressed and headed to work, kissing Marcello goodbye on his forehead as she left.

She stopped off home en route to pick up a clean pair of knickers, a top to wear...her jeans would do another day. Stassy had a spring in her step. Last night had been really fun and, well...just right. Marcello definitely had hidden potential. He was gorgeous, sexy, caring and lots of fun. Who knew? She didn't want to jump ahead of herself, but he could potentially be boyfriend material...a bold statement for her. She didn't feel like that about men. They were usually only good for one thing.

Stassy got into work, and it felt like there was more staring and more whispering than usual. She got to her desk and started working. The phone rang.

It was Sarah, shrieking. "OH MY GOD! Oh My God. Have you seen the The *Daily Planet* today?" she asked.

"No," said Stassy.

"Well, you are in it, lady," squealed Sarah, "...and I mean BIG TIME! Are you sitting down?"

"Yes...what the fuck has happened now?"

"Well, I don't know how to tell you this, honey, and you're not going to believe it, but apparently there's a video of the other night...the blackmail three-some...where you admit that you were lying and then you're, well, at it, with Marcello and me. I've been trying to download the video, but it looks like the website has crashed."

The *Daily Planet* was the equally feisty sister tabloid of the *Sunday Planet*. With Stassy and the other main players snubbing another chat with the paper, Raquel and co had not managed to get an official story together in time for their weekly Sunday edition. After deliberation between the two newsdesks, it was decided a piece, based on latest developments, would be run in the *Daily Planet* on Monday, to steal a march on the holding company's competitors.

"Fuck," said Stassy under her breath as she scanned the office. "By the looks I'm getting I think there might be a few people in this office currently downloading it."

"Marcello must have had a camera or cameras in his flat that night."

"That fucking little shit," stormed Stassy, failing to admit to Sarah that she was with him last night. "Right, that's it, I am taking legal advice," she announced.

Stassy called Chloe around ten minutes later from the car park. It must be serious.

"Can you talk?"

"Yes, give me a second. Let me find somewhere to chat."

Chloe slid into a meeting room and jumped back on the line. "What on earth is it, Stassy? You sound really distressed."

"I don't even know where to begin. This whole situation has descended into a total fucking living nightmare. Marcello, who works for *Nearer* magazine, found out I was lying and started blackmailing me...and I mean...sexually blackmailing me. On video! Now the *Daily Planet* have revealed the lie and mentioned the video. What a nightmare..."

Crucially, Stassy omitted at this stage to mention Sarah's involvement.

"OK," said Chloe. "Look, if you haven't given permission for this video to be shown and you are clearly the person in the video then you can claim damages from the people who have released it...so that means both Marcello and the company taking the revenue from the downloads."

"Right, OK..." said Stassy.

"Get on that website and find out as much as you can about the company peddling this stuff," instructed Chloe. "I would also get hold of Marcello and see if he can help you."

"I am not sure I want to contact Marcello, to be honest," said Stassy.

"I know, but it was probably him who sold the tape so he will know who's got it," reasoned Chloe. "We need to contact these people A-sap."

"I will think about it," said Stassy. "I can't believe what a fucking arsehole he's been...but thanks, though, lovely. I appreciate the advice. Are you around later if I need you?"

"Of course."

Stassy didn't really want to view the video at work, but it was becoming a critical piece of the puzzle. A lot had happened that night. She clearly needed to know exactly which bits were there for all and sundry to download.

She called Sarah.

"Any luck with the download yet?"

"It's going through now. I had to pay a fiver for the bloody thing. It's taking ages...I'll call you back when it's done."

Stassy went back to her desk. It was impossible to concentrate on anything. She had heard several gasps around the office. An advertising agency was probably one of the few workplaces where you were able to download porn safely these days.

She called Sarah back.

"So, what's the damage?"

"Well, you are clearly Marcello's favourite. You can't really tell it's me...but it's definitely you, sweetie. You can see bits of me but it's not that obvious, thank God, unless you look really closely or spot the tattoo on my bum – which, I guess, is clearly quite an identifiable feature – if you've...erm...been there. Sorry, I know that's no consolation for you, honey. Marcello has done a great job of editing himself completely out of it too, and has blurred his face in parts. Thankfully there's no coke in it. I have to say he could probably take it up as a profession. You look pretty hot baby, although it's probably not a look you are generally keen to share with the outside world."

There was a pause for several seconds. "Hmmm?" said Stassy eventually. "I'm glad I look hot in it, though."

"Uh-oh," said Sarah, coming back on the line. "It's saying 16,765 downloads."

"Fucking hell! I need to get my head around this," said Stassy. "Someone is going to pay for this. I am not going to lie down and take it."

"With all due respect, lying down and taking it is exactly what you have been doing!"

"Very funny. Fuck, I need to think this through ...speak later."

~

It was early evening at Marcello's flat and a loud knocking on his front door startled him as he sat in his pants, on his Playstation. He hadn't buzzed anyone up so he quickly threw on a pair of jeans and opened the door. Stassy barged past him, almost knocking him over in her rage. This was more 'Grand Theft Lesbo' than 'Auto'.

Marcello looked like a rabbit caught in headlights.

"Stassy, what are you doing here? You should have called?"

"And you should have told me that you were fucking recording me when I sucked your cock the other night..."

"Stassy...!!!"

"You are such a cunt!" screamed Stassy. "We had such a lovely night and then I get into work to find I was exposed in the *Daily Planet* for being a lying bitch. Now all my work colleagues have downloaded footage of me having a threesome. If you do this to people you really like I would hate to see what the fuck you do to your enemies."

Marcello sat down and put his head his hands, Preston Price-style.

"Stassy, I am so so sorry," he pleaded. "I don't know what to say. I had no idea about the *Daily Planet*. I have been busy today. I have been a fucking idiot. I lost my job and I got desperate. I originally took the footage as I wanted to capture the three of us together. After the first time I was addicted. I thought it would be a way to have more. After the second time I knew there wasn't going to be another time. I was hooked on you and I thought I would make myself something for my own pleasure. Then I got sacked because of the validity of your story and you didn't respond to my text. You fucking lied to me, and I lost my fucking job. I managed to get £20k for the video. I just thought it would disappear into the ether. I didn't think the *Sunday Planet* or *Daily Planet* or whoever would do a reveal...I know our magazine wasn't keen to expose it as a lie...and then we had such an amazing time last night. It's all such a mess, because I really like you...you know."

"Well, that's all very nice...thank you for your explanation, but you're still a cunt...," fumed Stassy, refusing to admit to Marcello that she had feelings for him too. "You are going to write down here exactly who you have sold it to, as I am going to take them to the fucking cleaners. And you will be lucky if I don't take you down with them. I want anything you have signed...ALL the paperwork."

~

Chloe was at the house when Stassy arrived home.

"I want us to start a legal process against these shysters... All-Star fucking Porn-Star, or whatever they're fucking called. Can you help?"

"Of course I can," said Chloe. "But to really have an impact I'll need to run it through my firm on letterheaded paper, etc, and that will mean charging a fee, but I can get you some good mates' rates... obviously."

"That's fine...whatever..."

"I will do my best, honey, I will do my best: first thing tomorrow. Wine?"

"Sure, I need a drink...a large one."

Alexa walked in about 30 minutes later. Staring at Anastasia, she remarked cattily: "Oh look...it's Debbie Does Dallas."

"Thanks, Alexa. She was pretty damn hot and now I'm pretty damn famous...actually, more famous than you, darling."

"Your aspirations are admirable, Anastasia."

"Fuck off, Alexa. You will appreciate I haven't had the best day. You rubbing it in isn't helping."

"You've rubbed all of it in yourself, darling," bitched Alexa, floating out of the room, delighted that Stassy had finally got her comeuppance and that she so far had been untouched by any fall-out.

Stassy poured another glass of wine.

~

The next morning Chloe worked on the necessary legal letters for Stassy, had them signed off from her boss and sent them out. They were strongly worded and she was sure they would inspire a response. Any settlement would depend on how well the tape was selling, but from some brief research, downloads seemed to be selling strongly – more than 25,000 copies had been downloaded directly from the *All-Star Porn Star* site – and free downloads were available on pirate sites, if you dug deep enough.

~

Stassy was desperate for her current contract to end. Work was becoming unbearable...all the whispering and pointing. She still couldn't bring herself to watch the sex tape. She was engrossed in her handover tasks when she got the call.

"Erm...hi," she said, the trepidation in her voice obvious.

"Hello, is that Stassy?" said an abrupt voice on the end of the line. "I work for a major talent agency, I.A.L...International Artists Limited...and we are very keen to sign you onto our books. You have caught our attention over the last few days and I really think we could capitalise on this situation if you are with the right agent. Would you come and meet us?"

Stassy was a little taken back, but had little to lose.

"Sure I will come and meet you," she whispered. "Where are you based?"

"Tottenham Court Road."

"Great, can I come this evening? 6ish?"

"Sure, see you then, I'll text you the full address."

~

As Stassy finished the call, Sarah phoned. She sounded exhausted.

"I haven't slept very well," she whined. "I am so worried about being exposed. It's only going to take one ex-boyfriend to recognise that tattoo and go to the press."

"Well, it's not like you to have been that promiscuous," said Stassy. "Fuck, if I was in your position, no pun intended, I would be screwed...again no pun intended. I can't even recall some of the people I have slept with."

"I'm not sure that makes me feel better. I can remember all of them, although a few are a bit sketchy...you know, the odd boozy one-night-stand, so not sure I can trust every one. Who could?"

"Well, there isn't a lot you can do about it now, Sarah. You just have to hope it will all die down. If not, you can always try and sue *All Star Porn Star*. It might even raise your theatre career...you know, PR and all that. I mean, to be honest, you are not even the star of the show and you haven't come out too bad. Although, time will tell."

"My family will be mortified."

"Well, hopefully they are not huge fans of porn and this will simply pass them by," said Stassy.

"Yeah, but can the internet pass them by? There's a load of stuff out there, you know."

"Nothing you can do, babe. Just hope it'll all be ok. You haven't killed anyone."

"Thanks babe...think I might try and get some sleep. I'm on stage later."

"Yes, don't let this mess up your big chance, babe," stressed Stassy.

"You're right...let me sleep it off...just gotta ride this out...no pun intended."

19

Stassy had managed to leave work a bit early. She couldn't bear being there any more. She arrived at the I.A.L offices and was greeted with feigned enthusiasm by the two agents waiting for her, one a petite bubbly blonde in leggings and heels, the other a middle-aged man wearing dark-rimmed glasses and a sharp suit.

Stassy was ushered into a meeting-room.

"Come through, come through," said the female. "I am Kirsten...and this is Jake."

"Hi, hi," said Stassy, shaking them each by the hand.

"Right, well, let's cut to the chase, shall we?" continued Kirsten.

The slick duo rattled through an impressive Power-Point presentation of how they were going to transform her from a dubious porn star to a reborn tabloid diva.

Their plan would start with a series of interviews where Stassy explained why she had lied to the press. This involved some tactical weeping and eating a huge slice of humble pie. The agency would pay for the right clothes, the right hair, the makeup (non-run mascara) and also acting lessons to help guide her through the whole process. There would be supervised rehearsals of her interview spiel to ensure her performance was finely tuned.

Phase two had her appearing in a high-profile reality show...next stop superstardom.

"Wow, that is pretty impressive," exclaimed Stassy. "Do you really think this is all possible?"

"Of course," beamed Kirsten. "That's our job."

"Well, it sounds like a great opportunity...gosh."

Jake took over. "We can say you filled out the survey to play a practical joke on your friend and as an impoverished graduate you just couldn't resist the lure of money...you have been badly treated and ridiculed for what is essentially a harmless lie. You have now been cruelly treated by the media, duped by a dashing reporter, who blackmailed you, used you for sex, recorded you without your knowledge and then sold you down the river for his own financial gain."

"Oooh, that's fantastic," squealed Kirsten. "Yes, she can be heartbroken at the rejection of the reporter... that cruel, manipulative hack...what was his name?"

"Marcello..." said Stassy.

"Oooh, yes...Marcello, 'The Callous Casanova'," said Kirsten.

"So, what do you think?" said Jake, bringing it back to business, as Kirsten added: "Yes Stassy, what d'ya say? Shall we get started on this?"

"Well, what does it involve me signing up to?" asked Stassy.

"Well, it's simple," said Jake. "We get you a shedload of work, a pot full of cash and we take just 30% of all your earnings."

"Erm, that seems a bit steep," bartered Stassy.

"Let's call it 20% for an exclusive arrangement," offered Kirsten.

"Done," said Stassy, who had hoped for exactly that compromise.

"Great, let's get pen to paper, then," said Jake.

Stassy signed a pre-agreement, giving I.A.L exclusivity until a full contract was drawn up. She left the meeting, her head spinning, but still not expecting anything to come of it. Just like a certain sex survey.

Stassy woke just after 3am in a hot sweat, a thousand thoughts flashing through her mind. She was in turmoil. Normally she felt invincible and nothing got her down. She usually brushed aside any mishaps or any minor controversies her love life caused, but this was bigger...much bigger than her.

Poor Preston had quit his job and was not loving Hull, his new temporary life a living hell. The doctors couldn't say if his Grandma would pull through and there was so much bad blood with his folks that surely things would never be the same with them again.

Stassy felt more dreadful about Preston than anyone else. She knew that she would come through all of this, all of it, even having a sex tape released, but for poor Preston it was just so much worse. Her head was spinning, a little voice reminding her over and over again that she had essentially killed Preston's Grandma. Manslaughter! Grandma-slaughter.

She could take no more of the tossing and turning, so she struggled out of bed and shuffled downstairs. She grabbed her laptop and downloaded the video. Unable to watch it up until this point, it was about time she faced up to what this sex tape was all about.

The first scene was her talking about the scam, pretty much admitting to lying. Then she was locked in a clinch with Sarah...kissing...groping...probing. Jeez! She didn't remember doing that, she thought...or that...and definitely not that, but she looked good – slim and sexy – and Sarah definitely looked like she was enjoying herself. Then she was with Marcello, who had pretty much totally edited himself out, apart from his vital parts. Stassy had to admit it was well produced, fast-paced and action-packed. She hadn't watched many porn movies but it was definitely much better than anything she had ever seen. At least she had given the performance of her life, helped, of course, by the drugs that thankfully weren't at all present in the film. Before she logged off, she noticed the figure of 68,814. Stassy nearly fell off her chair. Had all those people really downloaded the video and ogled her in all her glory? Ironic, of course, given her performance with Sarah, that just 'under' sixty-nine thousand people now had their own copy.

What next? she thought. Her mind was still racing. What exactly were the consequences? Family-wise, her mum was about as liberal as mothers come. She had dabbled with glamour modelling in the 1970s and also worked as a 'Playboy Bunny' in Park Lane in the late 1960s. Sure, this was on a whole other level, but at least her poor old dad, himself the consummate Playboy, was not around to witness it all. In fact, they weren't close to any of that side of the family, and her mum lived alone so there was no step-dad to deal with either. Yes, she felt humiliated and violated, but she would embrace this. Brazen it out. Own it. On paper, she seemed the perfect candidate to maximise this opportunity.

This was clearly going to go one of two ways. Either she would just have to ride the storm...or I.A.L would come up with something. The next steps were in the hands of others, and she would just let the situation play itself out.

~

Eventually 9am came, and Stassy got ready for work. On autopilot, she felt like a soldier as she diligently got dressed, shined her stilettos, stood to attention and marched out to work. Was it her, or was she instinctively dressing slightly more provocatively?

The last few weeks, let alone days, had been a whirlwind for Stassy. She had gone from filling in a sex survey for a giggle to a huge gaggle of voyeurs surveying her very own sex life. This had not been the plan.

She was now in the sex-tape hall of fame, up, or 'down there', with the likes of Pamela Anderson and Paris Hilton...laid bare to the world. A certain Kim Kardashian hadn't burst onto the sex tape scene quite yet, but would 'blow' up a couple of years later. How long she could stay in the spotlight would determine how long her star would shine and, most importantly, how much money she could make.

Of course, finance was not a major issue to Stassy right now. She wasn't wealthy, but she was cash rich. It was money that had landed her and Preston into this mess in the first place. Well at least, it was the offer of easy money that had stopped them revealing the survey had been a blag.

They might have 20-odd thousand pounds in the bank each, but it wasn't going to cure Preston's Grandma any day soon and it wasn't going to last for ever. She was more than capable of spending it as quickly and immorally as she had earned it.

The offer of a showbiz career on the back of this sordid episode in her life was extremely tempting, even though she was not at all sure she could handle the spotlight. Stassy famously liked operating under the radar. Unlike Alexa, she had never longed for fame.

Now tabloid, television and internet exposure of the most infamous kind had left her with a conundrum. Did she turn her back on it all, not look for a new freelance contract, and maybe go travelling for a year? Or take things up a notch, cash in her 'fifteen minutes of fame' chips and see where it took her?

As she sat at her desk at work pondering her next move, a steady stream of work colleagues ambled past...gawping, staring, whispering, sniggering. She felt like a caged animal at the local zoo. Surely it wouldn't be long before someone tossed her a banana. Except Marcello already had. Suck on that, bitch. And don't trip up on the way out.

An email appeared in her inbox. It was from Kirsten. I.A.L had already drafted up an official contract...the pre-agreement Stassy had signed the night before, not even giving her 24 hours to think about one of the biggest decisions of her life.

But right now, this thing didn't look or feel like it was going away any time soon. Even if she did turn her back on it all, it could take months, even years, to live down the shame and shun the fame.

Instinctively, Stassy opened the attachment, printed out the contract, signed on the dotted line and committed to an initial 12-month deal with I.A.L. She scanned the signed copy and emailed it to I.A.L. No turning back now.

First stop, a 'spoiler' interview with the *Sunday Planet*, first thing in the morning. Kirsten would call her shortly.

No time or need for sickies now. Stassy calmly tidied her desk, threw anything worth keeping into her shopper and strode out of the office, head held high, more jaws dropping as she left. It wasn't even lunchtime, but as she walked out through reception she phoned her line manager...the campaign she was working on was all but ready to air, so she asked if she could call it quits. She had some "personal issues" to resolve. She felt she had pretty much done most of the tie-up but she could always pop in for a day if needed. Her manager was fine and said he understood. He had downloaded Stassy's personal issues the night before and had already watched them several times.

Stassy took herself to the nearest coffee shop, and ordered a latte. No pub this time: she needed to keep her wits about her. The phone rang.

"Right, we are all good," said Kirsten sternly. "Thank you for sending over your signed contract. We've got that OK and now phase one of the plan is kicking in. The *Sunday Planet* spoiler is happening tomorrow, and will be out this weekend. This is all about the truth now."

"Right," said Stassy. "What truth and how is this going to run?"

Kirsten suddenly became even more serious. "Listen Stassy, and listen to me carefully. Our plan is to drive as much traffic to this sex tape as possible. Now I have had a chance to watch it, I have to say you are a bloody star. I don't mind telling you that I like my porn...and that's some premium stuff going on there. We will drive the traffic and then get you a TV deal which capitalises on it."

"OK, so you want me to go to the *Sunday Planet* and say what exactly?"

"You continually keep saying that the sex tape has been the lowest point of your life. How could someone you barely knew record you in that way? But you must keep mentioning the tape. I hate to say it but the sex tape is the strongest thread in all of this. This is an unusual one because you've already been in the *Sunday Planet* the first time around. If they don't do this 'spoiler' sensitively then someone else will get to the truth first and then we're in trouble."

So Stassy had a complete handle on the situation, Kirsten further explained: "Spoilers allow celebrities to tell the story in their own words and are designed to be sympathetic to their plight and to their cause. They're aimed at damage limitation, and usually the reluctant domain of love rats caught with their trousers down...and, of course, they spoil it for any other rival newspapers sniffing around."

Stassy, her own knickers proverbially around her ankles, was in the unique position of having already lied to the *Sunday Planet*, and had been paid for the pleasure. Her head was all over the place, but at least she was sober.

Before she had time to reconsider her options, Kirsten was back on the line. "Right, a car will be with you 9am sharp. I am organising hair and make-up, pre-interview, when we get there. You'll be picking me up on the way through. Until tomorrow."

The line went dead.

20

Kirsten clambered into the taxi, sat opposite a sleepy-eyed Stassy and was straight back on her sales pitch.

"Just make sure you mention the sex tape lots...and you must sound distressed about it. Our key objective is to actually drive traffic to *All Star Porn Star*: that's what will really make you a star, the vulnerable vixen with a really hot sex tape."

"Right, so why do I say I lied?"

"Don't mention the word lie? Just say it was necessary to bend the truth because, otherwise, you couldn't see a way out of it all. You were naïve and unsure and were then double-crossed when taken under Marcello's wing. Take no blame and ensure you bring across two aspects: naivety and the sex tape...and you will be on the road to stardom."

"How much will I get paid this time?" asked Stassy, now used to quick and fat payments for her time and elaborations.

"Mm-hmm. No money for this, darling," explained Kirsten, dismissively. "You can't be paid for deceit now, that's not how it works at this stage of the game. We have to play the game and your game is now the long game."

Stassy was not sure about Kirsten and her whole strategy, but she felt at a crossroads and that, given how bad everything was, she should go with the flow. However, she was under no illusion. She couldn't misrepresent the truth again.

As they arrived at the *Sunday Planet*, Jake was waiting outside. Stassy felt cute entering the paper's Whitechapel headquarters again, but this time flanked by her sharpshooter agents, she also felt almost invincible.

No Raquel this time. Hosting this interview would be the paper's showbiz editor Ben Bishop. He greeted Kirsten and Jake warmly and bantered with the duo. It was clear these three knew each other well. Stassy immediately felt more relaxed, and settled into the interview well. Ben was understanding about her situation, and it was agreed that she would donate her fee for this interview (after I.A.L's 20% was deducted) to an appropriate charity.

The story would explain that a practical joke had gone horribly wrong, and that Stassy now had egg all over her face after being 'shafted' by an unscrupulous journalist. If only said reporter had edited out the scene where she had something else all over her face!

The piece would put the record straight, almost, and would detail how Stassy had been the victim of a callous porn baron. She had now seen the error of her ways, and wanted to set up a foundation to raise awareness and money for "used and abused porn stars". She was about to issue High Court proceedings against this seedy organisation with downloads, at the time of going to press, now exceeding 100k.

She would explain how Preston's grandmother had suffered a heart attack after watching *Elevenses*, and that he had been forced to leave his job, as had she. All designed to highlight how accusations that the duo had profited handsomely were wide of the mark. Mentally and emotionally, there had been much more pain than gain here.

She told how she was forced into lesbian sexual

activity and used by a cruel reporter, then black-mailed. This was uncharted territory for the *Sunday Planet*, though. Newspapers hate discrediting reporters or their craft, so this would have to be handled sensitively. The paper had found a photo of Marcello, and he was known to them through him selling various tabloid exposures to them in the past, but they would take legal advice on how he was mentioned in the piece, if at all.

A photoshoot was arranged, this time with Stassy alone, in a sombre pose and mood, wearing an oversized pure white linen shirt to demonstrate her innocence.

Stassy had dutifully mentioned the sex tape at least ten times. She hoped she hadn't gone over the top, and knew full well the reporter, if he hadn't already, would be gawping at it afterwards. She felt both ashamed and empowered at the same time.

~

Before the night was out, Kirsten was back on the phone.

"Right, I have you lined up to do *Elevenses* the day after next…then back-to-back meetings with the other newspapers and a few more TV interviews which will take about three days out of your schedule."

"Sounds pretty busy," enthused Stassy. "Any money for any of this?"

Stassy felt that Kirsten perhaps needed some assistance in negotiation, but her agent added curtly: "We will get some money for some of it… but trust us, we know what we're doing. Your downloads are now well over 100,000, so this should be giving your legal team some great leverage. Do let us know if you want any help with that, because we can take care of those negotiations too."

"No, no, you're fine, my legal advisor is on the case. OK, well, just tell me where I need to be and when," said Stassy, shrugging her shoulders.

Stassy went home and tried to relax. At least she was getting somewhere near the truth now.

Chloe called.

"Hi lovely, I've had a reply from the porn people."

"Right, what have they got to say for themselves?"

"Well, you're not going to like it. They accept that they have used your image without your permission, and they're offering £5,000 for full and final settlement."

"Well, they can fuck off," fumed Stassy, understandably, her lack of fee from the *Sunday Planet* second time around still hurting. "They're clearly trying it on. Do they think I was born yesterday? Have you seen the amount of downloads? I will have my day in court with them. They're making a mint out of me right now."

"OK, I will go back to them and tell them to stick it...in legal speak, of course."

"Great. Thanks, hun, appreciate it."

~

Steve called Alexa. "Hey babe, how are you doing?"

"I am all good, sweetie...how are you?"

"Well, we've finally got an hour off. It's so intense doing these run-throughs. I hope they speed up. It's painfully slow and I am so hot under the lights. I am sweating like a..."

"...that's the price of fame, gorgeous," cut in Alexa.

"Yes, I guess I shouldn't complain. Could be doing worse things for a living."

"Yes, you could be," snapped Alexa, still envious

Steve was hosting a prime-time show, not her. "Stop whinging!"

"Anyway," continued Steve. "I was calling you because I have heard something about a sex tape that is doing the rounds...which involves Stassy and...erm... a lesbian lover. Apparently she fully admits making the whole thing up. Looks like your mate Sarah is with her on tape too, though. You can hardly tell it's her, but she has a tell-tale tattoo that...erm...I should imagine...gives her away."

Alexa felt her stomach churn.

"It's pretty graphic," said Steve. "That Stassy's a right goer, isn't she?"

"STEVE," shrieked Alexa. "I cannot believe you have watched this? And how the fuck do you know Sarah has a tattoo on her arse?"

"Erm? Did you know about the tape?" said Steve, trying to buy himself some time.

"Yes, I did, but I hadn't got my head around it all yet, and I didn't think you would watch it?"

"Umm...how do you know I have watched it? Did I say it was on her arse?"

"Well, how the fuck do you know the other girl in it is Sarah?"

There was silence on the other end of the line.

"Steve...Steve...," demanded Alexa.

"Erm..."

"Steve, I need an answer!"

"Ok...ok...you've got me. I, erm...well, erm... I recognised her tattoo."

"Sarah has one tattoo on her whole body and it's on her arse. I know this because I share a house with her, but how the fuck have you seen it?"

Steve took a deep breath. There was an awkward silence.

"Steve...I'm waiting."

"Erm...well."

"Erm...well...what?"

Several seconds, Steve later blurted out: "I think...I erm...slept with Sarah."

"What the fuck! When?"

"About six years ago."

Now a deathly silence replaced the awkward one.

Then ten seconds later, but what seemed like an eternity to Steve, Alexa growled: "You...think?"

"I am pretty sure, baby, I mean, I must have...to know she had a tattoo there, but I have slept with a lot of ladies before you...you know that. I don't remember every one of them. I just can't."

"Don't baby me, Steve. Why the hell didn't you tell me this before?"

"Well, I thought I recognised Sarah, when you first introduced us briefly and I wondered if something had happened with her, but I couldn't place her. I wasn't about to ask her, and she didn't seem to recognise me anyway, or tell you. It wasn't until I saw that video that it came back to me. It was a long time ago...it was a drunken one night stand, after a house-party in Maida Vale, if I remember rightly...and it meant nothing."

"I can't believe you shagged Sarah, one of my best mates," stormed Alexa.

More silence...and now it was more eerie.

"Does it mean nothing now you have watched her getting it on with Anastasia?"

"Yeah, but listen..."

"Did you not think about how I would feel with you watching that sex tape?"

"Well, I..."

"They are my housemates. I am very disappointed, Steve. How will you ever be able to look at Stassy...or Sarah...in the same way?"

"Well I won't...but baby, nothing compares to you."

"Oh, please...who do you think you are...Sinead fucking O'Connor? Give me a break!"

"Baby, please, one of the guys at the tennis club showed me," pleaded Steve. "What was I meant to do? And you've been in such a state about this whole sex survey thing that I wanted to hear Anastasia revealing the lies for myself so I could advise you about it...I am so sorry. Don't think this is the last we're going to hear about it. It's all over the internet. Going viral, don't they call it?"

"Well, Steve, I'm not happy," added Alexa. "I don't want you to see my friends like that. I say, friends...who the fuck do these cheap whores think they are? But I guess it's not your fault that their sex lives are plastered all over the internet. I've been on at them for ages about this, and they just don't listen. I've just about taken as much as I can."

"Well, I do think you should be berating other people, rather than me. Don't shoot the messenger and all that."

"To be honest, I am not even comfortable living here anymore. I can't believe Anastasia has sunk this low and as for Sarah...well, I thought better of her."

Steve quietly pondered whether he should ask Alexa to come and stay with him for a while. But then thought better of it. She was at the apartment several days each week, but actually asking her to move in might still be premature.

"I will make it up to you baby, I promise," said Steve. "I love you." He kissed into the phone as Alexa put down the handset firmly.

Alexa was absolutely gobsmacked. What the hell was Sarah doing? Stassy was just stupid, but Sarah...why had she let herself get into all of this? She was so angry with Stassy for starting it all and furious with Steve for watching it. Let alone the fact it was looking like he had slept with Sarah. Why hadn't she mentioned it? She didn't think she would ever be able to forgive Stassy for this, and she was still having to live with her. She needed to hatch a plan to move into Steve's penthouse...as soon as possible. Maybe this was her chance to suggest it?

~

Downloads were still rising steadily, so Chloe phoned Stassy. The porn company were now offering £20k, but they agreed to hold firm for the time being as the spoiler story would be in the *Sunday Planet* tomorrow and it was likely to have a further impact on downloads. Chloe would go back and ask for £100k on the back of the impending press and web traffic, telling *All-Star Porn-Star* there was more to come.

~

Steve picked Alexa up straight from the studio in the car the production company had arranged. She was still fuming, but she knew it was going to be hard to stay angry at Steve for long, especially as he was going up in the world. She wasn't the sort of girlfriend who was against her fella watching porn, just not when it involved her housemates!

"Hi, babe," said Steve, praying Alexa had calmed down, as the driver opened the door and she slid in.

"Hi," pouted Alexa, staring out of the window.

The driver started the engine. Steve undid his seat belt and shimmied across to Alexa.

"Baby."

"I am not happy, Steve."

"I understand, honey, but what can I do now? I can't reverse watching the tape. I can't reverse the fact I probably slept with Sarah. I love you…things have changed now, I don't want anyone else. I want you."

"Well, Steve," said Alexa, going in for the kill. "You have made me so uncomfortable about being at home now, maybe it's time I came and lived with you? So you can prove how much you love me. Because I just don't know what to do? How can I stay in that house with everything that has happened?"

"Baby, that's a big step. It's a huge step, in fact. We have only been dating a little while and, well…it's just a massive step, isn't it?"

"Hmmm…" sighed Alexa. "Well, I think I'm just going to go home then, Steve. My head is all over the place. I need time to think."

Steve was dismayed.

"No please, Alexa, don't go home. I have had a crazy day and I really need you with me tonight."

"My head is fried, Steve. I just think we should both have time to think…you know, after what has happened today."

"Alexa, you are coming back with me. I don't think I ever want you to leave, but you can't make me commit to that now. It's not fair. We can't mess this up, it's too important. This is all so new for me. I am falling in love with you, but this isn't something that comes easily. Can we just forget today for now."

Alexa's pout fell off her face and she turned to Steve.

"OK, OK, I understand. You are right. We don't want to rush things, but being in the house is tough at the moment…it is just tough."

"And you always have my place to hang out at, baby, now…let me take you home and I will really make it up to you."

The car drew up outside Steve's apartment block. He looked longingly into Alexa's eyes.

"Come with me, baby," he purred, slipping his hand between her thighs. "Come with me, baby," he reiterated, kissing her on the lips.

Steve took Alexa's hand, slowly pulled her out of the car and added: "Please let me make it up to you… again and again and again."

21

Stassy was woken by Kirsten's call at 10am on Friday morning.

"Hello," she said in a sleepy voice.

"Oh, jeez, darling, have I woken you?" said Kirsten, actually not sounding at all concerned...or surprised.

"Well, I am a lady of leisure these days," bragged Stassy.

"Not for long you won't be…," interrupted her agent.

"Erm, yes, you're right...," said Stassy, correcting herself, and sitting upright in the bed.

"Right, some good news for you this morning," said Kirsten assertively. "Your video is so going viral, on the back of the *Sunday Planet* article. More than 125,000 downloads already on the *All Star Porn Star* site and it's also available on several other sites too."

"And this is good news…"

"Well, yes it is," smiled Kirsten. "You are becoming an overnight sensation darling…'overnight' being the operative word!"

"Kirsten, I am just waking up...this is a lot for me to take in, to be honest. I have never had ambitions of being a porn star and this is what I seem to be becoming."

"Think of the end game, Stassy...the end game."

"What a happy ending…" smirked Stassy.

"With all due respect," interrupted Kirsten. "We're

not asking you to film any more porn, darling. That little episode will hopefully be a one-off."

"And so what's next..."

"Well, next week you're going to be busy busy. You are doing *Wake Up Britain* first thing Tuesday and then there is a series of interviews with radio and newspapers for the rest of the day. Then you are booked into do *Elevenses* again on Wednesday and then back to London in the afternoon for..."

Stassy began to zone out. She didn't realise quite how hard fame could be.

"...and then Friday we are in discussions about your autobiography, which we are hoping to have released next month."

"Autobiography!" exclaimed Stassy. "Really? Me? Have I enough content for an autobiography?"

"Listen darling, with your imagination, and a good ghostwriter, anything is possible."

"OK, OK, whatever...I'm just going to take it all as it comes..."

"Darling," quipped Kirsten. "It's you taking it as it comes that got you in this mess in the first place..."

"OK, OK, very funny Kirsten," said Stassy, at least warming to her biting wit. "What's the plan for today?"

"Today we need to take you shopping, and you're having your hair done at 3pm."

"OK, right, I can do that..."

"We think you need to go blonder," continued Kirsten. "You need to look good for all this press. We also need to brief you on the tone for each interview. So, you have an appointment with an acting coach, who will go through the different personae you need to adopt. The 'Anastasia' interviewed on breakfast TV won't necessarily be the same 'Anastasia' in the women's magazine feature you do later in the day."

"Fine, hun...just tell me where I need to be and when...and what to wear...and I am all yours."

"The car will be with you in around an hour."

"Great...see you then."

Stassy put down the phone, splashed some cold water on her face and called Chloe.

"Hiya."

"Right, the video is officially going viral. Apparently it is being downloaded and copied. I think now is the time to close down those arseholes at *All Star Porn Star* and get some cash...can you try and resolve it this week? Would you consider going over to their offices and hand-delivering some nasty legal shit? I want at least £50k out of this."

"Sure thing, boss," replied Chloe sarcastically.

"I am serious. This wanker is cashing in on ...on...well, on my arse. Literally."

"I understand. Let me talk to my superiors and see what we can do."

~

Stassy's request was a little unusual...Chloe wasn't really sure what to do. Nervously, she knocked on her boss's door.

"Come in," he said.

"Hi, Jim, erm...I've had my housemate Stassy on the phone. You know we sent a letter to a company that had released sexual video content of her without her permission on the internet for financial gain?"

"Oh, yes, vaguely..."

"Well, so far they have tried to settle with us for £20k, but, given the downloads, Stassy feels we should be looking at anything up to £100k. I agree. She wants me or someone from our firm to go down to the offices in Soho and close this out because apparently the video is going viral...which means it's all over the internet. She feels the chance to strike is now."

"Right...I probably need to see this content, so I can get some idea of her exposure, etc. It would also be good to get some feel for how much this company has gained from it so we can work out the right settlement. Can you send me a link to the video?"

"I'm not sure you will be able to download it at work, Jim. I think there are some restrictions on that type of material."

Jim's eyes seemed to light up and then he blushed slightly.

"Well, send me the link and I will ask I.T to give me authorisation to watch it. Have you seen it?"

"Erm, no, Jim. I am not sure I want to. She is my housemate."

"Well, I know it's sensitive, but I think we both have to watch it. How can we take these people to court if we don't know what we are taking them to court for? Email me the link and then come back to my office and we'll watch it together. Unfortunately the legal world is fraught with predicaments like this. We can't afford to be squeamish in this game."

Chloe felt physically sick. On one hand she couldn't think of anything worse than sitting with her boss watching her mate in some dirty home movie, but the prospect somehow also intrigued her. Chloe texted Stassy to send her the link and forwarded it on to Jim, who had duly been given clearance by I.T. She was sure those dirty bastards were copping a look too.

Half an hour later and Chloe was back in her boss's office, hovering nervously over his shoulder as he used his credit card to pay for the download, probably one of the strangest business expenses that would ever go through to accounts at Smedley, Smith and Sweeney.

As he sat attentively in front of his computer

monitor, Jim looked at the screen now with genuine fear in his eyes...and pressed play.

"*Lies, Champers, Action,*" said a vocoded voiceover ...and then it all began.

Jim tried to maintain an air of professionalism throughout the film. Chloe pointed out which one was Stassy, which was pretty clear, as the other two 'stars' of the show were difficult to recognise. Then it hit Chloe. THAT tattoo. How could she forget THAT tattoo. It was unmistakable, certainly if you know Sarah...and Chloe could clearly see it was Sarah.

Chloe was in total shock. Why hadn't Stassy mentioned this? They hadn't had much of a chance to talk to her since the release and, of course, she was probably trying to protect Sarah, but it was so uncomfortable watching two of her housemates in such compromising positions...going down on each other like that...kissing so passionately, even.

"I think you should make some notes," said a bumbling Jim, trying to give Chloe a pen, but handing her a tissue instead. Freudian slip!

Jim's well-chiselled face went a worrying shade of crimson and his furrowed forehead was starting to perspire. He took off his jacket and loosened his collar. Chloe instinctively mopped his brow with the tissue. Awkward!

"Hmmm?" he blustered. "It's really hot in here."

Grabbing a biro, Chloe put her head down and started writing notes, being careful not to implicate Sarah. She would clearly need to ask her what she wanted to do...whether she would also want to sue. Her case would not be as strong as she wasn't really in view, but Chloe could tell it was her, so it only needed an old flame to recognise that tattoo and leak the story to the press and she would be implicated in this whole debacle too.

Thankfully, the tape came to a close. Unfortunately, not before the money shot!

"Well," proclaimed Jim. "That certainly was an unusual start to a Friday morning. Can you bring me the file, so I can look at what we have done so far."

Chloe left the office, flustered but also feeling an attraction to Jim she had never felt before...and, ever so slightly, turned-on. Bloody hell Stassy, she thought. What have you created?

After an hour of 'analysis', Jim decided they had a strong case. The latest stats showed the video now already had more than 200,000 hits in a couple of days and therefore the company must have already netted close to £1.2m. The sex tape had even reached the States, with some 'downloads' a result of postings and shared links on a popular new college-wide social media platform in America called The Facebook. Given another *Sunday Planet* piece was due at the weekend, and a whole raft of TV and other magazine interviews were scheduled for next week, the forecast was that downloads could easily double...even treble by then. Now a settlement of £100k looked too low. Jim decided that £500k, based on *All-Star Porn-Star* netting almost £4m gross within the next ten days, was the fair and correct settlement at this juncture. Jim also decided that they needed to strike quickly. Once the company had done the bulk of the initial sales it could transfer rights and close down the existing company, making it harder to sue.

It was decided that Jim and Chloe would go down to the offices at close of business that day with a strong counter letter and push for some closure on the matter.

This was actually looking like it could net Smedley, Smith and Sweeney close to £75,000 in legal fees. Chloe was up for a nice bonus too. It had been a difficult start to the year for the company, and this could stave off some planned redundancies. It might even save Chloe's job. Her stock was rising fast.

~

Jim and Chloe strolled down to Greek Street and stood outside the backstreet offices of *All Star Porn Star*. She rang the bell.

"Hi," came a sultry female voice over the intercom.

"Could we come up?" asked Jim. "We have a business proposal we would like to discuss with Mr Jerry Jerkoff?"

"Erm...OK," said the lady, buzzing them in.

The 'receptionist' was pretty surprised to see the legal pair, as they were, in suits, probably not the usual clientele she was used to seeing in those offices.

"Jerry!" she screamed down the corridor. "There are some people to see you."

"Hi, what can I do for you?" said Jerry Jerkoff, scuttling towards Jim and Chloe, and ushering them into a room.

"Hello," said Jim. "We are here representing Anastasia Thomas. We are from the law firm Smedley, Smith and Sweeney. My name is Jim Smedley."

"Right..." said Jerry, twitching and looking at the receptionist and back at the legal pair again.

"We understand that you have now, or are about to, net more than £1m of revenue by using footage of our client, which you don't have pre-authorisation for."

"That's preposterous. We have had some money and I agree we need to settle, but if it was a million quid I would probably be sailing around the Caribbean by now."

"Well, the website clearly says you have had almost

quarter of a million downloads."

"Well...erm...umm, a lot of them will have been free for our monthly subscribers and then others are offered free as part of certain packages. It ain't that simple, mate."

"Well, I appreciate it 'ain't that simple'," retorted Jim. "But your latest offer of £20k is pretty paltry on the back of these figures and interest the tape has generated."

"Well...erm...yes...I can see that," stuttered Jerry, taking a seat to steady himself, and gesturing to Linzi to bring him a glass of water.

"We need a fair settlement for my client. Otherwise, we would have a strong case in a court of law. If you don't want to pay up, or discuss a settlement, then I would urge you to take the video down immediately, before we apply to the High Courts for an injunction for the same."

"And how much exactly are you thinking?"

"Well, based on the £1.2m to date, and then future sales of, let's say, at least another £2.5m...well, we believe our client is entitled to at least 10-15% of that revenue, so we are looking at a settlement figure in excess of £500k."

Jerry nearly fell off his chair.

"Look, I appreciate the visit in person and I see your point, but I ain't a lawyer and I just don't know what is fair. Given these amounts you are quoting, I need to instruct someone myself."

"I would do that over the weekend or as soon as possible," said Jim. "My client is extremely distressed about the speed this is moving across the internet and we will need to settle fast or move to court, as my client can't continue to let you benefit financially from this without a share of it herself. I am sure you understand that. This video is making you a lot of money, Mr Jerkoff, so we are just asking for a fair share of that pie."

"Ok...I will instruct my lawyers today."

"Could I have their names please?" asked Chloe.

Jerry scribbled down the the details and Jim and Chloe left the offices.

It had been the strangest day of Chloe's career to date. Her boss had gone up in her estimation, and it was great to see him in action. After witnessing Stassy in full flow earlier, Chloe was still in a state of shock, especially seeing Sarah and Stassy together in that way. She wasn't sure she would be able to look at either of them quite in the same way again...or Jim!

The colleagues emerged from the depths of the back-street office of *All Star Porn Star*, onto the bustling sun-drenched Soho streets.

Chloe gazed gooey-eyed at her boss, and gushed: "You were really impressive in there, Jim. You really showed them we meant business."

Jim smiled warmly back at Chloe.

"Well, you weren't so bad yourself, young lady," he added. "You brought this client to the table, remember. Do you fancy a tipple? It is Friday and it's been a tough week."

Chloe tried to stifle her excitement. Was Jim flirting with her?

"Good idea," she beamed. "We deserve a drink after that encounter!"

They found a basement cocktail bar barely 50 yards away. Jim held the door open for Chloe, his gold wedding band glistening in the bright sunlight and catching her eye as he ushered her inside.

Jim ordered a Sancerre Sauvignon Blanc. "SSS owe us a decent bottle for our efforts this week," said Jim, justifying the expense, as he tucked the V.A.T receipt away in his wallet.

With the crisp white wine flowing, the veteran solicitor and his protege started to relax in each other's company like never before.

"So, do you have a boyfriend, Chloe?" asked Jim, apparently cutting to the chase.

"Errrr no...I don't...I've just finished with someone I was seeing recently."

Jim's pupils seemed to dilate a little and he loosened his tie and undid the top button of his shirt.

"I see," he grinned. "It surprises me that someone as attractive as you hasn't been snapped up by now. This chap must have been a fool to let you go."

Tom was definitely a fool...and Jim was definitely coming on to her. His eyes, the relationship questions, the nervous fidgeting with his collar...all gave it away.

"How old are your children, Jim?" enquired Chloe, trying to steer the conversation into safer territory.

"The boys? They're six and nine. Becoming a bit of a handful now, the little blighters, but they're good lads. I must say, though, it's nice to have a couple of drinks after work, and get away from all that for a bit. Do you know what I mean, Chloe?"

As she stared back at Jim, impressed at how he had expertly navigated her question, and steered it back in 'her' direction...'their' direction, Chloe could feel her face burning up. Blushing.

Jim put his hand momentarily on her knee. Chloe blushed as their eyes locked intensely. The solicitor was definitely soliciting her now. Going in for the kill, it seemed.

Chloe's heart was racing. In a knee-jerk reaction she stood up.

"I am...just...going to the toilet," she blurted out, red-faced.

Once inside the safe confines of the ladies' loo she called Sarah, who was in make-up at the dressing-room at the theatre.

"Sarah, can you talk?..."

"Hi Chlo, you all right?"

"Listen, I need you to do me a favour. Can you call me in 15 minutes? I need to excuse myself from a drink with my boss...he's coming on to me."

"Is he fit? Do you like him?"

"Well, I am attracted to him, a rugged, good-looking older man, shall we say, but he is married and it's probably not a very smart career move. Give me a little while, but please call in a bit."

"Ok...call you in about 20 minutes."

"Perfect."

Chloe returned to the table, as Jim poured more wine from a second bottle he had ordered, and engaged in more flirtatious conversation. Jim was quite the comedian and Chloe couldn't stop laughing, feeling increasingly more attracted to him.

This situation was a dangerous one, though, and while also hoping Sarah's call wouldn't come that quickly, Chloe knew she needed to leave before things got out of hand. She wanted to be able to face Jim on Monday morning.

Around half an hour later, Sarah, who had mischeviously left it a bit longer on purpose, dutifully called. Chloe made her apologies and left Jim yearning for more. Treating him mean, keeping him 'Keane', even. They gave each other an over-zealous bear hug and, as she left, a kiss a little too close to the lips.

22

Fresh from escaping the clutches of genial Jim, Chloe certainly had that 'Friday night feeling'. Gagging for a drink after the ordeal she had been through, Stassy was the obvious choice. They had plenty to discuss. Chloe called her mobile.

"Hey, superstar," announced Chloe.

"Hiya," she replied, somewhat subdued."

"How are you doing, hun?" inquired Chloe.

"All over the place, to be honest," admitted Stassy. "According to my agent I am apparently about to 'blow up'...and I am not sure how I feel about it. I've just come from my acting lessons, if you don't mind."

"Acting lessons?" exclaimed Chloe. "What were they like?"

"Load of nonsense with some daft old lovey called Gerald."

"You might have to rephrase that, babe, when you're talking to Sarah..."

"Oops, yes...anyway, I'm already a porn star, well, inadvertently..."

"Have you managed to talk to your mum? You really should tell her what's going on. If anyone is going to understand, it's her."

"We've spoken. She is worried, but, as you know, she is quite open-minded. Look, I am in it now. This could actually work out really well for me and if it doesn't I will just fuck off travelling for a year and hope everyone has forgotten about it when I return. By then it will be old news."

"Well, before you decide to leg it, I have some potentially good news for you..."

"Right...I'm all ears."

"Well, after being subjected to watching 'the movie' with my boss, he finally saw that this could be a big case."

"You watched it? You watched it with your boss!"

"Yes, not my usual type of entertainment. And, of course, I knew that you would be taking a starring role, but I am very shocked to know that Sarah was in it with you. What the hell happened? How did all...THAT...happen? I need some explanation, Stassy. Can you imagine what it was like discovering my housemates got it on...while I was with my boss? I'm not sure I would have been so willing, but given her excitement, maybe I am the fool."

"Babe, babe...calm down. I can imagine it was a shock, darling, but, you see, one thing led to another...let me explain over a bottle of vino...I can't go through it on the phone. Please don't be upset...I know it must feel weird. It is weird...but it's nothing serious...it just kinda happened."

"OK, well, yes, let's talk about that later. With all the evidence in front of him...erm...like, in front of us both...my boss now thinks £100k is far too low. We are going to push for several hundred thousand."

"Shit!"

"Yes, shit indeed. We met the wonderful Jerry Jerkoff, and he is making a fat sum out of your small ass, and we are determined to secure for our client what she's due," continued Chloe, sounding like a backstreet lawyer in a low-rent TV movie.

"You met who?"

"Jerry Jerkoff, the porn baron who bought your

tape. We went to the *All Star Porn Star* offices today and put Jerkoff in a corner. That slimeball is going to have to pay up..."

"Amazing...this is so exciting," beamed Stassy. "That kind of money will certainly help the medicine go down."

"By the looks of the video, you didn't need any help getting anything down, darling," Chloe couldn't help adding.

"All right, all right...very good. Jeez, suddenly everyone thinks they're a comedian."

"Sorry, couldn't resist that...anyway, let's not get too excited until Jerkoff coughs up his cash, but it does look like you have a fucking good case. Shall we grab a few drinks on our way home? The local?"

~

Chloe and Stassy met at The Islington Shed and, after a hearty hug, ordered a bottle of Pinot Grigio.

"Anastasia Thomas? What have you been up to?" said Chloe, half tutting, half chuckling.

Stassy smiled coyly.

"So, do you want to tell me what happened?"

"Well, remember that night after we did the interview for *Nearer* magazine?"

"Kind of...you were both really hungover and had pulled some blokes?"

"Yeah, well, we actually ran into the reporter, Marcello, in the bar after the interview and we had a few drinks with him...well, quite a few drinks, in fact, including some Porn Star Martinis...they're amazing, by the way. Have you tried them?"

"No, they sound great, but carry on..."

"Well, then he suggested we went back to his. He was keen to see us in action. The interview had got him hot and horny. He is fit, I actually quite like him and for all his sins, when this is all over, I might try and see him again. Anyway, once back at his flat, what could Sarah and I do? We had just spent the last few hours telling him how much we enjoyed each other sexually. We were in a tight spot."

"You could have just said you didn't want to go back to his, rather than digging an even bigger hole for yourself?"

"Erm, yeah, but we were drunk...and..."

"Well..."

"...and...and...he said he'd sort us out another couple of thousand pounds on top of our fee..."

"What!...that's tantamount to...we need more wine... NOW!"

Chloe gestured to the bar for some table service.

"So, the second time?" probed Chloe.

"Well, we were blackmailed. A guy I had hooked up with recently phoned Marcello...and told him we were lying and Marcello blackmailed us for round two."

"Shit!"

"This time he was in charge...and he secretly recorded us, supposedly for his own pleasure, but then he decided to leak it to a porn site after he lost his job because of our fabricated story and because he thought I didn't want to see him again. He's really pissed off I lied to him."

"Fucking hell! Could your love life be getting any more frickin' complicated...and somehow you've become a minor celebrity out of all of it."

"Well, it didn't do Paris Hilton any harm..."

"So are you going to be starring in your own reality series next?"

"Who knows? My agents think I can do really well out of all this and carve out some kind of showbiz career. Fuck knows, what will happen. I am in it for the ride, to be honest...and what do I have to lose now? There is no way I can stop that sex video...it is all over the internet."

"That's true. We should be close to a settlement soon, because if you start profiting from it a court might be less sympathetic. I am going to try my best to wrap this up Monday or Tuesday for you..."

"Thanks, hun...don't think I'd be handling this so well if you weren't involved..."

"No probs. I'm flavour of the month with my boss right now. For various reasons, this weird grin appears on his face every time I speak to him. So, hopefully we'll all do well out of it...but one last question."

"What is it?"

"Do you fancy Sarah? Is it going to be awkward?"

"Look, I really don't know. It was fun. She was hot and it was a different experience, which I enjoyed. Look, I still love cock, like really love cock, so I can't see me switching anytime soon, but would it happen again, when I am horny? Maybe. There seems to be no stopping me. To be honest, more than anything, I keep thinking about Marcello. He's been a dirty dog, but there is something about him that I like. This whole thing brought us together. We went on a date before I knew about the tape. I do get the sense that, he and I, well, we're both victims in this, you know...as for Sarah, all is cool with her. We laughed it off, but I have to admit...it was hot."

"It looked it, Stassy, it really looked it. I think you should keep away from Marcello, though. You've always gone for bad boys. You're going to have to pick your men wisely from now on...certainly if all this money comes your way. The guys are going to be all over you — even more than before."

"Talking about bad boys, how is Tom?"

"Him? Hmmm? Well, he'd love to be a bad

233

boy...loser! Trying to avoid him at the moment and take my mind off it with other guys, which is fun, but I do miss him. He just can't commit to anything close to a normal relationship. I'm giving up trying to have any normal relationships, it is pointless."

"He is hopeless, agreed, but you guys were good together..."

"I can do better."

"Agreed, you can definitely do better than Tom."

At that point two regulars from the pub shuffled up.

"Alright darling, ain't you that bird that loves a bit of fanny...want to show us how you did it, love? Is this your girlfriend?"

"No," said Stassy.

"Naah what?" said the other one. "You ain't going to get it on with your mate? Or you ain't that bird?"

"It is her, mate," the first one reiterated. "She's been all over the papers. She loves the ladies, alright... and that tape is serious. You are gorgeous, my love, gorgeous...I would love a piece of..."

"Any more pearls of wisdom, boys?" said Stassy cuttingly.

"Well, how about a pearl...?"

"You'd be fucking lucky..." said Stassy, giving them a 'stare of death' as the guys sheepishly bowled off, kissing their teeth.

"Twats," fumed Stassy.

"One for the road?" asked Chloe, trying not to snigger.

"OK, JD and cokes."

"Done."

Chloe and her 'client' toasted to "health, wealth and happiness"...and to "cash, sex and milking the media for all it's worth"...and, after a few more rounds, to..."Jerry frickin' Jerkoff."

~

Saturday came and Alexa was once again getting ready for *Date With Destiny*. She was not sure she felt like sitting through another night's live filming, but Steve had been keen for her to attend and she felt she should play the dutiful girlfriend. It was important for her career too. The first episode had rated really well and Steve had been doing a lot of press. Alexa had been photographed a couple of times out with him since the first show, and in one magazine had been listed as his girlfriend. She had bought another dress for tonight, and managed to be ready in three hours.

~

Sarah was also on stage tonight but, for her, Saturday night only highlighted that she hadn't heard from Philippe all week...since he had left her bedroom on Sunday afternoon. He had satisfied her in virtually every way possible, even pleading with her to stay a little longer, and then had texted her almost straight after she left to say what an amazing night he'd had. She had painstakingly styled out her reply, waited several hours to return the text, but then had heard nothing from him since. The player had played her once more.

Chloe came into the kitchen to make a cup of tea. Sarah was gazing out of the window.

"You OK?" asked Chloe.

"Men...I don't get them."

"Men...or Philippe?"

"Well, men...but especially Philippe. He couldn't get enough of me last week and then this week it's like I don't exist. How can he blow so hot and cold? I'm thinking of heading to the club after I finish this evening's show to see if I can smoke him out. Do you fancy coming?"

"Yeah, OK, I have some drinks quite close by, so could head on afterwards. Let's meet there about 11ish?"

"Perfect. Should I text Philippe and let him know we're coming?"

"Yes, and make sure he puts us on the guest list. At least then you're telling him you're coming...without expecting to be on his arm all night."

"Good idea..."

Sarah texted Philippe.

Hey babe, working this evening, but planning to come to the club with a friend later - can you add me to the guest list + 1. Thanks Sarah x

It wasn't long before Philippe texted back:

I have missed you this week baby, sorry not been in touch, been running here, there and everywhere. Be great to see you ltr. Is Stassy your + 1, be great to see her Px

Philippe was immediately exonerated in Sarah's eyes. Of course that's why he hadn't been in touch...he has just been busy. But no, Stassy wasn't her + 1: she would leave him guessing on that front.

~

Chloe was already well on her way when Sarah arrived at the bar, buzzing from a good audience. Desperate to see Philippe, she insisted they order a cab to the club immediately and on arrival they strode straight to the front of the waiting queue, Sarah nodding at the bouncers authoritatively.

"We're on the list," she said brashly and loudly enough for those at the front to hear clearly.

Inside, Sarah soon spied Philippe and made a beeline for him.

"Hiya," she said.

"Watcha," replied Philippe, grabbing Sarah's hand and, in textbook fashion, kissing his and her joined knuckles simultaneously, but also looking around disappointedly when he realised it was Chloe with her.

As Chloe tried, unconvincingly, not to cringe, Philippe continued: "Good to see you baby...looking so lovely, as always."

He then whispered something in Sarah's ear, which she giggled at, and gave her a handful of drinks tokens.

"What was that about?" said Chloe, as they walked to the bar.

"He was just saying how he can't wait to get me back to his place tonight."

"Who said romance was dead?" said Chloe flippantly.

Sarah ordered mojitos and the pair found some people they knew.

With their tokens replenished sporadically by Philippe, as he darted around the club, the drinks flowed. Sarah and Chloe cavorted around the dancefloor in the basement club. Philippe would appear again, pay Sarah some attention, thrust some more tokens into her hand, and then disappear again, ensuring 'subject' and 'wing-woman' were always well-oiled.

That was, until around 2.30am, when Sarah began to look for her man. Not easy at a time when most promoters and DJs are holed up in 'the office' holding court or buried away backstage bantering. It had been a while since she had seen him and as the night was due to finish at 3am, she needed to locate him quickly.

Chloe also wanted to leave, before the end, and make sure they could get a taxi. Sarah had walked aimlessly around the club a few times, when she spotted Philippe through a gap in the door of what looked like a stock room. As she got closer, among the stacked bottles and barrels, she could see Philippe, with a textbook leggy blonde, who looked suspiciously like the barmaid who had been serving them earlier. As she edged towards the door it was clear Philippe was kissing her passionately and running his hands up her bronzed thighs.

"Hi, Philippe," bellowed Sarah, so she could be heard above the throbbing music.

Philippe prised himself away from the blonde, just enough to glimpse Sarah, but the leggy blonde was still draped over him, determined to spoil their view.

"Thanks for the guest list," said Sarah through gritted teeth. "I'm off now."

"Ok," said Philippe red-faced, but seemingly unrepentant.

Sarah shut the door behind her and, now inside the stock room, stood frozen to the spot.

"Thanks for coming, babe," continued Philippe brazenly. "Maybe you'd care to join us," he added cockily. "By the looks of that sex tape, you clearly have skills ideal for a menage-a-trois...or do you reserve that sort of stuff for Stassy?"

"You know?" asked Sarah naively.

"Of course...I haven't thought of much else for a while now. Are you sure you don't want to join us. Bethany won't mind."

"It's Tiffany," snapped the blonde indignantly.

Sarah yanked opened the stock room door and turned on her heel, tears streaming down her face.

She quickly found Chloe and screamed: "We need to leave…NOW."

Hurrying out of the club, and tumbling out onto the street, Chloe hailed a cab as Sarah blubbed behind her.

"I hate him," she wailed. "He's all over one of the barmaids down there. How can he come on so strong and then humiliate me like that?"

"Sarah, he is a shit," said Chloe, shaking her head. "Once a shit, always a shit. You need to move on."

"I know, but I like him so much and I thought he really liked me…"

"He does really like you, but he has always said it is not exclusive."

"I guess…"

"That means if there is some hot totty in the club he wants, he will go for it and you have no right to complain. You just need to walk away from him, darling…per-lease…you deserve so much better."

"I know you are right and after this I am going to… I promise."

"Let's go home and crack open a bottle of wine, babe?"

"Sounds good – what a fucking arsehole – what…a…cunting…fucking arsehole."

~

Another Sunday, another tabloid exposé for Stassy, but this time it had been handled by the professionals. Project-managed, as they call it in the trade. Clearly nothing that had gone before it could claim to have been managed that well. Crucially, though, Stassy and co had somehow 'managed' to get paid along the way.

This one was a freebie, and it rankled with our leading lady, as she read the paper in the cafe at Highbury Corner that had now become synonymous with this whole escapade. Think of the bigger picture, she told herself, Kirsten's words echoing in her ears as she had traipsed bleary-eyed to the paper shop just after it opened at 8am...more 'yawn star' than 'porn star'.

The headline 'MY SEX TAPE HELL' screamed out at Stassy as she flicked through the front pages of the *Sunday Planet*, munching on a slice of toast. There she was in all her glory again, pages four and five. A strapline header read 'SURVEY NO-NO FOR FAUX LESBO.'

The piece began...

Sex tape siren Anastasia 'Stassy' Thomas' life has been turned upside down by a seemingly harmless practical joke.

When she came across your No 1 Sunday Planet's *annual sex survey earlier this year, the freelance advertising executive thought nothing of submitting it on behalf of a friend.*

When our reporter contacted that pal, Preston Price, it kick-started a series of events, culminating in some saucy threesome footage featuring Stassy, becoming an overnight Internet sensation.

Price went along with the story, that she had left him for her lesbian lover, that he had fallen into his own gay relationship, but was now dating a woman again.

A quickly assembled cast, including best pal Sarah Phillips as her new girlfriend, was put together by the pair to keep up with the demand for press coverage, beginning with an exclusive interview in our magazine supplement.

All five even appeared on the Elevenses *sofa with Polly and Will.*

But it is where and how else that she appeared that

has traumatised Stassy, after footage of her taking part in a rampant threesome was sold to a porn website by a callous lover.

Stassy was incensed that Marcello had not been named and shamed, but the paper had seemed hesitant to do so during the actual interview earlier that week, so it came as no real surprise. Looking after their own, and all that.

The piece continued...

The sex tape is dominated by Stassy after her ruthless romeo cleverly edited himself out of proceedings, and features only the briefest glimpse from the waist down of another woman, sporting a Thai tattoo on her backside. Bizarrely, the literal definition of the inking, tattooed in the Thai writing system Abugida, is 'I like it on the bum'...and from further investigation we can confirm that this is not a known Thai proverb.

Stassy claims that the reporter introduced her to this mystery lady and she has no idea who she is. With such an unusual tattoo the Sunday Planet *hopes we can track down her 'friend fatale'.*

Meanwhile, with downloads of the aptly-titled 'Lies, Champers, Action' from allstarpornstar.com, at the time of going to press, now topping 200,000 hits, Stassy is reluctantly locked in a legal battle with the porn website, in a bid to get her rightful share of the spoils.

She told the Sunday Planet: *"A ruthless porn baron has put the video up for sale without making any effort to contact me. I can't walk down the street at the moment without somebody sniggering, or people nudging each other. It's only right that I protect my image rights.*

"I've now had lots of offers to appear in actual porn films, but porn isn't a business I want to work in. I'm actually in the process of setting up a foundation to raise awareness and money for exploited porn stars."

Cruelly, tragedy hit the group of pranksters when Preston's grandmother suffered a heart attack watching her grandson's revelations on Elevenses, *and he has been by her bedside in intensive care ever since.*

Stassy added: "We have been accused of profiting from this whole debacle because of the fees we have earned from the various articles and appearances, but what happened to Preston's grandmother has put the whole thing in perspective. He's holding a bedside vigil at the hospital right now and we just don't know if she'll pull through. Yes, we were paid for our stories, but when you consider the loss of reputations and, for some of us, our jobs, and, in Preston's case, the potential loss of family, you really can't put a price on that. I'm hoping now that by setting the record straight I might be able to bring some comfort to Preston's family at this difficult time."

Distracting Stassy, however, from yet another starring role across two pages was a stand-alone piece, within the spread, with the headline...ON A BUM NOTE. A strapline asked, 'Can you help us find the lady with the mysterious tattoo?' The piece went on to offer a cash reward, but this time, at least, for the truth.

As she trudged back to the house, Stassy couldn't help but smirk. Sarah would go ballistic when she found out her tattoo didn't mean Peace, Love and Harmony. Something had definitely been lost in translation at the tattoo parlour.

Stassy called Sarah.

"I've seen it!" screeched Sarah immediately. "What

the fuck? I can't believe it. I just can't fucking believe it."

"I don't know what to say, babe," said Stassy, desperately trying to stifle a chuckle on the other end of the line.

"You know, the thing is, I have broken a few hearts along the way. And they must all be scratching their heads now, wondering why they didn't manage to have anal sex with me. I mean, d'ya know how many people have asked?"

"Well, these things will happen if you get a tattoo done when you're wasted in Thailand," was all Stassy could muster in support, grateful it wasn't all about her for a nanosecond.

"Thank fuck I've never been into Thai boys," added Sarah.

23

Monday morning arrived, and Stassy was awoken by the ever-excitable tones of Kirsten.

"Right, baby. We have a BIG week for you? Hope you're ready for it? Let's get you out there...the taxi will be with you at 10am."

"Yeah, yeah...I'll be ready..."

Stassy had uncharacteristically given herself 90 minutes to get ready. She knew she had to take this seriously. She had to reinstate Saturday's hairstyle and the make-up she had been shown how to apply numerous times. When the taxi arrived she was, she hoped, looking her best.

The cab pulled up. Kirsten was inside, sporting a grin as wide as Highbury Corner.

"Hiya," said Stassy, as she slid into the taxi.

"Wow, you look really elegant!" said Kirsten, sounding and appearing surprised.

"Oh, thanks," said Stassy. "Where first?"

"First, we're back to *Nearer* to apologise for your lies, then onto *21 Again, Have A Rest, Biscuit Time, Daily Planet* - more apologies - and finally, press-wise, *Miss Eighteen*.

"Then on Tuesday we have you in a hotel near the *Wake Up Britain* studios for an 'On The Couch At Breakfast' special."

Kirsten came up for air, and checked her notes.

"Wednesday," she continued. "You are on the panel

of *Gossip Girls* and then in the afternoon I've lined you up with a production company to start conversations about your TV career. Then Thursday and Friday you have two whole days with your ghostwriter...to start your book."

"Wow," said Stassy. "Busy, busy! Let's do it."

As the taxi drew up to *Nearer*'s offices Stassy thought about Marcello. She had tried to put him out of her mind over the last few days, but she was finding it hard. He had really double-crossed her, but he must have been in a difficult place after losing his job and, however she tried to play it out in her head, it was clearly her fault. She had convinced him to believe her lies and, in many ways, had seduced him. Then he paid the price with his career. Although Stassy had been significantly exposed, and you can't get more exposed than that, it might now actually work in her favour. It was as if she and Marcello were joined at the hip by their deceit...like only they could truly understand each other's actions, and why they had betrayed each other. Maybe she would call him...maybe when this week was over.

~

Jerry Jerkoff had engaged a lawyer, Mark, which made Chloe's life a lot easier. Negotiating with a fellow professional rather than a porn baron was a relief. The lawyer also seemed to want to cut a quick deal. He appreciated the film had gone viral, that as a result Stassy was becoming hot property and that would mean she could soon demand an even higher price. Jerkoff was not being very forthcoming with sales data, but Mark knew that if they went to court Smedley, Smith and Sweeney would get access to everything eventually and by that time there would be even more sales to factor in.

By the end of the day, after going back and forward, Mark had come back with an offer just north of half a million pounds.

As soon as the details of the settlement came through, Jim insisted he called Stassy straight away. She was en route to her last interview with the *Daily Planet* and Jim wanted to give her the good news personally.

"Stassy?" he asked, as she picked up the phone.

"Yeah," said Stassy nonchalantly, so fed up with the barrage of calls she had been getting from various supposedly well-meaning parties.

"This is Jim from Smedley, Smith and Sweeney. We have some good news?"

"Smedley, Smith and what?"

"Jim sounded slightly insulted. People were usually thrilled with his settlement calls. It was something he prided himself on.

"The lawyers handling your legal action. I work with Chloe."

"Oh right...I see...do you have...erm...news?"

"Yes, we managed to settle for the princely sum of £525,000 pounds."

"Five hundred what?...are you off your fucking tree?"

"I have to say, I am not sure what being off your tree entails...but, yes, we have an agreement in principle and we have a contract ready for signature, signed by the other side. If you sign tomorrow morning, the money should clear by the latest the next day. Let's celebrate when the cash hits the account: it can always be a little touch and go when you're dealing with, shall we say, unsavoury characters...but, from the way our negotiations have developed over the last few days, I'm confident that they will pay up.

I just need your name on the agreement and we can remit you the funds...minus our deduction, of course."

"Shit, shit, shit," screamed Stassy, pound signs flashing in front of her eyes. "I love you guys, you are amazing."

"OK, OK," said Jim, now happy Stassy was doing the kind of gushing he was used to when delivering good news. "Well, I am pleased you're happy with this outcome," he continued. "Can you make it in tomorrow morning?"

"Too fucking right...11am OK?"

"Ahem, 11am it bloody well is, then," said Chloe's blushing boss, finally getting into the spirit. "Goodbye Stassy...see you tomorrow."

"She is quite a character, your housemate," added Jim, looking a little aghast.

"Hadn't you worked that out from her video?" said Chloe, looking equally shocked.

"Well...yes, of course," he stuttered.

"Anyway, it's an excellent result," beamed Chloe, trying to close off the conversation on a positive note. "I hope this lead will be recognised come bonus time," she added, smiling at Jim.

"Yes, yes, of course...it will, it will, as long as this money clears," confirmed Jim, slipping his arm around Chloe's waist. "There could even be an interim bonus coming your way. I have to say this is massive for Smedley, Smith and Sweeney...probably our biggest fee earner this year...this has very much been noted."

Chloe felt she had arrived. It was a good feeling.

~

Chloe left the office in a celebratory mood. She had brought that record-breaking piece of work to Smedley, Smith and Sweeney. As she walked down the street grinning, Chloe walked straight into Pathetic Pete...

"Hi, gorgeous," he said, his eyes lighting up. "How are you doing?"

"I'm well, thanks," said Chloe, warmly. "Just closed a big deal, so feeling pretty pleased with myself."

"Oh right...so what was that about, then?"

"Client confidentiality, Peter, client confidentiality. I can't tell you...you know that."

"Oh, yeah...wink, wink," he said blinking at Chloe in a really awkward and unattractive way. "How about a celebratory drink? My treat? Maybe a glass of bubbly?"

Chloe hesitated, but wanted to mark the occasion. "OK, Pete, why not? Where shall we go?"

"There is a nice cocktail bar...just around the corner."

"OK, Pete...lead the way..."

Chuffed Chloe and Pathetic Pete walked into the small dimly lit lounge. Pete ordered the drinks, while she found a quiet corner to sit in, genuinely surprised when he came back with a bottle of champagne.

"Oooh, Pete, you are really spoiling us," said Chloe, unnecessarily mimicking a certain chocolate advert.

"Bankers' bonuses have been pretty good this year," explained Pete. "I can afford to splash out, and I am happy to splash out on such a beautiful lady."

"Well, thank you Pete, but I hope you're not expecting anything in return. We've been down this path before, and I really don't think we should go over old ground."

"Look, I can buy a beautiful lady a drink, can't I?"

"Of course you can, Pete."

The former flames began chatting. The champagne kicked in. Chloe yet again started to feel attracted to Pete. They followed the champagne with JD and cokes.

Chloe was starting to feel a little lightheaded.

Pete leaned over and kissed her and held her hand.

"I have missed you," he said.

Chloe smiled, still not sure she really felt the same way, but it was nice for someone to find her attractive. Nice to feel a connection. Tom had long ceased making her feel that way.

"Do you want to come back to mine?" he asked.

"Umm, I'm not sure Pete. Is this really a good idea?"

"I have really missed you..."

Before she had time to protest much further, Chloe was being ushered out of the bar and a cab was being hailed.

They were soon back at Pete's place and in his bedroom, Pete brimming with an air of authority that Chloe didn't recognise...surprisingly sexy. What happened next was also very unexpected. Pete was in the kind of sexual form Chloe had never seen before, making a level of effort that just wasn't normal for him, literally leaving her screaming with pleasure and yelping for more.

"Pete," shrieked Chloe. "I can't take much more...oh my fucking God...not again."

Pete grinned and calmly said: "I think you'll find I'm not fucking pathetic any fucking more."

"That wasn't pathetic...Pete...that most certainly wasn't pathetic. I think it's time I grabbed a taxi."

"Can we do this again soon?"

"Maybe...Pete...maybe."

~

Chloe scurried out of Pete's flat and clambered into a black cab dropping someone off next door.

Bumping (and humping) into Pathetic Pete was like

walking into a wind tunnel of past emotions. Apart from their brief encounter on the day she was introduced to Tom, Chloe hadn't seen him for several years.

Back then, her relationship with Pete had all started so promisingly. She had woken up in his bed, the night after they had met at a friend's birthday, to the following note.

> *You were so luRvley last night...can't*
> *wait to see you again, sorry, had to*
> *leave for work, call me soon.*

Chloe cringed as she remembered how they paraded around the bar that night telling everyone they were in luRve with a capital 'R'. The next morning she entered his number into her phone as 'luRvely Pete' and left his flat.

They met the following week. He wasn't her usual type, but sweet and tender, so by their third date she was taken aback when he informed her he wasn't looking for a relationship.

How could someone who appeared so interested, dump her on date three?

"I am not dumping you exactly," he explained. "I still want to sleep with you."

Chloe didn't want to hear another word...and left before the main course arrived. As she got up from the table to leave Pete muttered, "er...so does this mean we can't sleep with each other again?"

"Yes, it does," replied Chloe defiantly and flounced off. Outside in the street she took out her phone and replaced 'luRvely' with 'Pathetic' in her contact list. That'll show him...and unfortunately it did.

Some months later, after a mutual friend's birthday, a group ended up back at her house. The girls were dancing, ribbing Pete to join in, but he was more interested in locating his phone. Picking up Chloe's handset to try and dial his own, his face turned white as the words 'CALLING PATHETIC PETE' flashed up on the screen.

At the time, nothing Chloe could say could placate poor Pete...the rumour that he was pathetic in bed was far-reaching, the constant mocking traumatising. Now Pete was back...and back with a bang. The expensive sex therapy had clearly paid off.

24

As the week played out Stassy seemed to be every-where. Every newsstand or newsagent had a magazine telling her story. The grainy photo of Chloe as the fake bridesmaid was also popping up in a few places. She was wearing a horrible dress. It wasn't ideal, but so far nobody at work seemed to have picked up on it.

Jerry Jerkoff had paid the money into the client account and the finance manager had remitted the money to Stassy. It would clear by the end of the week. After Smedley, Smith and Sweeney's standard 15% fee, she had netted the best part of five hundred thousand smackers; a pretty penny for an hour's work.

Shattered from the previous night's adventures, Chloe collapsed for an early night after watching some mindless TV with Sarah and Stassy. Some normality for once.

Her mind kept wandering to the night before. She still couldn't believe the performance that Pete had put in. He had been A-mazing. Did she want to see him again? Chloe really didn't know. She just didn't think she could face getting involved again, but after last night he definitely deserved a place back on her booty call list...at the very least.

Alexa was staying at Steve's. She was spending less and less time at the house, desperately trying to keep out of Stassy's way, who was getting far more press attention than Alexa these days.

Chloe was too exhausted, and freaked out, to tell the girls about Pete's performance. That could wait for another day, when she had enough energy to relive it.

~

By the time Stassy finally came face to face with Alexa it was Thursday night. She was shattered. It had been an intense few days of interviewing and continual smiling. She had also had a couple of sessions with her ghostwriter for her autobiography: working title *Porn To Be Wild*. As she walked into the kitchen Alexa was making a sandwich.

"Hiya," said Stassy tentatively.

"Hello," replied Alexa curtly.

"How are you?" asked Stassy, with genuine concern.

"Fine, thank you," replied Alexa in monosyllabic tones.

"I hear Steve is doing really well. The quiz show is a real hit, right?"

"Yes," was all Alexa could muster.

"So you are still pissed?" continued Stassy, cutting to the chase. "Even though, so far, there has not even been a sniff of a mention of your name? Is that a bad thing? Maybe you secretly wanted the press?"

"Fuck you, Stassy. Some of us don't want that kind of publicity...for sleeping with our girlfriends or sucking cocks."

"You saying you don't suck Steve's cock? Poor guy, blow jobs are great for a relationship, honey. You should try it. You might even enjoy it?"

"Fuck you, Stassy, at least when I suck cock it doesn't appear all over the internet. Your mum must be so proud. What does she think of your cock-sucking? Did she show you what to do?"

"Alexa, you fucking bitch. That's out of order. I don't know what your problem is? Get over yourself! It isn't hurting you and if you can't take the fact I am in the press more than you at the moment then have a word with yourself...you stupid fucking cow."

Incredulous, Alexa had heard enough, lashing out at Stassy, who struggled to push her away. It was too late. Blood was seeping from cuts on her face.

Stassy dabbed at the wound with her thumb. Seeing spots of blood on her hand, she pushed Alexa as hard as she could across the kitchen and stormed into the lounge.

"What the hell is going on?" asked Sarah, as she entered the room.

"Alexa just attacked me...vicious bitch."

Alexa spun into the room, her eyes ablaze with anger.

Chloe appeared. It was time to intervene.

"Alexa, what the fuck is the matter with you?" she fumed.

Alexa knew she was in the wrong. Rightfully worried about all the lies, now Stassy was gaining celebrity status from the press, Alexa simply couldn't handle it. She had worked really hard to become a Z-list celebrity and Stassy had become an overnight sensation...over one particularly mucky night, of course.

Alexa was jealous, but there was no need for violence.

Alexa looked around the room...at Chloe, at Sarah and at a scarred and emotional Stassy. And they glared back at her. Despite Stassy's own guilt in all of this, Alexa realised she had little defence.

"I can't condone lying," she mumbled. "I am going to Steve's."

Nobody said a word. Stassy was clearly in a state of shock. She had three Bruce Lee-like red scratch marks down the left side of her face, courtesy of their housemate's 'fist of fury'...but nothing her new expensive make-up couldn't disguise. Alexa walked out. She had made her point...the way of a dragon!

"She's out of order," stormed Stassy, almost in tears. "Way out of fucking order."

"She was...she is," replied Chloe, as Sarah concurred, and wrapped her arm around Stassy's shoulders.

The front door slammed. Alexa had left the building.

~

Alexa was fuming and had no intention of returning to the house. As far as she was concerned, Stassy had stepped over the line and there was no turning back. Now she just had to convince Steve that he needed her to be a permenant part of his penthouse lifestyle.

As she flew into his apartment, Alexa screamed: "Steve, Stassy is off her head. She is mental. I can't live with her any more. She is beyond belief."

"Babe...calm down, it can't be that bad?"

"I fucking hate her...I cannot live with her any more..."

"Well..."

Steve knew what was coming, and braced himself for the inevitable.

"Well, I want to move in here or move somewhere, anywhere but there. I am moving out and that's that."

"Right," said Steve.

"Well, thanks for your support," said Alexa.

"I don't know what to say," replied Steve. "I've tried

to tell you a number of times that I am really not looking to commit fully at the moment. I really like you,
Alexa. You should be pleased that I feel this way. It is
the first time I've just wanted to be with only one
person, but I still need time."

"That's commendable, Steve, well done, have a
fucking brownie point," said Alexa, scathingly, slump-
ing on his white leather sofa.

~

First thing Friday morning, with the Jerkoff pay-out
now cleared in her account, Stassy informed Sarah and
Chloe that she was organising a "girl's night out like no
other girl's night out."

In a certain person's absence, and before they could
get washed or dressed, Stassy called an "emergency
house meeting" and as they gathered wearily in the
kitchen, she paced up and down, explaining what was
in store.

With just around £450k burning a hole in Stassy's
pocket, Sarah and Chloe were about to be treated to
an-all-expenses night at one of the West End's most
exclusive clubs...when, in reality, they could have both
easily paid for the whole thing too.

Stassy was rich, but for once Sarah was not doing
too bad either...the icing on the cake was when her
'lesbo lover' generously announced that she was gift-
ing her £25k from her pay-off from *All Star Porn Star*.
In Stassy's words..."some booty for your booty."

"You beauty," quipped Sarah, planting a thank-you
kiss, far too sloppy for Chloe's liking, full on Stassy's
lips.

Sarah was more than happy with her pay-out. Of
course, Marcello's obsession with Stassy meant she
played a minor role in the sex tape and was only

recognisable, if at all, by THAT tattoo 'on the bum'. Now the *Sunday Planet* had revealed its true meaning, she was still in two minds about having it removed, but that could wait.

It was communally agreed, with Chloe as legal advisor/witness, that 25 large ones was a suitable buy-out for Sarah's 'services', as it takes two - or in this case, three - to tango.

In truth, Sarah was pretty sure she'd do the whole thing again for free...or at least for some more lines, champers and action.

Stassy took Chloe to one side and also slipped her a cheque for £25k..."for her troubles."

Happy days!

"Thank you so much," gushed Chloe.

"Not at all," said Stassy. "It's the least I can do. Couldn't have bagged that much without you."

Chloe was already feeling loaded. Her wage was a good one anyway, some months probably almost as much as freelancers Stassy, Sarah and Alexa put together, with her fat bonus for the sex tape negotiations about to drop too, any day soon.

Collectively, they were flush beyond flush, with Stassy pulling out all the stops to ensure this was a night none of them would forget in a hurry.

After scrapping with Alexa, Stassy was in the mood for a BIG night out...but then she was always in the mood for a big night out anyway.

"You know what," said Stassy, picking at the scratches on her face. "Before last night's episode I was going to let bygones be bygones and try to make my peace with Alexa...invite her out tonight even...but she can go fuck herself now. We may have made up a few things and everything may have got out of hand, but we haven't hurt anyone, not intentionally, and we've certainly never resorted to violence."

"No, honey bunch, we haven't," said Sarah, sidling up to Stassy, lifting up her nightdress and slapping her pert bum cheeks. "We're lovers, aren't we, darling? Not fighters."

"OK, OK," interrupted Chloe. "That's quite enough. Put Stassy down, Sarah."

Stassy blew a kiss at Sarah as she sat back down at the kitchen table.

"Right," said Stassy, through a mouthful of muesli. "Tonight, ladies, is going to be ma-hoosive. We are going to smash the shit out of it. Alexa is going to rue the day she ever got crossed off this guest list. Leave all the finer details to me. I have got everything in hand. Just report back in this kitchen at 8pm. You can now leave the table."

With that, Stassy turned and did a little skip and a jump, cheekily flashing her backside once more, as she strode out of the kitchen.

Sarah and Chloe looked at each other, giggled, embraced and shuffled out after Stassy, with more than a spring in their steps too.

~

Over at Steve Keane's flat Alexa's ears must have been burning. Indignant, she was certainly in no hurry to come back to the house, let alone out on the town with the girls, and "that slapper Stassy". She lay in bed alongside a snoring Steve, staring at the ceiling, contemplating the whole sorry saga, fuming at her self-imposed isolation.

~

Pathetic Pete texted Chloe on Friday afternoon, asking what she was up to...and Chloe was busy, she was extremely happy to inform him. Stassy had just announced she was taking Sarah and her to an exclusive club to celebrate her new windfall, added Chloe. He might be back on form, but Pete just couldn't compete with that…"potentially next week," she replied with a kiss.

25

Chloe appeared in the kitchen at the house promptly at 8pm...dressed to the nines. Her sex kitten friends sauntered in seconds later, Stassy wearing a bra which made her breasts look three times the size of her A cup, and a plunging neckline to match. At least Chloe needed no help in the chest department, her ample bosom splilling out of her dress. Sarah's figure-hugging ensemble, as ever, was to die for. Collectively, they looked hot...hot to trot.

A loud car horn sounded outside.

"Ladies, our carriage awaits," boomed Stassy. "Let's be having you!"

Outside a silver stretch Hummer awaited, but this was no ordinary stretch Hummer. This one came complete with an outside terrace area at the back, with heaters and a disco ball. Just in case the girls didn't want to sit inside with the buff topless waiters. One each. All holding silver-plated butler dishes complete with lids. As the trio settled into the sumptuous cream leather interiors, they were encouraged to take a glass of freshly poured champagne. As they toasted "to us", the waiters removed the silver lids to reveal neat lines of white powder and rolled-up £50 notes. Shades of Marcello and the revenge threesome, but certainly taken to a whole new level. Sarah and Chloe looked to Stassy, who winked back at them and boomed: "All part of the service, girls, help yourself..."

As the Hummer pulled away, the girls shuffled around the back of the limo, struggling to snort the lines, bumping into each other, spilling champagne and cocaine over them and their hunky helpers. At that point, they thought they'd pretty much made it.

In fact, they hadn't made it out of their road yet. As the Hummer turned on to Upper Street and wound its way towards Kings Cross, Stassy took control once more and attempted to run through a provisional itinerary.

"Right, sisters," exclaimed Stassy, with a puff of white powder on the end of her nose. "Tonight...we are doing it for ourselves. Standing on our own two feet, ringing on our own bells..."

"Ringing on our own bells?" asked Sarah.

"Not my lyrics, darling," said Stassy. "Ask Annie Lennox."

Stassy woofed up another line of coke, and continued: "What I mean is...no blagging any drinks from guys tonight. No hanging around the bar, waiting for a fella to buy us a cocktail. We are solvent, we are in control of our own destiny and we are going to smash it tonight like never before."

Chloe piped up, and tried to grab Stassy's attention...well, as best as she could with her view now largely obscured by the buff barman currently sitting on her lap.

"Excuse me," said Chloe.

"Who said that?" said Stassy, now astride her own hunky helper.

"Me...over here," replied Chloe, peering in between a bulging bicep and an oiled 'pec'. "I think you'll find," she continued, "that I'm always standing on my own two feet, and always ring my own bell when I'm out."

"Well, you earn more than us," interrupted Sarah, as she ventured out on to the 'terrace', her waiter on her arm.

In a moment of clarity, Chloe asked Stassy: "Anyway, how the hell did you organise this little lot?"

Sheepishly, she replied: "Let's just say, there are some interesting links on the *All Star Porn Star* website..."

"Stassy!" shrieked Chloe.

Before Chloe could say "buy-out" or "legal restrictions", Sarah peered back in from the 'terrace' and asked: "Stass, did you also book the paparazzi boys following us?"

Stassy and Chloe rushed towards the rear of the Hummer, their buff barmen tumbling to the floor as they went. When they emerged into the night, on what could be loosely described as a terrace – more like a trailer bolted on – the limo had made its way through Leicester Square, via Holborn, and was driving around Trafalgar Square, circumnavigating Nelson's Column ...a euphemism if ever there was one.

Several paps rode alongside on the back of scooters, snapping away as Stassy and Sarah posed, almost instinctively, for seductive shots, draping themselves over the buff barmen...Chloe desperately trying to hide behind them.

"Right," said Stassy, attempting to get a grip of the situation...seemingly oblivious to the attention and possible conequences. "I thought we'd take the scenic route...down Shaftesbury Avenue..."

"And you would know all about going down Shaftesbury Avenue," interjected Sarah.

"Down Shaftesbury Avenue," continued Stassy, smirking. "On to Trafalgar Square, along Piccadilly, and on to Mayfair, and then we will have reached our destination....Bourbon Haze."

"Bourbon Haze!" exclaimed Sarah and Chloe in unison.

"Wow, you really are going to town," added Sarah.

"And, yes," pointed out Chloe. "Through the busiest part of central London too. Loving the route, babe, loving the route."

"Fucking right," said Stassy. "There have to be some perks to becoming an overnight, internet, porn-star sensation."

That this ostentatious limo ride was bordering on crass, was beyond Stassy. After taking *All Star Porn Star*'s grubby cash, she had no option but to embrace the whole debacle and play the game. Stassy would come to realise that while the rules can change, the game always remains the same. Sex sells.

For one night only, however, they would suspend belief, forget how they got there and, as Stassy quite rightly put it, "smash it".

The limo pulled up outside Bourbon Haze, where more paparazzi were stationed. Three burly bouncers stood discreetly outside the unassuming entrance, defined only by the smallest of red carpets and discreet VIP ropes. A glamorous female door picker appeared from nowhere, clipboard in hand, and whisked the group through to the foyer. Someone was missing, though. Chloe ran back outside to find Sarah attempting to put her tongue down the throat of her buff barman, who she had pinned down on one of the Hummer's cream leather seats. Chloe managed to drag her off. "We'll be here for the ride home, madam," the barman informed them. "Enjoy your evening."

"Ride home? I'll hold you to that," giggled Sarah, as she sauntered into the club.

The three girls reunited, they were led through a set of double doors. They caught just a glimpse and a feel of the 'communal' nightclub area, before being escorted through a side door, along a dark corridor, lit only by cat-eyes lighting on the floor, up a small flight of stairs and through some more doors. 'Lights, champers, action', this time. They were now in the club's exclusive VIP Pod, which overlooked the dancefloor.

A pumping mix of funky house was the soundtrack to the night...the club full of smartly dressed guys and glammed-up babes. The girls were shown to their table, the 'reserved' sign removed as they sat down. A bottle of Cristal champagne was brought to them as they made themselves comfortable.

"Cristal? Did you arrange that too?" asked Chloe.

"No, I didn't," said Stassy, looking bemused. "I asked for Bolly."

"Compliments of Mr Leeson," said the waiter, gesturing across the pod.

They looked up and saw controversial England football captain Mark Leeson sitting at a table with his entourage. Such was his own recent tabloid exposure, Leeson was unmistakable, even to Sarah and Stassy, who had no interest in football at all. Also the captain of the newly formed and Russian oligarch-owned London United team, Leeson was renowned for his partying and penchant for sex with more than one female fan at a time. It seemed that 'Threesome Leeson', as he been dubbed by the press, had come to the right place.

"Oh my God," said Stassy. "It's him...the footie player who got caught in bed with two Brazilian hotties the night before a big match at the World Cup."

"Yes, you're right," said Sarah... "It's 'Threesome Leeson'."

"You couldn't make it up," sighed Chloe.

Stassy and Sarah fluttered their eyelashes at the football legend, and then back at each other, the significance of it all suddenly dawning on their shallow selves.

"Fuck it," said Stassy, raising her glass of bubbly back at the star's table. "Thanks guys, cheers."

Leeson and his cronies all raised their glasses back, the reflections on their huge watches catching the lasers and almost blinding the girls as they did.

The champagne slipped down quickly.

"This is some lifestyle," beamed Chloe.

As they neared the end of the bottle, 'Threesome Leeson' appeared at the girls' table.

"Did you enjoy the champers, ladies?"

"Very kind of you," said Chloe.

"Yes, it was lovely," smiled Sarah.

"Well, only the best for you three pretty ladies...did YOU enjoy it?" demanded Leeson, now fixating his eyes on Stassy.

"Yes, thank you," responded Stassy a little pointedly.

"Why don't you join us?" asked Leeson. "I'm not sure if you know who I am, but I'm Mark Leeson. I play football for London United and I also captain the England team. With me are two of my London team mates...Roberto Alonsi and Mikael Farossa."

"I see," said Stassy. "I'm not really into football."

"OK, well, will you join us anyway?"

"What do you think ladies?" said Stassy, looking at Chloe and Sarah. "We are meant to be having a girly night out tonight? Sisters doing it for themselves, and all that..."

Chloe wanted to scream. Of course they did. Not only were these men highly paid well-known footballers, but they also had bodies to die for.

"I guess we could spend an hour or so with them," muttered Stassy, as Sarah and Chloe stared back at her forthrightly.

"Yes, I don't mind having a drink over there," confirmed Sarah.

"OK," said Stassy, looking up at Leeson. "Looks like you boys are in luck."

They gathered their purses and moved over to the footballers' table, where they were quickly introduced to Roberto and Mikael.

Typically, it felt like the men had already allocated their partners before they had joined them. Mark was careful to ensure Stassy sat next to him. Mikael seemed to take an instant liking to Sarah and Roberto, a fan of the voluptous form, began talking to Chloe.

More champagne was ordered, although now the girls' 'services' had been secured, it appeared a cheaper variety had been chosen.

Chloe didn't think she would have a lot to talk about with Roberto, but he was charming, constantly complimenting her and, despite going into great detail about London United's busy end-of-season fixture list, really good fun.

Stassy seemed to be connecting with Mark in more ways than one, his hand placed firmly on her knee helping to melt her initially icy exterior.

Meanwhile, Mikael was making headway with Sarah, who every now and then blushed coyly at him.

The drinks continued to flow. It was now 1am.

Leeson interjected: "Ladies, I use a great VIP concierge service. I can organise a suite for us to go back to and have a little soiree? I can make sure anything your heart desires is laid on?"

"Don't you have a match on Sunday afternoon?" asked Chloe, now totally up with the London United schedule.

"Details, darling, details," said Leeson arrogantly. "You let us look after the football, girls."

"Where would we be heading?" said Sarah

"I will need to make a call," said Leeson. "But not far...central."

"Why the hell not?" said Stassy. "We're out now, I certainly wasn't planning an early night."

"I am in," said Sarah.

"Me too."

"Great," said Mark, swaying slightly. "I will make the call and the cars will be here shortly."

The night had taken an exciting, if somewhat dangerous turn. Stassy texted the limo driver to release him and the stretch Hummer for the night. The topless waiters had been rebuffed.

~

Two Mercedes S-Class cars with blacked-out windows pulled up outside the club. A suited and booted white-haired chauffeur appeared from the second car, lifting his hat.

"Good evening to you, Mr Leeson. Hello Mr Alonsi...Mr Farossa. Good evening ma'am, ma'am, ma'am. How would you like to travel, Mr Leeson?"

"Let Roberto and Mikael travel in this first car with these two lovely ladies...and I will follow behind with Stassy in your car."

"Of course, sir."

The chauffeur leapt out of the first Merc and opened the doors. Sarah, Roberto, Mikael and Chloe climbed in. Out of nowhere, two reporters appeared in front of Stassy and Mark and started flashing their cameras at them.

"Quick," said, Mark, pushing Stassy into the car behind. "Let's get out of here."

As Stassy got into the limo, a gust of wind blew her dress up. Wearing a G-string, her bum became momentarily exposed and the camera lights flashed furiously. Mark pulled her dress down and bundled them both into the back seat of the car. The first vehicle had driven off and Mark screamed: "Drive, drive, drive."

The chauffeur sped off with multiple flashlights piercing the darkened windows of the Mercedes.

"You will need to put your foot down, driver," said Mark, firmly. "We don't want those boys following us back to the suite."

The chauffeur sped up, furiously checking his mirrors.

By now the first Merc had pulled up outside the penthouse and the driver got out and greeted the concierge at reception.

"Welcome," said a smartly dressed man. "Let me show you up."

The group were taken to the lift and then up to the 15th floor.

"Welcome to the penthouse suite," the smartly dressed manager said, opening the door. "We have stocked the bar with all of Mr Leeson's favourite drinks and snacks."

The apartment had three en-suite bedrooms, each with a jacuzzi, a plush expansive lounge area with views across central London and a to-die-for open-plan kitchen. A separate adjoining room boasted the suite's own bar area, complete with pool table and state-of-the-art stereo system with a huge range of CDs.

"What you fancy, ladies?" asked Roberto. "What music you like? Mikael, can fix some drinks?"

"Champagne, ladies?"

"Yes, please," said Sarah. "There can never be enough champagne."

Music pumping and the bubbles flowing, the after-party was in full flow. Sarah and Chloe were loving the free hospitality and hanging out with famous footballers. After around 20 minutes Chloe noticed there still wasn't any sign of Stassy. It was a little odd.

Her and Leeson had left directly after them and it was his concierge service, after all...

Chloe slipped off to the bathroom and called Stassy, but her phone was going straight to voicemail.

As she came back into the lounge area Chloe turned to Roberto: "Do you have Mark's number? I am getting a bit worried about Stassy. Her phone is going straight to voicemail?"

"Sure, no problemo...I give call pronto," said Roberto, rummaging around his jacket for his phone. There was no answer either.

"What do you think has happened?" asked Chloe.

"I no know," said Roberto, shrugging his shoulders. "Strange...he was quickly after us?"

"I zink he taking ze diversion to lose ze paps," interrupted Mikael. "I am sure they fine, don't worry."

Mikael's explanation seemed plausible...the last thing anyone wanted was the paps swarming around this suite. The chauffeur had probably taken a long route to put them off the scent.

The music was turned back up and the fizz started to flow again. The next time Chloe grabbed her phone it was an hour and a half later. Time had flown by. They were clearly having fun. There was still no sign of Stassy and Mark.

Chloe was beginning to get really worried. They had all left the club at 1am and it was now 3.30am. She wondered why Mikael and Roberto didn't seem bothered by Leeson's disappearance. Muttering between themselves, they simply assumed he had gone to his back-up penthouse – the booking of a second even more private suite for his own one-on-one sessions was a late-night party trick Leeson was well-known for among his team-mates.

Chloe tried to call Stassy again, but her phone was still going to voicemail. Roberto called Mark again, but still no answer.

What compelled Chloe to turn on the *24 News Now* channel in the bedroom she couldn't explain, her jaw dropping as she saw the BREAKING NEWS banner flash along the bottom.

'MARK LEESON AND FEMALE COMPANION ARRESTED'

"FUCK FUCK FUCK," screamed Chloe. "SHIT! Sarah come here...come here now!"

Sarah couldn't hear Chloe over the music and Mikael seemed to be going in for the kill. Not wanting to ruin Sarah's moment of pulling a Superior League football star, Chloe grabbed hold of Roberto, who was looking a little lost, and pulled him into the bedroom.

"Hey baby, let's get...," he slurred lurching towards Chloe.

"Maybe later, Roberto. Look at the TV...LOOK!"

"Am I on the TV?" he asked nonchalantly.

"No, Roberto - look at the bottom of the screen," urged Chloe.

"Va funcolo ... cazzo.. cazzo.... shit... Mikael Mikael, get here, get here!"

Mikael tumbled in, a dishevelled Sarah following. "What! What?" he exclaimed.

"Mark has been arrested," Chloe shrieked. "With Stassy...look at the TV...look."

"Oh my God," screamed Sarah. "Turn the volume up, they must bring the news story on at some point."

Chloe, Sarah and the football stars perched on the end of the bed anxiously and waited a few minutes: a more surreal moment you'd be hard-pushed to find.

"Try another news channel," yelled Sarah.

Roberto grabbed the remote control and scrolled through to *Planet News*. There was a reporter pictured standing outside Paddington Green Police Station.

The news anchor said:

"So Mike, can you tell us what you know?"

"Well, Geoff, we are currently trying to piece the story together. It seems England football captain Mark Leeson and his lady friend, who we understand to be Stassy Thomas, who has recently been in the tabloid papers for a sex tape scandal, were brought into the station at around 2am this morning. Our sources report that the couple were chased from outside the Mayfair nightclub Bourbon Haze by tabloid paparazzi on motorbikes. Although they were being chauffeured from the club, we understand for some reason Mark took over driving the car. They were stopped by the police and Mark Leeson was found to be above the legal alcohol limit. We understand that Stassy, who was travelling with him, has been arrested for allegedly being being drunk and disorderly and also in relation to the assault of a police officer. We understand the chauffeur had to be taken to hospital in an ambulance. We have no more details at present, but, of course, as soon as we do we will bring you the latest from here in Paddington."

"Thanks Mike, we will be back with that story as soon as we know more...and to discuss the implications for Sunday's big game. Now let's go to Lucy with the weather."

"I think we should go down to the station and see what the hell is going on?" said Sarah.

Mikael stood up: "I no think we need the media," he said. "Any us."

"Mark need lawyer now," said Roberto.

"Well, I am a lawyer," admitted Chloe, "but not criminal. It isn't really my field, but we do have some criminal lawyers in our firm. I could make a call."

"Let me try our agent," said Roberto. "Mark and I... we use same...he needs to know. I call him." Roberto grabbed his phone from the other room and dialled a number, surely waking up his agent in the process.

"It's almost 4am, Howard, I know, sorry. Mark has been arrested, he at Paddington Green police station."

The sleepy agent sprang into action. It was time for him to justify his large commissions. He arranged for a lawyer to go down to the station and then started fielding press calls. Howard arranged for a legal representative to see Stassy, too.

In separate calls the lawyer and the agent advised the players and their good-time girls to sit tight. Nothing would happen until the morning. Mark and Stassy would be locked up for a few hours yet and they would probably be trying to sleep it off.

"Let's get some kip too," reasoned Chloe, more bedtime than good time now. "There is nothing we can do and turning up to a police station drunk isn't going to do anyone any favours." The others agreed.

The girls were certainly no longer in the mood for anything more than some sleep. Sarah crashed in one of the rooms with Mikael and Chloe in another with Roberto. Both players were clearly worried about the repercussions, and soon forgot about their previous intentions.

Chloe quickly fell asleep. She was shattered, and drifted off, feeling secure, her head on the chest of a superstar striker, wondering what the hell had happened? How had the chauffeur ended up in hospital? Why did Mark start driving a car when he knew he was clearly well over the limit and why would Stassy slap a policeman? She had her faults, but was not normally violent when she drank.

Chloe stirred just after 7.30am and woke Sarah. They needed to go to the police station now. They were not exactly appropriately dressed to be seen on the London streets in daylight, let alone in the reception of the local cop shop, but they washed their faces and brushed their hair and did the best they could to scrub up for one helluva walk of shame. Mikael appeared as they were leaving, so Sarah asked if she could borrow his slim-fit blazer in a last-ditch attempt at looking respectable.

"Sure," he winked. "But I will need your number so you can return it."

Sarah scribbled her details enthusiastically on the room service menu and tossed it at Mikael, blowing him a kiss as the girls rushed out of the apartment.

Roberto was still asleep.

"Can I have your number, Mikael?" asked Chloe. "We might need the agent or lawyer's details and we'll let you know as soon as we know anything."

"Of course," said Mikael. "I'll text Sarah now...please tell me. You know, I would come, but I will...how you say...all over the news. Mark is enough trouble with management. No need us all being dragged..."

"We understand," said Chloe. "Please say goodbye to Roberto for me. Come on Sarah, let's go. We should be able to get a taxi outside."

~

Sarah and Chloe arrived at Paddington Green Police Station. The officer looked them up and down and smirked.

"Ladies, how can I help?"

"We understand you may be holding our friend?"

"Oh and who is your friend? Let me guess, her name wouldn't be Anastasia, would it?"

"Yes," said the pair in unison.

"Well, I think she may have sobered up a little by now," whispered the officer.

"Are you planning to hold her for much longer?" demanded Chloe.

"I shouldn't think so."

"Well, has she been charged?"

"Not yet..."

"Will you be charging her?"

"Probably not..."

"Well, can you just release her? We are here now. We will take her home."

"Let me go and see if she's awake...you realise we will need to caution her. You just can't go around hitting policemen!"

"Well, I am sure there was a reason she reacted like that and, officer, we can only apologise on Stassy's behalf."

"I can't really comment on all the details. Let me go and see if your friend has stirred?"

Chloe and Sarah waited patiently in the foyer of the police station. Twenty minutes later Stassy was led through a door and into their open arms. She looked dishevelled and in a bad way, but, in reality, no different than she did when she came home most weekends, and she'd certainly had more sleep than usual.

Stassy collected her personal effects from the front desk and signed some paperwork to say she understood she had been cautioned.

"What's going to happen to Mark?" demanded Stassy. "He shouldn't be here!"

"Well, I'm afraid that's out of your hands, darling," said a rather patronising constable.

"Come on, Stassy," said Chloe. "Mark's agent has the best lawyer in the country. I'm sure he's in good hands."

Stassy reluctantly gave up and the girls swept out of the door and quickly hailed a taxi.

"What the fuck?" raged Chloe.

"Fucking press, I fucking hate them," fumed Stassy. "They are all shits."

"Start from when we left you, sweetie. From the top?" said Sarah.

"Well, here goes then," said Stassy. "But it's been a long night. It ain't easy trying to get your head down in there."

"I bet," replied Chloe. "Can't say I've ever had the pleasure."

"So when we left," continued Stassy, as the girls got into a black cab. "All those paps were on us. We kept asking the chauffeur to drive faster, and he was taking loads of side streets. It was like something out of *The Dukes Of Hazzard*. Faster and faster, more side streets …and then he only fucking went and had a fucking heart attack. Mark wanted to get him to a hospital. I was calling an ambulance trying to find out where was the best place they could meet us. Mark shouldn't have driven, but the paps were closing in and the chauffeur was, like, dying in the car. I was desperately trying to give him CPR, but I have only ever seen it one of those TV dramas. It was awful. Then the police turned up…thankfully the ambulance wasn't long after. Mark was breathalysed and the coppers started goading me. One only brought up the sex tape. I just lost it…and slapped the cheeky wanker. Next thing I know I am cuffed and in the back of the police car along with Mark…then the paps had caught up and were flashing away as we're sitting there. They have me pulling the England captain, flashing my arse and my arrest. It's a fucking car crash. What a fucking night!"

"Car crash," giggled Sarah. "You've got to laugh, Stass."

"Well, I can't see the funny side just yet, darling," said Stassy. "What about the chauffeur? Does anyone know if he made it?"

"I don't know," said Chloe. "We picked the story up on *Planet News*...they didn't say what had happened to the driver."

Not in a Hummer this time, the three dirty stop-outs arrived home, knackered and humming. Mark was still in the cells, an expensive celebrity lawyer trying to negotiate his release. The girls were glued to the news bulletins for the rest of the day.

London United's management were not happy, and had released a strongly worded statement. There was a huge match on Sunday, which the England captain needed to be fit for. He shouldn't have even been in a nightclub, drunk on a Friday night, let alone getting arrested for drink driving. Threesomes aside, Mark Leeson was meant to be a role model for the nation. News was finally through on the chauffeur, though. He was in a serious condition, but he was stable. The feeling was he would pull through. Powerless to influence the situation any further, the girls all sloped off to bed.

26

Stassy slept the rest of Saturday, conveniently surfacing around 5pm as the tea time TV news aired. Mark Leeson had finally been released and the chauffeur was thankfully making good progress. As he had driven in the role of a 'Good Samaritan', the media seemed to have sympathy with Mark's situation. Not so understanding were his club's bullish Russian owners. Hanging out in nightclubs until the early hours on the Friday night before a huge Sunday top-of-the-table 'Superior League' clash was unacceptable. The England captain being charged with drink driving would be frowned upon by the club's top brass, but then Threesome Leeson clearly had a penchant for scandal...and, Stassy aside, the odd brass too.

Stassy called Mark.

"Er, hi," he answered, sounding shattered.

"It's Stassy."

"Oh, hi, baby...how are you? The police said you managed to get out this morning and your mates picked you up? I am so sorry how things panned out."

"It isn't your fault, Mark," said Stassy. "Those reporters are bastards. I don't know how you cope day to day with that."

"Gee, I guess I'm used to it. I haven't helped myself in the past, and they say you create your own luck and all that, but let's wait and see what the 'Sundays' bring baby. I don't think this furore is over just yet, but you like a bit of tabloid action yourself, don't you Stassy?"

"Haha, yes, well, that's as may be...and, yes, waiting for the 'Sundays' has become a bit of a habit for me too recently, Mr Leeson."

"Listen, I would love to see you again," continued the superstar footballer. "I am gutted we didn't get back to the suite. I really wanted to hang out with you. Let's meet again soon, baby, some time next week, perhaps? Right now I need sleep and to be match fit for tomorrow. It's going to be tough. If I play, that is. The club usually back me, whatever I get up to, but you never know with those Russians..."

"Well, good luck, honey," said Stassy, suddenly getting all W.A.G. "I will be rooting for you. Hope the nasty Russians don't come down too hard on you, babe!"

"I hope so, darling, I hope so. Speak soon, gorgeous."

~

Chloe woke up at 11am on Sunday feeling better. The media were having a field day with the story and everyone was speculating about whether the England captain would play in London United's live top-of-the-table clash against Manchester Rovers later that afternoon. The club's bosses were furious, but remained fiercely loyal to their talisman Leeson. He was likely to be reprimanded, but surely a player of his calibre wouldn't be left out of the squad altogether?

How could a player who had spent Friday night in a nightclub and the whole of Saturday in a cell be on top of his game, though? Current champions London United needed to win this against their fierce rivals if they were to keep their title bid on-track...so it would be a big decision that would only be made minutes before kick-off.

Chloe went to the kitchen to make a cup of tea. Sarah was standing by the fridge, looking vacant.

"Sarah?...you OK?"

Sarah span around.

"Sorry, I didn't mean to startle you."

"No, it's me," she explained. "My head is all over the place. Life has been a bit of a roller coaster recently. I am so confused about what has happened with Stassy, petrified of people finding out I was in a sex tape...a sex tape with a woman, for fuck's sake. Everyone is searching for 'this girl with the strange tattoo'. And now all this latest shit...jailed Superior League footballers, Stassy getting arrested too, the whole thing plastered all over the news...you couldn't fucking make it up, hun."

"Relax, babe," reassured Chloe. "It will all blow over for you, maybe not Stassy, but it will for you. This has all been life-changing for many of us in so many ways, but, you know, somehow I always thought this could happen to Stassy. Anyway, it's Sunday...a day to chill. Shall we go to The Islington Shed? We can get some brunch, try and avoid the papers...and watch the match?"

"Sounds good, although not sure watching the match will take my mind off it all that much," said Sarah, before she snapped out of her malaise, and continued defiantly. "Fuck it, yes, let's go down there and see what these guys are made of. They have got great legs. We at least have a vested interest now. And I need a drink. Let me get a face on and awake 'Her Majesty' from her post-jailhouse slumber."

~

They were at the pub by 2.30pm, the main bar starting to fill ahead of kick-off at 4pm. Whether Leeson was playing would soon be known. Stassy had appeared and the trio asked for a Full English and a Bloody Mary each...definitely what the doctor ordered.

Stassy was getting strange looks from a few people, so she put her baseball cap and sunglasses on and slid further down into the sofa group area they had commandeered.

"Really?" exclaimed Chloe. "You're not Victoria-bloody-Beckham!"

"I just can't be arsed with people asking me whether they know me or where they know me from," raged Stassy. "It's so tedious. Plus, if you had managed to look at the front pages of some of the tabloids today, you might have observed that I have assumed my usual position...'LEESON'S MYSTERY, FEISTY BRUNETTE?', 'THREESOME LEESON'S DRINK DRIVE RAP', 'A BOOZY, FLOOZY NIGHT IN THE LIFE OF THE ENGLAND CAPTAIN'...so sorry, darling, I might want to try and be incognito today."

Chloe conceded. Stassy was better undercover.

Brunch finished, more Bloody Marys were ordered. It was 3.30pm and the pub was heaving. Everybody seemed to be talking about whether Leeson would play. Stassy slipped further down into her high-backed leather armchair, pulled the collar of her jacket up and the peak of her cap further over her face.

"My round, but can't really go up there, girls," she argued. "I'll get lynched. Here's some money, can someone go for me?"

Sarah and Chloe looked at each other in despair. Chloe snatched the twenty-pound note being waved in their direction and headed to the bar.

At 3.40pm the teams were announced. Leeson

wouldn't start the game, but he was on the bench.

Stassy was still getting bemused looks, either because of her spiralling notoriety or maybe due to her somewhat bizarre behaviour.

The match started. Within minutes London United were one-nil down.

"You're shitting me!" exclaimed Stassy, who up to now had been relatively subdued.

"Get a load of Stassy, London United's newest fan," taunted Keith the landlord.

"Get Leeson on!" a few people started chanting. "She's already got it on with Leeson," said one wag.

Stassy shook her head and buried her face in her pint, frustrated that Keith had dared to utter her now-notorious name.

Finally London United had a free kick outside of the box. Mikael lifted his shorts up and stepped up.

"Fuck, he has got great thighs," drooled Sarah. "He texted me, you know," she added, now whispering. "We are meeting next week, hopefully."

"Good. Nice to see you dating someone other than that player Philippe...'player of the ball' must be better than 'player of the ladies'," chortled Chloe to herself.

"Shame he can't get his ball on target," sighed Sarah, as it flew over the goal.

It was 4.25pm. London United were not looking good at all...Manchester Rovers with most of the possession and looking like they might grab a second goal. Would Leeson be brought on? At 4.30pm he began warming up. By 4.35pm he was on the pitch. A rare first-half substitution. Could he make a difference? Seemingly not before the half-time whistle went.

Chloe ordered more beers.

The second half began and London United looked like they had been given the hairdryer treatment. They were on fire. Roberto had come on at half-time and was linking up well with Leeson. The full Friday night squad was now on the field. "Come...on...London," squealed Chloe. "C'mon Mark, c'mon Mark," muttered Stassy under her breath.

Then right on cue: the breakthrough. The pace quickened. London United swept through, Leeson scoring to finish off a stunning counter-attack.

"Whoop, whoop," cheered Stassy, before once again burying her head under her cap as a shout of "Oi, love, bet you wouldn't mind Leeson smashing the back of your net" crudely rang out from the back of the pub.

The scores were level...1-1...it was all to play for. The commentator was singing the praises of Leeson, who was apparently proving he could have it all.

Seventy minutes in and Leeson took his second, expertly heading the ball in from a corner.

Stassy whooped, then composed herself and gave Chloe cash to get another round.

"Thank you, lady muck," scoffed Chloe, also still not used to Stassy being so free-flowing with her spends.

The pub was packed now so Chloe pushed her way through to the bar. She was served relatively quickly, one of the advantages of being a regular. Carrying a tray of three beers back wasn't as easy.

Just as she got back to the table, Leeson scored again with the last kick of the game. 3-1 to London United.

"Leeson gets a hat-trick," roared the commentator.

"Well, three is his lucky number," the co-commentator quipped.

"Yes, three is certainly not a crowd for Leeson," added the anchorman cheekily.

~

Monday morning, just after 10am and Stassy was yet again woken by Kirsten.

"I am going to start calling you 'alarm clock'," said Stassy sarcastically.

"Well, that would be a first, but enough of all that," said Kirsten, quickly cutting to the chase. "You're such huge news right now, darling. You've had a good weekend and I've got some very good news for you. You'll thank me in a minute."

"Right, OK, well, come on then, spill the beans ...what news? Don't tell me...my arse is going to feature on another front page of another fucking paper...or maybe someone's got some footage of me giving the American president a fucking blow job. For the record, I did not have relations with him, OK?"

"Ha, ha, very funny...now, back to business, you got some really good coverage this weekend. The whole Leeson thing was a really good move. Hooking up with the England football captain is pure gold. It really upped your profile. And it didn't affect his performance or yesterday's result. It was a win win...literally. You should string it along if you can. It is great publicity."

"Well, if I see him again, it will be because I want to see him," said Stassy defiantly. "Not just to up my profile."

"OK, OK, understood," said Kirsten, totally not understanding.

"Anyway, what is this good news?"

"You have been asked to host a 'segment' on Louie Mitchel's prime-time chat show."

"Wow!"

"They want you to start filming this week. Are you in?"

"I guess...is the money good?"

"Yes, it's good enough and it could be the start of a

beautiful thing."

"OK, so when and where do I begin?"

"This weekend. Saturday night...primetime live TV, darling."

Wow, thought Stassy. Saturday night primetime entertainment! Things were looking up...and on the rival channel, although a slightly later slot and with much better viewing figures, to Steve Keane's new show. Alexa would be pleased! The plot thickened...

~

The others could brag all they wanted about hanging out with Superior League footballers, but Steve's penthouse was THE original penthouse and Alexa was going to make sure it became hers too.

She and Steve had been frosty over the weekend. The honeymoon period was over. He had recorded his show, but she hadn't attended this week. She had moped around the apartment, stewing at Steve for being so non-committal.

Tuesday night...and she was going back in.

"To be honest I am moving out of the girls' house with or without you," she told him. "The way you are talking...sounds like I should leave you too."

"No baby, no....that's not what I want..."

"Well, you are sending me confusing messages. I am fucking out of there, Steve. I have had enough of Stassy and I need somewhere else."

"Alexa, you are the first woman I have felt like this about in ages. I just don't know whether I am ready for this next step. It's a big move."

"Well, whatever. Make your mind up Steve. I am in or out. Into your penthouse or out of your life completely. I need to move and quite frankly if you aren't ready for me to do it now, then you will never be ready."

"Alexa!"

"Look, I am going to find somewhere else to stay tonight."

"Please don't…"

"So you are saying you are happy for me to move in?"

"Erm…"

"Well?"

"I guess so…"

Alexa breathed a huge sigh, stepped forward and hugged Steve, the resulting embrace reminiscent of the closing scene of a tacky TV soap opera…the resignation on his face a total contrast to the beaming smile belonging to his relieved girlfriend as her head nestled into his shoulder.

~

Wednesday was Sarah's day off and she had slept in, had a late breakfast and then taken herself to Oxford Street for some extremely well-funded and much-needed retail therapy. Laden down with shopping bags, she was about to head to the tube when her phone rang.

"Hi, babe," said Alexa.

Sarah was a little surprised. Alexa hadn't called her for a while. The romance with Steve and the ongoing arguments with Stassy had inadvertently affected their friendship too.

"Hi, Alexa, it's nice to hear from you. Is everything OK?"

"Yes, it is good, actually…things are going well. Do you want to meet for a drink this evening?"

"I am in Oxford Street. I was about to head home."

"I could meet you there in around 40 minutes. We

could go to that little bar that we like near Pop Store?"

"OK, I can always kill more time. See you there about 5.45pm?"

"Cool."

Sarah had already ordered a bottle of red wine when Alexa arrived...grinning from ear to ear.

"What's got into you Alexa?" probed Sarah, while pouring the Merlot into two huge 'goldfish bowl' glasses.

"Steve has asked me to move in," announced Alexa, being somewhat creative with the truth.

"Gosh, that's amazing," cooed Sarah.

"I know. It's the real thing. He wants me to live with him in his penthouse. His bachelor days are over. Make way for Mrs Keane!"

"Amazing! Should I start looking for a hat?"

Alexa blushed.

"Well, this is the first step. Hopefully, the next one will be a huge rock on this," said Alexa, wiggling her wedding finger.

Remembering the exact terms in which she had 'moved in', Alexa composed herself and continued: "Anyway, that will be a while off yet, Steve will have to do a few more quiz shows before he can afford a ring large enough!"

"So we need to find a new housemate, Alexa?" said Sarah. "You will be hard to replace."

"I know, but I'm sure Stassy will be happy..."

"Look, I know you two haven't seen eye-to-eye recently," continued Sarah. "But you used to be so close. I'm sure you'll get over it. Maybe it will be easier if you aren't living together."

"Hmmm?..." growled Alexa.

"Have you heard? You're not going to believe it...she has been offered a weekly segment on *The Louie Mitchel Show*?" said Sarah, unable to resist telling Alexa the latest Stassy news. "She is filming this weekend for his live Saturday night show. She's over the moon."

Alexa tried desperately to contain her jealousy.

"Oh," she said. "Has she now?"

"You don't seem pleased for her, Alexa?"

"I have to admit, I am jealous. I have worked so hard to try and make it to primetime. I have had to put so much skin into this game and Stassy seems to have managed it overnight by shaking her tits, sucking some cock and getting it on with her best mate..."

Sarah blushed.

"Sorry," said Alexa, reaching out for Sarah's hand.

"None of this was really intentional, Alexa," said Sarah, welling up. "Sometimes life has a way of taking you on a path and there is not a lot you can do about it. It wasn't planned. It wasn't predicted. Who knows what will happen to Stassy next? It could still all be over in a flash."

"I guess...maybe I am just not cut out for this game," said Alexa, sounding unusually defeatist. "I'm just not sure what I would do if I didn't do this. It is all I really have ever known."

"Things will sort themselves out, Alexa, and anyway you are about to move in with a gorgeous prime-time TV star. You will be living in a penthouse. Things are really not that bad."

"Yeah, you're right Sarah," said Alexa, not meaning it at all.

Couldn't she just enjoy Steve's success for a while? Now Stassy had landed a job on a bigger and more-watched Saturday night show. You just couldn't make it up. Yet, Stassy had...all of it!

27

Preston was still in Hull and, after racking up a huge bill at the Vacation Lodge, largely from miserable lonely nights drowning his sorrows in the hotel bar, he had now dumbed down to a grubby £20-a-night B&B. Marooned in the grim coastal market town in the East Riding of Yorkshire, he had largely missed the sex tape furore...it took these things longer to reach the outer reaches of the UK in the mid-Noughties. By the time he had caught up with Stassy and Sarah's ridings of north London, the downloads had gone through the roof.

His old nan was still in the local hospital and showing little signs of progress. The final indignation came for Preston when he was caught 'watching' the footage on his laptop by his strict matron-like landlady. Caught red-handed and red-faced in his room, Preston had been to Hull and back all right - caught with his pants down in so many ways recently.

Stitched up at the very start by his beloved Stassy, at least Preston had finally seen her in full swing, even if it was remotely. He wouldn't be surprised if that wasn't Sarah in the tape too. That distinctive tattoo looked strangely familiar...flashbacks to glimpses of it at the London Fields Lido last summer came and went. He had ambitiously tried his luck with both of those lovely ladies in the past, on several occasions, and the one consolation for him out of all this mess, as well as the hard cash he had earned, was the hardcore action he had witnessed between the pair. That he now possessed that on his hard drive for prosperity, he reckoned, was probably just about preferable to a lucky drunken 'one-off' with either of them in the past.

Philippe, meanwhile, had higher ambitions than that. He wanted both Sarah and Stassy, and together, clearly seeing himself up there with the England football captain in terms of pulling and sexual prowess. He was one of the main men in Shoreditch clubland, no doubting that...on top of his own game...and despite Sarah catching him with his 'fingers in the till' at the club that night, he was confident he could smooth that over one day, and determined, maybe when this whole thing finally died down, to emulate Marcello to achieve his 'Sarah-on-Stassy' goal.

~

Chloe decided it was time she had a drink and her own catch-up with Alexa, especially after her exclusion from the mother of all nights out. Things had been really strained in the house recently. It was all pretty uncomfortable.

They met in the local wine bar for drinks early evening on Thursday. Chloe ordered a bottle of Sauvignon Blanc.

"Hey, lovely, how's tricks?" asked Chloe.

"Pretty good," said Alexa. "Life is treating me well. Steve and I are totally loved up, I am really into him. I'm sure you've heard, but I'm moving in with him... officially. You know, after the other night...the scrap with Stassy...I just can't come back."

"I thought Steve was a bit of a player," said Chloe.

"Well, so far so good. He says I am different and I do believe him."

"Well, good for you Alexa, good for you...and how is work?"

"I'm getting enough to keep me fed. Could be better but the regular column and a few other ad hoc appearance fees are keeping the wolf from the door."

"And you and Stassy? It's obviously way out of hand now."

"I am just so fucked off that she has lied so much to the press. I don't see the point of exposing yourself like that. I am worried about the implications for me, of course, but I think she and Sarah are so misguided trying to play the media. And as for that sex tape? Well, it's just so crass..."

"Hopefully, it will all blow over soon enough," suggested Chloe. "And you will be able to see the funny side."

"Yes, let's hope so, but it will take me a long while before I am laughing...that's for sure. Thank God, I've got Steve. He's doing really well, he's big time now, with the new show, so we're both really happy. It's a relief to have moved in."

Alexa didn't mention Stassy's imminent foray into the 'primetime arena' she craved so much...even though she knew that Chloe knew...and that she also knew that Chloe knew she knew.

"Anyway, tell me more about Steve," asked Chloe. "I want to hear more about this tantric sex yoga you've been practising."

"Well, it's just this irresistible mix of pain and pleasure," explained Alexa. "You have to be pretty agile to do it, but I have been having the most wonderful time and experiencing the most amazing orgasms. It has been quite a journey."

"Sounds brilliant. Tell me more, tell me more."

Alexa went into great detail, giving Chloe an insight into her new world of tantric sex.

~

Chloe's catch-up with Alexa had left her feeling quite frisky. This called for desperate measures. Horny and helpless, and throwing caution to the wind, she decided to call her old sparring partner Tom...to see if he was up for a late-night visit. It was out of the blue, alright, and considering how ruthless Chloe had been when she booted him into touch barely five weeks earlier, it was about as desperate as booty calls get.

Tom, the randy old bugger, as expected, readily agreed and said he'd be there "within the hour". Experience told Chloe to double that as, in his weed-addled state, time often stood still for Tom. With Stassy out on the lash celebrating her big break on *The Louie Mitchel Show*, Sarah on stage and Alexa finally having masterminded her move to Steve Keane's place, the house was Chloe's for the night, so the coast was fairly clear for what she had in mind.

Naturally, Tom readily agreeing to a reunion romp left Chloe wondering – for the briefest of moments – if there might just be something left between them.

When Tom arrived he was typically stoned. Would this be a help or a hindrance, pondered Chloe. Only one way to find out. He would be supple and malleable, at the very least. Unable to understand basic instructions, at the worst. She expected the result to be akin to a fruity game of drunken Twister at Christmas, so expectation levels were not high, but then they never were with Tom.

Chloe fumbled around in the depths of the fridge for a bottle of wine and Tom offered her a toke on his joint. She swigged at the large glass of Pinot Grigio she had poured, but declined a drag of skunk, fearful that the potent stuff Tom smoked would throw her elaborate plans into chaos. She now wished she had puffed the lot and passed out.

As Chloe glugged the wine, and topped up another glass-full, Tom asked her what he "owed the pleasure" to and why she had sounded so flustered on the phone. Chloe wasn't aware she had, but could well imagine she did. Alexa spilling the beans on her unconventional love life had certainly got her hot under the collar. Her sex life had been sporadic since she parted company with Tom.

So here they were again, but this was going to be different.

Chloe started going into detail about what Alexa had revealed, the penthouse apartment, the positions and amazing climaxes that they achieved. Like all of her male friends, Tom had more than a soft spot for Alexa and was asking for a little too much detail on her role for her liking. He was clearly distracted. Chloe decided to take control and ushered him up the stairs and through to her bedroom.

Inside, the scene was set for some extreme yoga romance. Well, sort of...Chloe had lit the one, almost empty, Bo Stallone candle she owned and a stick of incense found on the floor behind her dressing table. She had also given the large rug at the foot of her bed a 'shake-out'. The resulting dust-storm was still lingering in the air, helping to create the required tantric ambience she imagined was vital: totally by chance, of course.

Completely ignoring everything she had said in the kitchen, Tom was quickly on top, clumsily pushing and pulling at her, trying to get them into their usual position – mercenary...sorry, missionary. He had forgotten Chloe's instructions already.

Position-wise, Chloe had decided on 'The Plough'. It was the one she could remember in the most detail, and now her plan would swing into action.

Chloe quickly broke away from the headlock she found herself in and lay flat on the floor, with the back of her head at the foot of the bed, and her arms by her side.

Chloe nearly knocked Tom flying as she swung her legs over her head, in an attempt to rest her feet on the bottom of the bed...above her head. In her drunken state Chloe had forgotten to remove her jeans, so Tom didn't need asking twice when she gave him that little task, clumsily dragging off her knickers in the process too.

Whether it was the wine, the skunk or Tom's general haste/waste, it was becoming impossible to explain or execute the desired position.

It soon became clear the strain Tom was placing on Chloe wasn't right. Steve Keane's version involved the man taking his weight on his arms, not on the female currently in 'The Plough' position.

Chloe really must have had too much to drink because, in a snap decision, she decided her room was just too cramped for this elaborate attempt at fornication.

"Outside," Chloe ordered Tom.

"What?" said Tom. "In the garden?"

"No, you fool! On to the landing. C'mon, let's be having you."

And have her he would, if he hadn't lost interest, or his mojo, by now.

Now, it had always been a bugbear of Chloe's that the square footage of the landing was actually bigger than any of the bedrooms in their house. Its lack of furniture also made it the ideal place to attempt extreme adult sports. Having the place to yourself would obviously be a prerequisite.

They tumbled out of the bedroom, Chloe in just her bra, Tom's Calvins chomping at the bit.

They assumed the position. Lying on the floor, Chloe, with her arms by her side, flipped her legs over her head. This time Tom was able to manoeuvre expertly, hovering above her, without any unnecessary pressure.

The result must have resembled a mucky mixed doubles version of the wheelbarrow race. Chloe was beginning to completely regret having ever told Tom about Steve Keane's methods. This was painful, she wasn't enjoying it at all, but Tom seemed extremely excited and there was little chance of her getting him to stop now. Chloe gritted her teeth through the pain and imagined she was lying on a Caribbean beach... seductively filming a Bounty advert on the remote island of Tortola. In her head she was willing Tom to finish. Why was it all over too quickly when you didn't want it to be, and now it seemed to be taking an eternity. In truth the whole episode hadn't lasted long and was over in a matter of frantic tantric minutes, before Tom unceremoniously crumpled in a heap on top of her.

Then disaster. A crippling cramp! As Chloe tried to wriggle free, her legs above her head, she span around on her back like an X-rated female breakdancer. She required such a burst of strength to shove Tom aside that when Chloe did finally manage to break free, she catapulted herself across the sliperry laminate landing flooring, spinning furiously as she crashed through the bannisters.

Chloe's whole life flashed in front of her as she hurtled towards what she could only imagine was, her imminent demise. But that thought was suddenly suspended...because she was exactly that...suspended.

As she disappeared from view, her knight in shining armour, in what could only have seemed like particularly slow motion, somehow found an inner strength, threw out his arms and managed to grab, first one ankle, then the other...and held on for dear life as he himself slid closer to the bannisters. Who'd have thought Tom could have acted so instinctively, been so agile and so strong?

However, Chloe's ordeal was nowhere near complete. As she swung gently over the downstairs hallway, her head still a good four feet from the floor...Tom above her, steadfastly unable to let go - she heard the worst sound in her life. Keys in the front door!

Please let it be Sarah, Chloe pleaded to herself. She would be the most sympathetic and discreet. Otherwise, Stassy. Her legal issues meant she definitely owed her one right now. And then the door was flung open. Returning to collect her belongings, Alexa, with Steve Keane, stood in front of her – a mixture of bemusement, horror and delight all over their faces.

From nowhere, Stassy and Sarah, who had hooked up in the West End for a nightcap (or four), appeared in the hallway from their hiding place in the kitchen. Amazing, a full house...what were the chances?

And then the icing on the cake. With perverse comedy timing Chloe's bra finally gave way, and one by one her considerable breasts popped out to say hello, clattering each side of her face as they fell.

Steve Keane had seen some sights in his time, but nothing quite like this. Taking command, he gallantly stood beneath Chloe, beckoning Tom to let go. He was ready, he could handle this. With Alexa rooted to the spot in shock, Steve raised his arms quickly above his head and not so much caught her, as broke Chloe's fall as she smothered the slight yoga guru.

Then Alexa screamed, blood pouring from her face. Steve had inadvertently elbowed her as he assumed the 'catch' position.

"You fucking idiot," wailed Alexa. "I think I've

broken my nose."

As Steve tried, but failed to extricate himself from beneath Chloe, there were muted chortles and chuckles at his humiliating expense.

However, Alexa was clearly not amused and in enormous pain herself. "This could be the end of my career," she whined, yet again, as Sarah dabbed at her nose with a tea towel.

How long had Stassy and Sarah been in the house? A matter of minutes, it turned out, having heard strange noises from the landing when they came home minutes before, then dived into the kitchen in a fit of giggles.

But this was now serious. Chloe had unceremoniously pinned Steve to the exposed wooden floorboard and now realised she couldn't lift her neck. She tried to get up, but couldn't raise her head and her spine felt frozen. Then the pain intensified even more and she started screaming.

"I can't move, I can't move," spluttered Steve. "Get an ambulance...quick...my back doesn't feel right."

The laughter subsided. Tom, now by Chloe's side, fluttered around like a headless chicken, the most animated she'd ever seen him. "Don't move, don't move," he shouted, desperately trying to pull on his jeans, but failing miserably, and crumpling in a heap on the floor.

Stassy stood there motionless, still trying not to laugh, while Sarah took the lead, and phoned for an ambulance.

Alexa, incensed at her facial wound - and that her whimpering boyfriend had been incapacitated by her naked flatmate - raged inappropriately: "Why did you think you could catch her, Steve? You're a yoga guru not a fucking bodybuilder."

"I need something to cover me up," wailed Chloe.

"For God's sake, please...a towel, a sheet..SOME-THING! ANYTHING!"

Springing into action, Sarah ordered: "Don't move, either of you. Not until the paramedics arrive."

Stassy appeared with a throw, which she draped over Chloe's naked body. How macabre! She expected someone to appear with a stick of chalk any moment and draw an outline around her and Steve.

This had to be the most embarrassing moment of Chloe's life. Steve continued to groan and moan underneath her. The sheer indignation was one issue....the agony something else altogether.

After what seemed like an eternity the ambulance arrived. First the paramedics placed Chloe in a neck brace and then carefully lifted her off Steve and onto a stretcher.

Then they concentrated on Steve, also placing him into a neck brace and strapping his leg, as it was pretty clear from the level of the swelling that he had broken it.

The paramedics were trying hard not to laugh. It was clear they had recognised who Steve was...and also Stassy.

It was pretty obvious this was sex gone wrong.

"Don't worry, love," said the ambulance man reassuringly. "It is actually more common than you would think."

Tom went crimson.

"What about me? What about me? I'm injured too," stormed Alexa, as one of the paramedics finally began treating her.

The stretchers were loaded into the waiting ambulance, and Chloe's fellow yoga sex novice kindly escorted her to the hospital. Alexa had no choice but to accompany Steve.

Chloe was quickly taken into A&E and X-rayed. She

had done some damage to her back and neck, but nothing permanent. A few days in bed in traction and she would be able to start moving again. They thought she would need to be in hospital for a few days. She wasn't going anywhere tonight, that was for sure. She couldn't even lift her head up and she was put on a drip to keep her hydrated. There was a level of amusement around the hospital staff too: news of how she had been found had clearly spread.

The chaos of Chloe, Steve and Alexa's arrival at the hospital in the early hours of Friday morning and the seemingly colourful and 'familiar' characters hanging around was causing a stir at the hospital, and tongues began wagging.

Steve had fared worse. His broken leg was in plaster, and he would be in a neck brace for the next few months...his fledgling TV career possibly on hold. He had been placed in the private room next to Chloe. Stassy and Sarah were milling around trying to be helpful, while Alexa was treated in A & E. It was later confirmed she had indeed broken her nose and would require an operation in two weeks' time.

Chloe felt miserable and alone. The painkillers were starting to kick in, though, and she fell asleep, dosed-up and disorientated.

~

Saturday morning came in a blur. Chloe was served a truly dreadful breakfast. Alexa appeared sheepishly. She had been sleeping in a chair in Steve's room for the past two nights and looked awful, two black eyes emerging on her face, her nose heavily bandaged. She also felt really bad as Chloe had been injured from her suggested position, but Steve was cursing Tom, saying he should have read one of his books rather than just assume he could execute these complex moves. He argued that 'The Plough' was an advanced position that needed to be undertaken after careful tuition and that being sober was also essential. Poor Tom, it wasn't his fault. If anyone had been reckless, it was Chloe...reckless, randy and, now, rueful.

Stassy arriving with Sarah meant her presence, combined with Steve's, was causing increased commotion on the ward. She had become quite the celebrity in the last few weeks and her impending slot with Louie Mitchel was about to catapult Stassy even further into the public eye.

The nurses were all vying for a view of the 'celebs' and also staring intently at Chloe.

The paparazzi photographer came from nowhere. He mumbled to the charge-nurse about visiting someone. Distracted, the staff didn't pay much attention to the name he gave. With camera expertly produced and quickly poised, he first snapped Steve, who was slow to react, sleepy from the cocktail of strong painkillers and anti-inflammatory drugs he had been administered. Then the photographer quickly came at bedridden Chloe, unable to excape...the other three leading ladies unable to get out of shot either.

In a flash, the pap had done a runner, with the nurses squealing about patient privacy. Holy fuck, mouthed Chloe. Whatever next?

28

Being asked to go on *The Louie Mitchel Show* was a big deal. The camp chat show host had stolen a lead on rival channels by attracting some of the biggest A-listers in show business, and usually had a huge star from the States on his sofa each week.

Stassy was under no illusion that being offered a regular slot on the ratings-winning live primetime Saturday night programme was a golden opportunity. Anyone she told simply looked at her in awe. Her 'slot' involved 'mingling with the public', Kirsten informed her, and would be called 'Challenge Stassy'.

Dressed in a figure-hugging jumpsuit, Stassy would appear in front of the sofa and Louie Mitchel would identify a specific topic discussed that night by the celebrity panel of guests. Then she would be filmed running out of the studio, tasked with finding a member of the public to bring back and sit on the 'big purple stool' to tell a related story.

Coincidentally, a certain Mark Leeson was now one of this week's star guests. What were the chances? Well, the show's celebrity bookers knew exactly what they were doing, as did Kirsten, thought Stassy. The footballer's management team were also keen to get their client as much positive PR after the recent 'incident', which he was under strict instructions not to speak about. Cheeky chat show legend Louie Mitchel might have had other ideas, but he was also being urged behind the scenes to try to help show Leeson's sensitive side.

Also on the sofa was Dom Bruise, the American action-film megastar, renowned for performing all his own stunts and never one to shy away from a potentially life-threatening scene. His latest movie 'The Edge Of Improbable' had him leaping from exploding motorbikes and scaling cliff faces professional rock climbers would shiver just thinking about.

Louie Mitchel had been bantering well with Leeson and Bruise ahead of the new segment. Waiting in the wings with a cameraman in tow, Stassy adjusted the plunging neckline on her jumpsuit by pulling the zipper down a little bit more. Armed with an oversized microphone, she leapt on to the set, winking at Leeson when momentarily her back was to the audience and the camera. The ever-gobby Bruise was for once lost for words. Louie Mitchel held a stopwatch in his left hand and bellowed: "On your marks, get set...Stassy...GO!"

Stassy sped out of the studio, the cameraman desperately trying to keep up, unaware his new colleague had been a county sprint champion in her teens.

"'Challenge Stassy' has exactly ten minutes to find someone willing to sit on the big purple stool and talk about a sporting story with a saucy twist. Will she find someone? We'll find out straight after we've spoken to Dom Bruise about his new film...so Dom, I understand this is your most action-packed film yet?..."

Stassy was running aimlessly through the streets of west London, in search of someone who would fit the bill. She decided to knock on a few doors. Why hadn't she organised for one of her mates to be on standby? Definitely next week.

Eventually: light in the doorway of a ground-floor flat in a Victorian town house. A handsome, strapping

Australian student stood in front of Stassy, looking her up and down, staring suspiciously into the camera.

"Hi, I'm from *The Louie Mitchel Show*. Do you play sport?" asked Stassy hopefully. "You look like you do...with those...erm...big muscles."

"Yeah, I play a bit of rugby," replied the hunk with an Australian accent.

"Great," said Stassy trying to encourage her first conquest out into the street. "And I bet you and the lads have...erm...enjoyed your fair share of...erm...romance...along the way? What goes on tour, stays on tour, and all that."

"Well, I couldn't comment," he replied.

"Excellent. Will you come on TV and enlighten us?"

"Erm...well...I'm not sure about that, mate."

"Per-lease," begged Stassy, flashing her best smile, thrusting her cleavage a little further forward.

"Go on then," said the hunk, quickly giving in to Stassy's charms, like so many before him.

Louie Mitchel was back in her ear-piece now.

"I hear Stassy has someone out there...oooh, he looks just the ticket...bring him back, Stassy. Let's hear what he has to say for himself."

Stassy ran full pelt, grasping the young lad firmly by the arm...the cameraman struggling to keep up. We will need someone fitter next week, she decided, now beginning to enjoy this. Back in the studio with the burly stud in tow, Leeson could not help feeling a pang of jealousy. Stassy looked stunning in lycra.

"And who is this?" asked Louie Mitchel with a glint in his eye.

"I am Brett and I am 23 years old."

"Come and sit on my big purple stool, Brett."

Stassy escorted Brett over to the chair.

Leeson could not help staring at Stassy's bum. She had 'Challenge' spread across each cheek, something that had not escaped Dom Bruise either.

Louie Mitchel quizzed Brett and he did relatively well for someone who had been chosen randomly from the street minutes earlier, telling a naughty dressing room story about one of his teammates. A final round-up, then music from an earlier guest.

"That's a wrap," said the producer.

The credits began to roll and Louie Mitchel asked Stassy and all the guests, including Brett, to the green room.

"Let's go and get some drinks, folks," he said.

"Would you mind if my friend Sarah comes?" chanced Stassy, pointing her out in the audience. "She came to support me today."

"Sure," said Louie Mitchel, eager to please his new recruit after her impressive debut. "Bring her along."

Stassy beckoned Sarah to join her on stage and they all drifted into the Green Room, Sarah beaming at Dom Bruise.

Drinks were handed out by the production runner and everyone was gushing about Stassy's debut performance.

"You were wonderful, Stassy," said Sarah, kissing her on the lips and squeezing her.

Stassy felt a rush come over her. "Thanks darling... thanks for coming to support. It means a lot."

"Hi," said Leeson to Stassy, a little awkwardly. It was the first time they had seen each other since the police station, when they were thrown into separate cells, although they had spoken several times on the phone.

He was so good looking, thought Stassy, still baffled at how she had managed to pull the hunky England Captain.

"You look amazing," cooed Leeson.

"Thanks," said Stassy smiling seductively back at Leeson.

"Hi Sarah," added Leeson. "Great to see you again."

Dom was quick to introduce himself to Stassy, who felt immediately star struck, having seen all his films.

Brett was tucking into the free bar, intrigued by the gazes of Louie Mitchel, who had clearly taken a shine to him.

~

Chloe was still in hospital on Sunday morning, and had missed Stassy's TV appearance the night before, drowsy from the potent 'meds' she was being force-fed. She had seen more than enough of madam and the media for now, and was sure she'd hear all about it.

When the nurses brought over a copy of the *Sunday Planet* to her bed, Chloe's face was staring back at her, the only person in this whole crazy saga who had been determined not to appear in the papers, splashed all over the front page. A picture of her hospitalised, alongside the headline...YOGA SEX GOES TITS UP.

In a smaller column running down the main piece a sub-heading read...BAD BREAK FOR TANTRIC GURU. An inset photo of Steve, with his leg in traction, topped the article, which suggested possible 'career conse-quences' for the 'controversial presenter and his model girlfriend'. Chloe wasn't even aware that he was controversial, but, apparently, he was now, after an 'unsupervised attempt' at one of his 'extreme sexual positions' had almost left her 'paralysed'. Shit! Paral-ysed? That's not what the doctors were saying. Chloe certainly didn't feel 'paralysed' when she just hobbled to the loo and back. More tabloid nonsense.

At the bottom of the page was a cut-out photo of the full cast on the *Elevenses* sofa - Stassy, Sarah,

Preston, Ralph...even Serendipity made it on to the front page.

Alexa, looking like she was about to explode, appeared at the foot of the bed, pointing at the cruel 'before and after' mugshots the *Daily Planet* had chosen to run of her, with the caption...*Steve Keane's model girfriend suffered a broken nose in the aftermath of the tantric sex accident.*

"You're alluded to darling," said Chloe, offering a crumb of comfort.

"Yeah, as a 'model girlfriend'...a model 'bloody' girlfriend." said a bunged up Alexa, struggling to speak and shattered after two very sleepless and breathless nights. "They've also managed to leave my name out of the whole piece. I mean, it could only happen to me. And if you only read that caption, you'd think I was involved in the sex accident too."

Alexa crumpled in a heap in the chair beside Chloe's bed. 'Alluded to' wasn't the idea, nor was that "horrid picture" of her puffy, swollen face. She was even happy with the 'before' photo.

Alexa's self-prophesied downfall was complete, but, ironically, not necessarily or directly because of Stassy. In contrast to her nemesis sex had sold out Steve, and his fame-hungry girlfriend, and sold them out good.

Not that Stassy was aware of the latest column inches she had secured in the *Sunday Planet* ...the Louie Mitchel green room after-show drinks had gone on all night. They had left the green room, that she remembered. They been in the West End...and Shoreditch... and some after-hours place in north London...and she had at least made it home. Now, as midday on Sunday approached and she lay in her bed, staring at the ceiling, she wasn't quite sure who that was snoring peacefully under the sheets...and she daren't even look.

~

"Champagne, madam?" said the impeccably dressed, model-esque stewardess, as Dom Bruise's private jet sped across the Atlantic.

"Don't mind if I do," said Sarah, oblivious to her part in the latest tabloid revelations. She looked across at a beaming Dom, sitting in the deep leather seat next to him. He had promised her the world last night and so, without a thought, she'd texted her director at the theatre and told him she was heading to Hollywood. Regrets? She knew she'd have had a few, if she'd refused.

~

Louie Mitchel ordered an overly priced organic Full English breakfast and a bottle of expensive Italian lager for Brett, and his favourite Eggs Benedict and a white wine Spritzer for himself. He was a regular face at the exclusive 'food store' on Portobello Road, the staff used to seeing him on a Sunday morning, often with guests who had appeared on his show the night before. They hadn't seen the blonde Aussie lad before, though. "Can we have an extra sausage over here, please?" asked Louie Mitchel, admiring Brett's appetite, as he wolfed down his food.

~

Stassy carefully extracted herself from the duvet and tiptoed around the bed. Heading for the door and some time in the kitchen to compose herself, she glanced back at the lump in her bed. The bunch of keys on the bedside table distracted her, the gleaming London United keyring staring back at her. "Oh

...my...fucking...God," she mouthed under her breath. Quickly outside on the landing, a little louder now, she muttered to herself: "The England fucking football captain...it can't be...in my fucking bed?" She opened the door again...still no movement...back outside again. "What the fuck?" Then a noise, someone was stirring, and a gravelly voice.

"Stass?"

Stassy took hold of the door handle once more and slowly turned it...a familiar creaking as she nervously entered her bedroom, to reveal, not the London United captain, but one of the club's season ticket holders...a huge fan of both the Superior League champions and the captain's recent conquest.

"Morning," said Marcello.

SIX MONTHS LATER...

SARAH is not going to be the next Mrs Bruise but she did make a huge splash Stateside, thanks to action-star Dom's connections. She landed the role of a dizzy English rose in a prime-time major TV network sit-com, her critically acclaimed performance ensuring the show was commissioned for a second series. Living on a strict macro-botic diet, which also allows copious amounts of white wine, she still has that tattoo. Sarah's publicist in LA decided that revealing what it actually means was a great career move, and it was, instantly making her a favourite on the lucrative TV talk show circuit.

Dropped from her *Sunday Planet* beauty column when Steve launched (unsuccessful) defamation proceedings against the tabloid, **ALEXA** has had a total of four nose operations following 'complications' from initial surgery, which caused cartilage damage and her septum to deviate. Not ideal for a 'model girlfriend'. She is living in Walthamstow with two other wannabees, and has been shortlisted for a reality TV series. Separated from Steve for three months, she reluctantly works in a department store in Oxford Street as a cosmetic sales assistant. Still trying to snare her dream high-profile, well-connected man, Alexa vehemently refused a £10,000 hand-out from Stassy recently, and has only infrequent contact with Chloe and Sarah.

PRESTON is still in Hull, engaged to the duty manageress of the Vacation Lodge, and is himself now the bar manager at the hotel. With several thousand pounds still in the bank, a new steady income, free accommodation...and all just down the road from his nan, Preston's whirlwind romance with feisty fiancée Charlotte was a no-brainer. Right now, laying low in the north of England seems the perfect antidote to his notoriety down in London. He was devastated to hear that he had been written out of his grandma's will, at the advice of his parents, the executors.

Voluptuous fledgling lawyer **CHLOE** continues to find herself in the 'wrong relationships'. Her illicit affair with boss Jim means booty calls with Tom are now finally off the menu, but regular liaisons with a rejuvenated Pathetic Pete are a firm fixture again…very firm. Usually assigned the plum cases on offer, Chloe's career is continually on the rise at Smedley, Smith and Sweeney. Her starring role on the front page of the *Sunday Planet* was fortunately a one-off.

The success of his *Elevenses* appearance led to **RALPH** modeling globally for major hair product brand, Lock Wash…the perfect poster boy to flog their mission statement 'silkiness like you've never felt before'.

PHILIPPE is still pining for that Sarah-and-Stassy menage-a-trois…busying himself by running east London clubland in the meantime. An ego almost as huge as Old Street Roundabout has seen him engineer several threesomes with fawning club babes in the last six months, but still the 'S-A-S' eludes him.

TOM continues to struggle with his array of online start-ups, largely due to his unwavering skunk habit …and because he hotfooted it to Thailand two months ago, where the internet connection is awful. He is living with a local woman on the remote island of Koh Samui, and is also the subject of a civil law suit by Steve Keane for misrepresentation of trade.

PATHETIC PETE's one-man crusade to demonstrate to everybody that he is pathetic no more is…well, frankly…pathetic.

Living in a man-made tunnel under the proposed

site of a new super highway in north west London, **SERENDIPITY** currently works as a chugger on Upper Street for hugatree.com. Few people stop to fill in her questionnaire; those that do rarely hang around long once that unmistakable odour kicks in.

JIM SMEDLEY has taken on more revenge porn cases, becoming a leading expert in the field. He has recently renewed his annual subscription to *All Star Porn Star*.

Doctors were amazed when **NANA PRICE** suddenly came out of her coma days after Stassy's first appearance on *The Louie Mitchel Show*. She was discharged from hospital two months later, returning triumphantly to the nursing home, where barely weeks later she peacefully passed away in her sleep while watching *Elevenses* one morning. However, not before she had left several thousand pounds in her will for Donal and his family, with instructions to let an unaware Preston have it once he reached the age of 40...if by then he had stayed away from any further controversy.

Being smothered by Chloe was the start of all **STEVE KEANE**'s problems. TV bosses announced he had been 'relieved of his duties indefinitely while he recovers from his largely self-inflicted injuries'. He would never return, his replacement an instant hit with much higher viewing figures throughout the rest of the series, and a three-season contract in the bag. Steve, jobless and with a huge legal bill, has rent arrears on his precious penthouse and is currently teaching yoga at the local community centre.

MARK 'THREESOME' LEESON succeeded where Philippe hasn't (yet), scoring that coveted 'S-A-S' after flying Stassy out to see Sarah in LA. When he discovered a jumped-up Shoreditch club promoter was trying to steal his crown he pulled out all the stops, organising a pre-season all-expenses jaunt to Hollywood where the girls repaid him...in kind...with the kind of kindness he likes.

Business is good for **JERRY JERKOFF** and Linzi. Their perseverance and determination to survive in the ever-evolving porn industry has paid off. Despite the hefty settlement to Stassy, the remaining royalties from *Lies, Champers, Action* allowed the couple to relocate to Jamaica, from where they run *All Star Porn Star* remotely. The duo have launched their own adult phone-in TV channel, JerkStation, which broadcasts in the UK and online. A second channel, Jamaican Jerk Station will launch soon.

When his *All Star Porn Star* fee ran out, **MARCELLO** was offered a stint of freelance phone hacking by an old colleague, now masquerading as 'The Fraud Lord', but preying on celebrities Stassy worked or socialised with was too low for even his moral compass. Full of remorse over his shady sex-tape deal, Marcello gallantly took a press officer job working for a home-less charity, which helps get drug-addicted sex workers off the streets. He is very much in love with Stassy and fiercely loyal, promising never to deceive her again.

Her dalliance in LA with Leeson and Sarah was a one-off and the only time **STASSY** has been unfaithful to Marcello since she 'found' him in her bed...but, hey, it was a threesome she couldn't really get out of...she was sure he'd understand. Currently living with the rogue reporter in a spacious loft apartment in Canary Wharf, Stassy presents two primetime terrestrial TV shows, as well as her slot on *The Louie Mitchel Show*. A regular panelist, showbiz commentator and asked to attend more glitzy events than she can schedule, Stassy is very much in demand. She lives by the old adages that 'no press is bad press' and that, without question, 'Sex Sells!'

Also on MT Ink

Mr Pikes - The Story Behind The Ibiza Legend - Tony Pike

The playboy who built himself a playground reveals all in his electric memoir.

The iconic hotelier reflects on a life of hedonism and the globe-trotting backstory that influenced his creation of pioneering Balearic boho bolthole, Pikes.

Pike talks candidly about his relationships with hotel guests and friends including George Michael, Freddie Mercury, Julio Iglesias and lover Grace Jones...and also goes exclusively behind the scenes at the Club Tropicana video shoot.

The Life & Lines of Brandon Block

Brandon strips back his dramatic life as we chart the meteoric rise of a cocky schoolboy from Wembley who became an Ibiza legend along the way. A symbol for an acid house generation of excess, Brandon headlined a clubland era that changed the lives of millions.

His spiralling drug habit peaked at an amazing ounce of cocaine a day but somehow he survived to tell the tale. Includes extra chapters published in 2017 as Brandon prepared to enter the Celebrity Big Brother house.

Half Man Half Misfit - Dave Kidd

● What happens when a man statistically proven to be the happiest person on the planet reaches the point of optimum euphoria?

● Can love possibly flourish between an agoraphobic fraudster and a hypochondriac Eskimo?

● When a middle-aged couple visit a bric-a-brac shop in the Cotswolds, what effect will a woollen Guatemalan peasant doll have on their miserable marriage?

At mt-ink.co.uk or all Amazon sites

Also on MT Ink

DJ Whore - Jaqi Loye-Brown (Pts 1 - 4)

In pre-Millennial London Heavenly Angel, the alter-ego of disillusioned Yvonne-Leigh, worships at the altar and ego of DJ Starkey Moran.

Jaqi Loye-Brown's debut four-part series DJ Whore is set in the late 1990s, peering over the shoulders of the movers and shakers, fakers and takers.

Through her Portobello Novella series, Jaqi explores the frayed hem of a cutting edge era, tiptoeing through a club-scene rarely explored in a chick-lit.

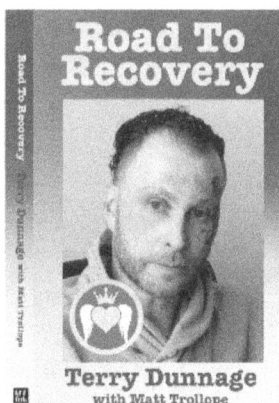

Road To Recovery - Terry Dunnage

Terry Dunnage had been scooped up...and dumped in Hell. His favourite uncle flicked at a cigarette lighter, trying to ignite more petrol. The fire felt like a bomb had gone off. A huge swirling backdraft engulfing both of them, Uncle Vince defiantly resisting Terry's desperate attempts to drag him...them...from the suffocating flames.

An inspirational comeback from deep depths of life-threatening burns, trauma, dispair, family tragedy, bitter legal battles, financial ruin and depression.

One More: A Definitive History of UK Clubbing - 1988 - 2008 - Matt Trollope

The story behind the superclubbing generation features the era's resident DJs including Jeremy Healy, Sasha, Judge Jules, Danny Rampling, Graeme Park, Brandon Block and many more.

With promoters behind clubs like Venus, Renaissance, Hacienda, Golden and Miss Moneypenny's they answer the question: If tonight was your last ever gig, what would be your 'One More' track?

At mt-ink.co.uk or all Amazon sites